The Lost Naval Papers

by Bennet Copplestone

Copyright©2018 by Ashed Phoenix Library

All rights reserved.

Ashed Phoenix Library

All Rights Reserved ©2018 Ashed Phoenix.
First Printing: 2018.

The editorial arrangement, analysis, professional commentary and glossary are subject to this copyright notice. No portion of this book may be copied, retransmitted, reposted, duplicated, or otherwise used without the express written approval of the author, except by reviewers who may quote brief excerpts in connection with a review.

United States laws and regulations are public domain and not subject to copyright. Any unauthorized copying, reproduction, translation, or distribution of any part of this material without permission by the author is prohibited and against the law.

Disclaimer and Terms of Use: No information contained in this book should be considered as financial, tax, or legal advice. Your reliance upon information and content obtained by you at or through this publication is solely at your own risk. Teumessian Fox Library or the authors assume no liability or responsibility for damage or injury to you, other persons, or property arising from any use of any product, information, idea, or instruction contained in the content or services provided to you through this book. Reliance upon information contained in this material is solely at the reader's own risk. The authors have no financial interest in and receive no compensation from manufacturers of products or websites mentioned in this book.

Created in the United States of America

Title: The Lost Naval Papers
Author: Bennet Copplestone
Language: English
Proofreaders

THE LOST NAVAL PAPERS

By

BENNET COPPLESTONE

1917

CONTENTS

PART I

WILLIAM DAWSON

CHAPTER

I A STORY AND A VISIT

II AT CLOSE QUARTERS

III AN INQUISITION

    IV SABOTAGE

    V BAFFLED

    VI GUESSWORK

    VII THE MARINE SENTRY

    VIII TREHAYNE'S LETTER

PART II

MADAME GILBERT

IX THE WOMAN AND THE MAN

X A PROGRESSIVE FRIENDSHIP

XI AT BRIGHTON

PART III

SEE IS TO BELIEVE

XII DAWSON PRESCRIBES

XIII THE SEEN AND THE UNSEEN

XIV A COFFIN AND AN OWL

PART IV

THE CAPTAIN OF MARINES

XV DAWSON REAPPEARS

XVI DAWSON STRIKES

XVII DAWSON TELEPHONES FOR A SURGEON

PART I

WILLIAM DAWSON

CHAPTER I

A STORY AND A VISIT

At the beginning of the month of September, 1916, there appeared in the *Cornhill Magazine* a story entitled "The Lost Naval Papers." I had told this story at second hand, for the incidents had not occurred within my personal experience. One of the principals—to whom I had allotted the temporary name of Richard Cary—was an intimate friend, but I had never met the Scotland Yard officer whom I called William Dawson, and was not at all anxious to make his official acquaintance. To me he then seemed an inhuman, icy-blooded "sleuth," a being of great national importance, but repulsive and dangerous as an associate. Yet by a turn of Fortune's wheel I came not only to know William Dawson, but to work with him, and almost to like him. His penetrative efficiency compelled one's admiration, and his unconcealed vanity showed that he did not stand wholly outside the human family. Yet I never felt safe with Dawson. In his presence, and when I knew that somewhere round the corner he was carrying on his mysterious investigations, I was perpetually apprehensive of his hand upon my shoulder and his bracelets upon my wrists. I was unconscious of crime, but the Defence of the Realm Regulations—which are to Dawson a new fount of wisdom and power—create so many fresh offences every week that it is difficult for the most timidly loyal of citizens to keep his innocency up to date. I have doubtless trespassed many times, for I have Dawson's assurance that my present freedom is due solely to his reprehensible softness towards me. Whenever I have showed independence of spirit—of which, God knows, I have little in these days—Dawson would pull out his terrible red volumes of ever-expanding Regulations and make notes of my committed crimes. The Act itself could be printed on a sheet of notepaper, but it has given birth to a whole library of Regulations. Thus he bent me to his will as he had my poor friend Richard Cary.

The mills of Scotland Yard grind slowly, yet they grind exceeding small. There is nothing showy about them. They work by system, not by inspiration. Though Dawson was not specially intelligent—in some respects almost stupid—he was dreadfully, terrifyingly efficient, because he was part of the slowly grinding Scotland Yard machine.

As this book properly begins with my published story of "The Lost Naval Papers," I will reprint it here exactly as it was written for the readers of the *Cornhill Magazine* in September, 1916.

* * * * *

I. BAITING THE TRAP

This story—which contains a moral for those fearful folk who exalt everything German—was told to me by Richard Cary, the accomplished naval correspondent of a big paper in the North of England. I have known him and his enthusiasm for the White Ensign for twenty years. He springs from an old naval stock, the Carys of North Devon, and has devoted his life to the study of the Sea Service. He had for so long been accustomed to move freely among shipyards and navy men, and was trusted so completely, that the veil of secrecy which dropped in August 1914 between the Fleets and the world scarcely existed for him. Everything which he desired to know for the better understanding of the real work of the Navy came to him officially or unofficially. When, therefore, he states that the Naval Notes with which this story deals would have been of incalculable value to the enemy, I accept his word without hesitation. I have myself seen some of them, and they made me tremble—for Cary's neck. I pressed him to write this story himself, but he refused. "No," said he, "I have told you the yarn just as it happened; write it yourself. I am a dull dog, quite efficient at handling hard facts and making scientific deductions from them, but with no eye for the picturesque details. I give it to you." He rose to go—Cary had been lunching with me—but paused for an instant upon my front doorstep. "If you insist upon it," added he, smiling, "I don't mind sharing in the plunder."

* * * * *

It was in the latter part of May 1916. Cary was hard at work one morning in his rooms in the Northern City where he had established his headquarters. His study table was littered with papers—notes, diagrams, and newspaper cuttings—and he was laboriously reducing the apparent chaos into an orderly series of chapters upon the Navy's Work which he proposed to publish after the war was over. It was not designed to be an exciting book—Cary has no dramatic instinct—but it would be full of fine sound stuff, close accurate detail, and clear analysis. Day by day for more than twenty months he had been collecting details of every phase of the Navy's operations, here a little and there a little. He had recently returned from a confidential tour of the shipyards and naval bases, and had exercised his trained eye upon checking and amplifying what he had previously learned. While his recollection of this tour was fresh he was actively writing up his Notes and revising the rough early draft of his book. More than once it had occurred to him that his accumulations of Notes were dangerous explosives to store in a private house. They were becoming so full and so accurate that the enemy would have paid any sum or have committed any crime to secure possession of them. Cary is not nervous or imaginative—have I not said that he springs from a naval stock?—but even he now and then felt anxious. He would, I believe, have slept peacefully though knowing that a delicately primed bomb lay beneath his bed, for personal risks troubled him little, but the thought that hurt to his country might come from his well-meant labours sometimes rapped against his nerves. A few days before his patriotic conscience had been stabbed by no less a personage than Admiral Jellicoe, who, speaking to a group of naval students which included Cary, had said: "We have concealed nothing from you, for we trust absolutely to your discretion. Remember what you have seen, but do not make any notes." Yet here at this moment was Cary disregarding the orders of a Commander-in-Chief whom he worshipped. He tried to square his conscience by reflecting that no more than three people knew of the existence of his Notes or of the book which he was writing from them, and that each one of those three was as trustworthy as himself. So he went on collating, comparing, writing, and the heap upon his table grew bigger under his hands.

The clock had just struck twelve upon that morning when a servant entered and said, "A gentleman to see you, sir, upon important business. His name is Mr. Dawson."

Cary jumped up and went to his dining-room, where the visitor was waiting. The name had meant nothing to him, but the instant his eyes fell upon Mr. Dawson he remembered that he was the chief Scotland Yard officer who had come north to teach the local police how to keep track of the German agents who infested the shipbuilding centres. Cary had met Dawson more than once, and had assisted him with his intimate local knowledge. He greeted his visitor with smiling courtesy, but Dawson did not smile. His first words, indeed, came like shots from an automatic pistol.

"Mr. Cary," said he, "I want to see your Naval Notes."

Cary was staggered, for the three people whom I have mentioned did not include Mr. Dawson. "Certainly," said he, "I will show them to you if you ask officially. But how in the world did you hear anything about them?"

"I am afraid that a good many people know about them, most undesirable people too. If you will show them to me—I am asking officially—I will tell you what I know."

Cary led the way to his study. Dawson glanced round the room, at the papers heaped upon the table, at the tall windows bare of curtains—Cary, who loved light and sunshine, hated curtains—and growled. Then he locked the door, pulled down the thick blue blinds required by the East Coast lighting orders, and switched on the electric lights though it was high noon in May. "That's better," said he. "You are an absolutely trustworthy man, Mr. Cary. I know all about you. But you are damned careless. That bare window is overlooked from half a dozen flats. You might as well do your work in the street."

Dawson picked up some of the papers, and their purport was explained to him by Cary. "I don't know anything of naval details," said he, "but I don't need any evidence of the value of the stuff here. The enemy wants it, wants it badly; that is good enough for me."

"But," remonstrated Cary, "no one knows of these papers, or of the use to which I am putting them, except my son in the Navy, my wife (who has not read a line of them), and my publisher in London."

"Hum!" commented Dawson. "Then how do you account for this?"

He opened his leather despatch-case and drew forth a parcel carefully wrapped up in brown paper. Within the wrapping was a large white envelope of the linen woven paper used for registered letters, and generously sealed. To Cary's surprise, for the envelope appeared to be secure, Dawson cautiously opened it so as not to break the seal which was adhering to the flap and drew out a second smaller envelope, also sealed. This he opened in the same delicate way and took out a third; from the third he drew a fourth, and so on until eleven empty envelopes had been added to the litter piled upon Cary's table, and the twelfth, a small one, remained in Dawson's hands.

"Did you ever see anything so childish?" observed he, indicating the envelopes. "A big, registered, sealed Chinese puzzle like that is just crying out to be opened. We would have seen the inside of that one even if it had been addressed to the Lord Mayor, and not to—well, someone in whom we are deeply interested, though he does not know it."

Cary, who had been fascinated by the succession of sealed envelopes, stretched out his hand towards one of them. "Don't touch," snapped out Dawson. "Your clumsy hands would break the seals, and then there would be the devil to pay. Of course all these envelopes were first opened in my office. It takes a dozen years to train men to open sealed envelopes so that neither flap nor seal is broken, and both can be again secured without showing a sign of disturbance. It is a trade secret."

Dawson's expert fingers then opened the twelfth envelope, and he produced a letter. "Now, Mr. Cary, if we had not known you and also known that you were absolutely honest and loyal—though dangerously simple-minded and careless in the matter of windows—this letter would have been very awkward indeed for you. It runs: 'Hagan arrives 10.30 p.m. Wednesday to get Cary's Naval Notes. Meet him. Urgent.' Had we not known you, Mr. Richard Cary might have been asked to explain how Hagan knew all about his Naval Notes and was so very confident of being able to get them."

Cary smiled. "I have often felt," said he, "especially in war-time, that it was most useful to be well known to the police. You may ask me anything you like, and I will do my best to answer. I confess that I am aghast at the searchlight of inquiry which has suddenly been turned upon my humble labours. My son at sea knows nothing of the Notes except what I have told him in my letters, my wife has not read a line of them, and my publisher is the last man to talk. I seem to have suddenly dropped into the middle of a detective story." The poor man scratched his head and smiled ruefully at the Scotland Yard officer.

"Mr. Cary," said Dawson, "those windows of yours would account for anything. You have been watched for a long time, and I am perfectly sure that our friend Hagan and his associates here know precisely in what drawer of that desk you keep your Naval Papers. Your flat is easy to enter—I had a look round before coming in to-day—and on Wednesday night (that is to-morrow) there will be a scientific burglary here and your Notes will be stolen."

"Oh no they won't," cried Cary. "I will take them down this afternoon to my office and lock them up in the big safe. It will put me to a lot of bother, for I shall also have to lock up there the chapters of my book."

"You newspaper men ought all to be locked up yourselves. You are a cursed nuisance to honest, hard-worked Scotland Yard men like me. But you mistake the object of my visit. I want this flat to be entered to-morrow night, and I want your Naval Papers to be stolen."

For a moment the wild thought came to Cary that this man Dawson—the chosen of the Yard—was himself a German Secret Service agent, and must have shown in his eyes some signs of the suspicion, for Dawson laughed loudly. "No, Mr. Cary, I am not in the Kaiser's pay, nor are you, though the case against you might be painted pretty black. This man Hagan is on our string in London, and we want him very badly indeed. Not to arrest—at least not just yet—but to keep running round showing us his pals and all their little games. He is an Irish-American, a very unbenevolent neutral, to whom we want to give a nice, easy, happy time, so that he can mix himself up thoroughly with the spy business and wrap a rope many times round his neck. We will pull on to the end when we have finished with him, but not a minute too soon. He is too precious to be frightened. Did you ever come across such an ass"—Dawson contemptuously indicated the pile of sealed envelopes; "he must have soaked himself in American dime novels and cinema crime films. He will be of more use to us than a dozen of our best officers. I feel that I love Hagan, and won't have him disturbed. When he comes here to-morrow night, he shall be seen, but not heard. He shall enter this room, lift your Notes, which shall be in their usual drawer, and shall take them safely away. After that I rather fancy that we shall enjoy ourselves, and that the salt will stick very firmly upon Hagan's little tail."

Cary did not at all like this plan; it might offer amusement and instruction to the police, but seemed to involve himself in an excessive amount of responsibility. "Will it not be far too risky to let him take my Notes even if you do shadow him closely afterwards? He will get them copied and scattered amongst a score of agents, one of whom may get the information through to Germany. You know your job, of course, but the risk seems too big for me. After all, they are my Notes, and I would far sooner burn them now than that the Germans should see a line of them."

Dawson laughed again. "You are a dear, simple soul, Mr. Cary; it does one good to meet you. Why on earth do you suppose I came here to-day if it were not to enlist your help? Hagan is going to take all the risks; you and I are not looking for any. He is going to steal some Naval Notes, but they will not be those which lie on this table. I myself will take charge of those and of the chapters of your most reprehensible book. You shall prepare, right now, a beautiful new artistic set of notes calculated to deceive. They must be accurate where any errors would be spotted, but wickedly false wherever deception would be good for Fritz's health. I want you to get down to a real plant. This letter shall be sealed up again in its twelve silly envelopes and go by registered post to Hagan's correspondent. You shall have till to-morrow morning to invent all those things which we want Fritz to believe about the Navy. Make us out to be as rotten as you plausibly can. Give him some heavy losses to gloat over and to tempt him out of harbour. Don't overdo it, but mix up your fiction with enough facts to keep it sweet and make it sound convincing. If you do your work well—and the Naval authorities here seem to think a lot of you—Hagan will believe in your Notes, and will try to get them to his German friends at any cost or risk, which will be exactly what we want of him. Then, when he has served our purpose, he will find that we—have—no—more—use—for—him."

Dawson accompanied this slow, harmlessly sounding sentence with a grim and nasty smile. Cary, before whose eyes flashed for a moment the vision of a chill dawn, cold grey walls, and a silent firing party, shuddered. It was a dirty task to lay so subtle a trap even for a dirty Irish-American spy. His honest English soul revolted at the call upon his brains and knowledge, but common sense told him that in this way, Dawson's way, he could do his country a very real service. For a few minutes he mused over the task set to his hand, and then spoke.

"All right. I think that I can put up exactly what you want. The faked Notes shall be ready when you come to-morrow. I will give the whole day to them."

In the morning the new set of Naval Papers was ready, and their purport was explained in detail to Dawson, who chuckled joyously. "This is exactly what Admiral —— wants, and it shall get through to Germany by Fritz's own channels. I have misjudged you, Mr. Cary; I thought you little better than a fool, but that story here of a collision in a fog and the list of damaged Queen Elizabeths in dock would have taken in even me. Fritz will suck it down like cream. I like that effort even better than your grave comments on damaged turbines and worn-out gun tubes. You are a genius, Mr. Cary, and I must take you to lunch with the Admiral this very day. You can explain the plant better than I can, and he is dying to hear all about it. Oh, by the way, he particularly wants a description of the failure to complete the latest batch of big shell fuses, and the shortage of lyddite. You might get that done before the evening. Now for the burglary. Do nothing, nothing at all, outside your usual routine. Come home at your usual hour, go to bed as usual, and sleep soundly if you can. Should you hear any noise in the night, put your head under the bedclothes. Say nothing to Mrs. Cary unless you are obliged, and for God's sake don't let any woman—wife, daughter, or maid-servant —disturb my pearl of a burglar while he is at work. He must have a clear run, with everything exactly as he expects to find it. Can I depend upon you?"

"I don't pretend to like the business," said Cary, "but you can depend upon me to the letter of my orders."

"Good," cried Dawson. "That is all I want."

II. THE TRAP CLOSES

Cary heard no noise, though he lay awake for most of the night, listening intently. The flat seemed to be more quiet even than usual. There was little traffic in the street below, and hardly a step broke the long silence of the night. Early in the morning—at six B.S.T.—Cary slipped out of bed, stole down to his study, and pulled open the deep drawer in which he had placed the bundle of faked Naval Notes. They had gone! So the Spy-Burglar had come, and, carefully shepherded by Dawson's sleuth-hounds, had found the primrose path easy for his crime. To Cary, the simple, honest gentleman, the whole plot seemed to be utterly revolting—justified, of course, by the country's needs in time of war, but none the less revolting. There is nothing of glamour in the Secret Service, nothing of romance, little even of excitement. It is a cold-blooded exercise of wits against wits, of spies against spies. The amateur plays a fish upon a line and gives him a fair run for his life, but the professional fisherman—to whom a salmon is a people's food—nets him coldly and expeditiously as he comes in from the sea.

Shortly after breakfast there came a call from Dawson on the telephone. "All goes well. Come to my office as soon as possible." Cary found Dawson bubbling with professional satisfaction. "It was beautiful," cried he. "Hagan was met at the train, taken to a place we know of, and shadowed by us tight as wax. We now know all his associates—the swine have not even the excuse of being German. He burgled your flat himself while one of his gang watched outside. Never mind where I was; you would be surprised if I told you; but I saw everything. He has the faked papers, is busy making copies, and this afternoon is going down the river in a steamer to get a glimpse of the shipyards and docks and check your Notes as far as can be done. Will they stand all right?"

"Quite all right," said Cary. "The obvious things were given correctly."

"Good. We will be in the steamer."

Cary went that afternoon, quite unchanged in appearance by Dawson's order. "If you try to disguise yourself," declared that expert, "you will be spotted at once. Leave the refinements to us." Dawson himself went as an elderly dug-out officer with the rank marks of a colonel, and never spoke a word to Cary upon the whole trip down and up the teeming river. Dawson's men were scattered here and there—one a passenger of inquiring mind, another a deckhand, yet a third—a pretty girl in khaki—sold tea and cakes in the vessel's saloon. Hagan—who, Cary heard afterwards, wore the brass-bound cap and blue kit of a mate in the American merchant service—was never out of sight for an instant of Dawson or of one of his troupe. He busied himself with a strong pair of marine glasses, and now and then asked innocent questions of the ship's deckhands. He had evidently himself once served as a sailor. One deckhand, an idle fellow to whom Hagan was very civil, told his questioner quite a lot of interesting details about the Navy ships, great and small, which could be seen upon the building slips. All these details tallied strangely with those recorded in Cary's Notes. The trip up and down the river was a great success for Hagan and for Dawson, but for Cary it was rather a bore. He felt somehow out of the picture. In the evening Dawson called at Cary's office and broke in upon him. "We had a splendid trip to-day," said he. "It exceeded my utmost hopes. Hagan thinks no end of your Notes, but he is not taking any risks. He leaves in the morning for Glasgow to do the Clyde and to check some more of your stuff. Would you like to come?" Cary remarked that he was rather busy, and that these river excursions, though doubtless great fun for Dawson, were rather poor sport for himself. Dawson laughed joyously—he was a cheerful soul when he had a spy upon his string. "Come along," said he. "See the thing through. I should like you to be in at the death." Cary observed that he had no stomach for cold, damp dawns and firing parties.

"I did not quite mean that," replied Dawson. "Those closing ceremonies are still strictly private. But you should see the chase through to a finish. You are a newspaper man, and should be eager for new experiences."

"I will come," said Cary, rather reluctantly. "But I warn you that my sympathies are steadily going over to Hagan. The poor devil does not look to have a dog's chance against you."

"He hasn't," said Dawson, with great satisfaction.

Cary, to whom the wonderful Clyde was as familiar as the river near his own home, found the second trip almost as wearisome as the first. But not quite. He was now able to recognise Hagan, who again appeared as a brass-bounder, and did not affect to conceal his deep interest in the naval panorama offered by the river. Nothing of real importance can, of course, be learned from a casual steamer trip, but Hagan seemed to think otherwise, for he was always either watching through his glasses or asking apparently artless questions of passengers or passing deckhands. Again a sailor seemed disposed to be communicative; he pointed out more than one monster in steel, red raw with surface rust, and gave particulars of a completed power which would have surprised the Admiralty Superintendent. They would not, however, have surprised Mr. Cary, in whose ingenious brain they had been conceived. This second trip, like the first, was declared by Dawson to have been a great success. "Did you know me?" he asked. "I was a clean-shaven naval doctor, about as unlike the army colonel of the first trip as a pigeon is unlike a gamecock. Hagan is off to London to-night by the North-Western. There are two copies of your Notes. One is going by Edinburgh and the east coast, and another by the Midland. Hagan has the original masterpiece. I will look after him and leave the two other messengers to my men. I have been on to the Yard by 'phone, and have arranged that all three shall have passports for Holland. The two copies shall reach the Kaiser, bless him, but I really must have Hagan's set of Notes for my Museum."

"And what will become of Hagan?" asked Cary.

"Come and see," said Mr. Dawson.

Dawson entertained Cary at dinner in a private room at the Station Hotel, waited upon by one of his own confidential men. "Nobody ever sees me," he observed, with much satisfaction, "though I am everywhere." (I suspect that Dawson is not without his little vanities.) "Except in my office and with people whom I know well, I am always some one else. The first time I came to your house I wore a beard, and the second time looked like a gas inspector. You saw only the real Dawson. When one has got the passion for the chase in one's blood, one cannot bide for long in a stuffy office. As I have a jewel of an assistant, I can always escape and follow up my own victims. This man Hagan is a black heartless devil. Don't waste your sympathy on him, Mr. Cary. He took money from us quite lately to betray the silly asses of Sinn Feiners, and now, thinking us hoodwinked, is after more money from the Kaiser. He is of the type that would sell his own mother and buy a mistress with the money. He's not worth your pity. We use him and his like for just so long as they can be useful, and then the jaws of the trap close. By letting him take those faked Notes we have done a fine stroke for the Navy, for the Yard, and for Bill Dawson. We have got into close touch with four new German agents here and two more down south. We shan't seize them yet; just keep them hanging on and use them. That's the game. I am never anxious about an agent when I know him and can keep him watched. Anxious, bless you; I love him like a cat loves a mouse. I've had some spies on my string ever since the war began; I wouldn't have them touched or worried for the world. Their correspondence tells me everything, and if a letter to Holland which they haven't written slips in sometimes, it's useful, very useful, as useful almost as your faked Notes."

Half an hour before the night train was due to leave for the South, Dawson, very simply but effectively changed in appearance—for Hagan knew by sight the real Dawson—led Cary to the middle sleeping-coach on the train. "I have had Hagan put in No. 5," he said, "and you and I will take Nos. 4 and 6. No. 5 is an observation berth; there is one fixed up for us on this sleeping-coach. Come in here." He pulled Cary into No. 4, shut the door, and pointed to a small wooden knob set a few inches below the luggage rack. "If one unscrews that knob one can see into the next berth, No. 5. No. 6 is fitted in the same way, so that we can rake No. 5 from both sides. But, mind you, on no account touch those knobs until the train is moving fast and until you have switched out the lights. If No. 5 was dark when you opened the peep-hole, a ray of light from your side would give the show away. And unless there was a good deal of vibration and rattle in the train you might be heard. Now cut away to No. 6, fasten the door, and go to bed. I shall sit up and watch, but there is nothing for you to do."

Hagan appeared in due course, was shown into No. 5 berth, and the train started. Cary asked himself whether he should go to bed as advised or sit up reading. He decided to obey Dawson's orders, but to take a look in upon Hagan before settling down for the journey. He switched off his lights, climbed upon the bed, and carefully unscrewed the little knob which was like the one shown to him by Dawson. A beam of light stabbed the darkness of his berth, and putting his eye with some difficulty to the hole—one's nose gets so confoundedly in the way—he saw Hagan comfortably arranging himself for the night. The spy had no suspicion of his watchers on both sides, for, after settling himself in bed, he unwrapped a flat parcel and took out a bundle of blue papers, which Cary at once recognised as the originals of his stolen Notes. Hagan went through them—he had put his suit-case across his knees to form a desk—and carefully made marginal jottings. Cary, who had often tried to write in trains, could not but admire the man's laborious patience. He painted his letters and figures over and over again, in order to secure distinctness, in spite of the swaying of the train, and frequently stopped to suck the point of his pencil.

"I suppose," thought Cary, "that Dawson yonder is just gloating over his prey, but for my part I feel an utterly contemptible beast. Never again will I set a trap for even the worst of my fellow-creatures." He put back the knob, went to bed, and passed half the night in extreme mental discomfort and the other half in snatching brief intervals of sleep. It was not a pleasant journey.

Dawson did not come out of his berth at Euston until after Hagan had left the station in a taxi-cab, much to Cary's surprise, and then was quite ready, even anxious, to remain for breakfast at the hotel. He explained his strange conduct. "Two of my men," said he, as he wallowed in tea and fried soles—one cannot get Dover soles in the weary North—"who travelled in ordinary compartments, are after Hagan in two taxis, so that if one is delayed, the other will keep touch. Hagan's driver also has had a police warning, so that our spy is in a barbed-wire net. I shall hear before very long all about him."

Cary and Dawson spent the morning at the hotel with a telephone beside them; every few minutes the bell would ring, and a whisper of Hagan's movements steal over the wires into the ears of the spider Dawson. He reported progress to Cary with ever-increasing satisfaction.

"Hagan has applied for and been granted a passport to Holland, and has booked a passage in the boat which leaves Harwich to-night for the Hook. We will go with him. The other two spies, with the copies, haven't turned up yet, but they are all right. My men will see them safe across into Dutch territory, and make sure that no blundering Customs officer interferes with their papers. This time the way of transgressors shall be very soft. As for Hagan, he is not going to arrive."

"I don't quite understand why you carry on so long with him," said
Cary, who, though tired, could not but feel intense interest in the
perfection of the police system and in the serene confidence of

Dawson. The Yard could, it appeared, do unto the spies precisely what Dawson chose to direct.

"Hagan is an American citizen," explained Dawson. "If he had been a British subject I would have taken him at Euston—we have full evidence of the burglary, and of the stolen papers in his suit-case. But as he is a damned unbenevolent neutral we must prove his intention to sell the papers to Germany. Then we can deal with him by secret court-martial.[1] The journey to Holland will prove this intention. Hagan has been most useful to us in Ireland, and now in the North of England and in Scotland, but he is too enterprising and too daring to be left any longer on the string. I will draw the ends together at the Hook."

[Footnote 1: Author's Note: This conversation is dated May, 1916.]

"I did not want to go to Holland," said Cary to me, when telling his story. "I was utterly sick and disgusted with the whole cold-blooded game of cat and mouse, but the police needed my evidence about the Notes and the burglary, and did not intend to let me slip out of their clutches. Dawson was very civil and pleasant, but I was in fact as tightly held upon his string as was the wretched Hagan. So I went on to Holland with that quick-change artist, and watched him come on board the steamer at Parkeston Quay, dressed as a rather German-looking commercial traveller, eager for war commissions upon smuggled goods. This sounds absurd, but his get-up seemed somehow to suggest the idea. Then I went below. Dawson always kept away from me whenever Hagan might have seen us together."

The passage across to Holland was free from incident; there was no sign that we were at war, and Continental traffic was being carried serenely on, within easy striking distance of the German submarine base at Zeebrugge. The steamer had drawn in to the Hook beside the train, and Hagan was approaching the gangway, suit-case in hand. The man was on the edge of safety; once upon Dutch soil, Dawson could not have laid hands upon him. He would have been a neutral citizen in a neutral country, and no English warrant would run against him. But between Hagan and the gangway suddenly interposed the tall form of the ship's captain; instantly the man was ringed about by officers, and before he could say a word or move a hand he was gripped hard and led across the deck to the steamer's chart-house. Therein sat Dawson, the real, undisguised Dawson, and beside him sat Richard Cary. Hagan's face, which two minutes earlier had been glowing with triumph and with the anticipation of German gold beyond the dreams of avarice, went white as chalk. He staggered and gasped as one stabbed to the heart, and dropped into a chair. His suit-case fell from his relaxed fingers to the floor.

"Give him a stiff brandy-and-soda," directed Dawson, almost kindly, and when the victim's colour had ebbed back a little from his overcharged heart, and he had drunk deep of the friendly cordial, the detective put him out of pain. The game of cat and mouse was over.

"It is all up, Hagan," said the detective gently. "Face the music and make the best of it, my poor friend. This is Mr. Richard Cary, and you have not for a moment been out of our sight since you left London for the North four days ago."

When I had completed the writing of his story I showed the MS. to Richard Cary, who was pleased to express a general approval. "Not at all bad, Copplestone," said he, "not at all bad. You have clothed my dry bones in real flesh and blood. But you have missed what to me is the outstanding feature of the whole affair, that which justifies to my mind the whole rather grubby business. Let me give you two dates. On May 25 two copies of my faked Notes were shepherded through to Holland and reached the Germans; on May 31 was fought the Battle of Jutland. Can the brief space between these dates have been merely an accident? I cannot believe it. No, I prefer to believe that in my humble way I induced the German Fleet to issue forth and to risk an action which, under more favourable conditions for us, would have resulted in their utter destruction. I may be wrong, but I am happy in retaining my faith."

"What became of Hagan?" I asked, for I wished to bring the narrative to a clean artistic finish.

"I am not sure," answered Cary, "though I gave evidence as ordered by the court-martial. But I rather think that I have here Hagan's epitaph." He took out his pocket-book, and drew forth a slip of paper upon which was gummed a brief newspaper cutting. This he handed to me, and I read as

follows:
"The War Office announces that a prisoner who was charged with espionage and recently tried by court-martial at the Westminster Guildhall was found guilty and sentenced to death. The sentence was duly confirmed and carried out yesterday morning."

* * * * *

Two months passed. Summer, what little there was of it, had gone, and my spirits were oppressed by the wet and fog and dirt of November in the North. I desired neither to write nor to read. My one overpowering longing was to go to sleep until the war was over and then to awake in a new world in which a decent civilised life would once more be possible.

In this unhappy mood I was seated before my study fire when a servant brought me a card. "A gentleman," said she, "wishes to see you. I said that you were engaged, but he insisted. He's a terrible man, sir."

I looked at the card, annoyed at being disturbed; but at the sight of it my torpor fell from me, for upon it was written the name of that detective officer whom in my story I had called William Dawson, and in the corner were the letters "C.I.D." (Criminal Investigation Department). I had become a criminal, and was about to be investigated!

CHAPTER II

AT CLOSE QUARTERS

Dawson entered, and we stood eyeing one another like two strange dogs. Neither spoke for some seconds, and then, recollecting that I was a host in the presence of a visitor, I extended a hand, offered a chair, and snapped open a cigarette case. Dawson seated himself and took a cigarette. I breathed more freely. He could not design my immediate arrest, or he would not have accepted of even so slight a hospitality. We sat upon opposite sides of the fire, Dawson saying nothing, but watching me in that unwinking cat-like way of his which I find so exasperating. Many times during my association with Dawson I have longed to spring upon him and beat his head against the floor—just to show that I am not a mouse. If his silence were intended to make me uncomfortable, I would give him evidence of my perfect composure.

"How did you find me out?" I asked calmly.

His start of surprise gratified me, and I saw a puzzled look come into his eyes. "Find out what?" he muttered.

"How did you find out that I wrote a story about you?"

"Oh, that?" He grinned. "That was not difficult, Mr.—er—Copplestone. I asked Mr.—er—Richard Cary for your real name and address, and he had to give them to me. I was considering whether I should prosecute both him and you."

"No doubt you bullied Cary," I said, "but you don't alarm me in the least. I had taken precautions, and you would have found your way barred if you had tried to touch either of us."

"It is possible," snapped Dawson. "I should like to lock up all you writing people—you are an infernal nuisance—but you seem to have a pull with the politicians."

We were getting on capitally: the first round was in my favour, and I saw another opportunity of showing my easy unconcern of his powers.

"Oh no, Mr.—er—William Dawson. You would not lock us up, even if all the authority in the State were vested in the soldiers and the police. For who would then write of your exploits and pour upon your heads the bright light of fame? The public knows nothing of Mr. ———" (I held up his card), "but quite a lot of people have heard of William Dawson."

"They have," assented he, with obvious satisfaction. "I sent a copy of the story to my Chief—just to put myself straight with him. I said that it was all quite unauthorised, and that I would have stopped it if I could."

"Oh no, you wouldn't. Don't talk humbug, Mr. William Dawson. During the past two months you have pranced along the streets with your head in the clouds. And in your own home Mrs. Dawson and the little Dawsons—if there are any—have worshipped you as a god. There is nothing so flattering as the sight of oneself in solid black print upon nice white paper. Confess, now. Are you not at this moment carrying a copy of that story of mine in your breast pocket next your heart, and don't you flourish it before your colleagues and rivals about six times, a day?"

Alone among mortal men I have seen a hardened detective blush.

"Throw away that cigarette," said I, "and take a cigar." I felt generous.

Our relations were now established upon a basis satisfactory to me. I had no inkling of the purpose of this visit, but he had lost the advantage of mysterious attack. He had revealed human weakness and had ceased for the moment to dominate me as a terrible engine of the law. But I had heard too much of Dawson from Cary to be under any illusion. He could be chaffed, even made ridiculous, without much difficulty, but no one, however adroit, could divert him by an inch from his professional purpose. He could joke with a victim and drink his health and then walk him off, arm in arm, to the gallows.

"Now, Mr. Dawson," said I. "Perhaps you will tell me to what happy circumstance I owe the honour of this visit?"

He had been chuckling over certain rich details in the Hagan chase—with an eye, no doubt, to future enlarged editions—but these words of mine pulled him up short. Instantly he became grave, drew some papers from his pocket, and addressed himself to business.

"I have come to you, Mr. Copplestone, as I did to your friend Mr. Cary, for information and assistance, and I have been advised by those who know you here to be perfectly frank. You are not at present an object of suspicion to the local police, who assure me, that though you are known to have access to much secret information, yet that you have never made any wrongful use of it. You have, moreover, been of great assistance on many occasions both to the military and naval authorities. Therefore, though my instinct would be to lock you up most securely, I am told that I mustn't do it."

"You are very frank," said I. "But I bear no malice. Ask me what you please, and I will do my best to answer fully."

"I ought to warn you," said he, with obvious reluctance, "that anything which you say may, at some future time, be used in evidence against you."

"I will take the risk, Mr. Dawson," cried I, laughing. "You have done your duty in warning me, and you are so plainly hopeful that I shall incriminate myself that it would be cruel to disappoint you. Let us get on with the inquisition."

"You are aware, Mr. Copplestone, that a most important part of my work consists in stopping the channels through which information of what is going on in our shipyards and munition shops may get through to the enemy. We can't prevent his agents from getting information—that is always possible to those with unlimited command of money, for there are always swine among workmen, and among higher folk than workmen, who can be bought. You may take it as certain that little of importance is done or projected in this country of which enemy agents do not know. But their difficulty is to get it through to their paymasters, within the limit of time during which the information is useful. There are scores of possible channels, and it is up to us to watch them all. You have already shown some grasp of our methods, which in a sentence may be described as unsleeping vigilance. Once we know the identity of an enemy agent, he ceases to be of any use to the enemy, but becomes of the greatest value to us. Our motto is: Ab hoste doceri." He pronounced the infinitive verb as if it rhymed with glossary.

"You are quite a scholar, Mr. Dawson," remarked I politely.

"Yes," said he, simply. "I had a good schooling. I need not go into details," he went on, "of how we watch the correspondence of suspected persons, but you may be interested to learn that during the three weeks which I have passed in your city all your private letters have been through my hands."

"The devil they have," I cried angrily. "You exceed your powers. This is really intolerable."

"Oh, you need not worry," replied Dawson serenely. "Your letters were quite innocent. I am gratified to learn that your two sons in the Service are happy and doing well, and that you contemplate the publication of another book."

It was impossible not to laugh at the man's effrontery, though I felt exasperated at his inquisitiveness. After all, there are things in private letters which one does not wish a stranger, and a police officer, to read.

"And how long is this outrage to continue?" I asked crossly.

"That depends upon you. As soon as I am satisfied that you are as trustworthy as the local police and other authorities believe you to be, your correspondence will pass untouched. It is of no use for you to fume or try to kick up a fuss in London. Scotland Yard would open the Home Secretary's letters if it had any cause to feel doubtful of him."

"You cannot feel much suspicion of me or you would not tell me what you have been doing."

"You might have thought of that at once," said Dawson derisively.

I shook myself and conceded the round to Dawson.

"It has been plain to us for a long time that the food parcels despatched by relatives and 'god-mothers' of British prisoners in Germany were a possible source of danger, and at last it has been decided to stop them and to keep the despatch of food in the hands of official organisations. Since there are now some 30,000 of military prisoners, in addition to interned civilians at Ruhleben, the number and complexity of the parcels have made it most difficult for a thorough examination to be kept up. We have done our utmost, but have been conscious that there has existed in them a channel through which have passed communications from enemy agents to enemy employers."

"I can see the possibility, but a practical method of communication looks difficult. How was it done?"

"In the most absurdly simple way. Real ingenuity is always simple. I will give you an example. An English prisoner in Germany has, we will suppose, parents in Newcastle, by whom food has been sent out regularly. He dies in captivity, and in due course his relatives are notified through the International Headquarters of the Red Cross in Geneva. He is crossed off the Newcastle lists, and his parents, of course, stop sending parcels. Now suppose that some one in Birmingham begins to send parcels addressed to this lately deceased prisoner, his name, unless Birmingham is very vigilant, will get upon the lists there as that of a new live prisoner. The parcels addressed to this name will go straight into the hands of the German Secret Service, and a channel of communication will have been opened up between some one in Birmingham and the enemy in Germany. Prisoners are frequently dying, new prisoners are frequently being taken. Under a haphazard system of individual parcels, despatched from all over the British Isles, it has been practically impossible to keep track of all the changes. For this, and other good reasons, we have had to make a clean sweep and to take over the feeding of British prisoners by means of a regular organisation which can ensure that nothing is sent with the food which will be of any assistance to the enemy."

"That is a good job done," I observed. "Have you evidence that what is possible has in fact been done?"

"We have," said Dawson. "Not many cases, perhaps, but sufficient to show the existence of a very real danger. It is, indeed, one particular instance of direct communication which has brought me to you to-day. Orders were given not long since that all new cases, that is, all parcels addressed to prisoners whose names were new to local lists, should be opened and carefully examined. Some six or seven weeks ago parcels began to be sent from this city addressed to a lieutenant in the Northumberland Fusiliers. There was nothing remarkable in that, for though we are some distance here from Northumberland, young officers are gazetted to regiments which need them irrespective of the part of the country to which the officers themselves belong. In accordance with the new orders all the parcels for this lieutenant—which usually consisted of bread, chocolate, and tins of sardines—were examined. The bread was cut up, the chocolate broken to pieces, and the tins opened. If the parcel contained nothing contraband, fresh supplies of bread, chocolate and sardines to take the place of those destroyed in examination were put in, and the parcel forwarded. For the first two weeks nothing was found, but in the third parcel, buried in one of the loaves, was discovered a cutting from an evening newspaper which at first sight seemed quite innocent. But a microscopic search revealed tiny needle pricks in certain words, and the words, thus indicated, read when taken by themselves the sentence, 'Important naval news follows.' At this stage I was sent for. My first step was to inquire very closely into the antecedents of this lieutenant of Northumberland Fusiliers. I found that his friends lived at Morpeth, that he had been taken prisoner during the Loos advance of September 1915, and that he had died about a year later of typhoid fever in a German camp. His friends, as soon as they had been informed, of the death, had stopped sending parcels of food out to him. They were not told the object of the inquiries. It would have caused them needless pain. It was bad enough that their only son had died far from home in a filthy German prison."

Dawson's rather metallic voice became almost sympathetic, and I was pleased to observe that his harsh profession had not destroyed in him all human feeling.

"After this you may suppose that the parcels addressed to our poor friend the late lieutenant were very eagerly looked for. The alleged sender, whose name and residence were written upon the labels, was found not to exist. Both name and address were false. It was a hot scent, and I was delighted, after a week of waiting, to see another parcel come in. This would, in all probability, contain the 'important naval news,' and I took its examination upon myself. I reduced the bread and the chocolate to powder without finding anything."

"Excuse me," I cried, intensely interested, "but how could one conceal a paper in bread or in chocolate without leaving external traces?"

"There is no difficulty. The loaves were of the kind which have soft ends. One cuts a deep slit, inserts the paper, closes up the cut with a little fresh dough, and rebakes the loaf for a short time, till all signs of the cut have disappeared. The chocolate was in eggs, not in bars. The oval lumps can be cut open, scooped out, a paper put in, and the two halves joined up and the cut concealed by means of a strong mixture of chocolate paste and white of egg. When thoroughly dried in a warm place, chocolate thus treated will stand very close scrutiny. I did not trouble to look for signs of disturbance in either loaves or eggs; it was quicker and easier to break them up. I then addressed my attention to the sardine tins, which from the first had seemed the most likely hiding-places. A very moderately skilled mechanic can unsolder a tin, empty out the fish and oil, put in what he pleases in place, weight judiciously, and then refasten with fresh solder. I opened all the tins, found that all except one had been undisturbed, but that one was a blissful reward for all my trouble, for in it was a tightly packed mass of glazier's putty, soft and heavy, and at the bottom the carefully folded paper which I have now the honour of showing to you."

Dawson handed me a stiff piece of paper, slimy to the touch and smelling strongly of white lead. Upon it were two neatly made drawings and some lines of words and figures. "It is just what I should have expected," said I.

"You recognise it?"

"Of course," said I. "We have here a deck plan showing the disposition of guns, and a section plan showing arrangement of armour, of one of the big new ships which has been completed for the Grand Fleet. Below we have the number and calibre of the guns, the thickness and extent of the armour, the length, breadth, and depth of the vessel, her tonnage, her horse power, and her estimated speed. Everything is correct except the speed, which I happen to know is considerably greater than the figure set down."

"You have not by any chance seen that paper before?" asked Dawson, with rather a forced air of indifference.

"This? No. Why?"

"I was curious, that's all." He looked at me with a queer, quizzical expression, and then laughed softly. "You will understand my question directly, but for the moment let us get on. What sort of person should you say made those drawings and wrote that description?"

I am no Sherlock Holmes; but any one who has had some acquaintance with engineers and their handiwork can recognise the professional touch.

"These drawings are the work of a trained draughtsman, and the writing is that of a draughtsman. One can tell by the neatness and the technique of the shading."

"Right first time," said Dawson approvingly. "At present I have that draughtsman comfortably locked up; we picked him out of the drawing office at ——" he named a famous yard in which had been built one of the ships of the class illustrated upon the paper in my hands.

"Poor devil," I said. "What is the cause—drink, women, or the pressure of high prices and a large family?"

"None of them. His employers give him the best of characters, he gets good pay, is a man over military age, and has, so far as the police can learn, no special embarrassments. He owns his house, and has two or three hundred pounds in the War Loan."

"Then why in the name of wonder has the *schweinehund* sold his country?"

"He declares that he never received a penny for supplying the information upon that paper, and we have no evidence of any outside payments to him. He did not attempt to conceal his handwriting, and when I made inquiries of his firm, he owned up at once that the paper was his work. He said that for years past he had given particulars of ships under construction to the same parties as on this occasion. He admitted that to do so was contrary to regulations, especially in wartime, but thought that under the circumstances he was doing no harm. I am not exactly a credulous person, and I have heard some tall stories in my time, but for once I am inclined to believe that the man is speaking the truth. I believe that he received no money, and was acting throughout in good faith."

"I am more and more puzzled. What in the world can the circumstances be which could induce an experienced middle-aged man, employed in highly confidential work in a great shipyard, not only to break faith and lose his job, but to stick his neck into a rope and his feet on the drop of a gallows. Reveal the mystery."

"You are sure that you have never seen that paper before?" asked Dawson again, this time slowly and deliberately.

"Of course not!" I said. "How could I?"

"That is just what I have to find out," said Dawson. He stopped, took out a knife, prodded his nearly smoked cigar, puffed once or twice hard to restore the draught, and spoke. "That is what interests me just now. For, you see, this very indiscreet and reprehensible swinehound of a draughtsman, who is at present in my lockup, declares that he was without suspicion of serious wrong-doing, because —because— the particulars of the new battleship upon that paper were supplied to YOU."

CHAPTER III

AN INQUISITION

Perhaps I ought to have seen it coming, but I didn't. For a moment, as a washerwoman might say, I was struck all of a heap. Then the delicious thought that I—by nature a vagabond, though by decree of the High Gods the father of a family and a Justice of the Peace—had to face the charge of being a German spy shook my soul with ribald laughter. I had been dull and torpid before the arrival of Dawson; he had awakened me into joyous life. I arose, filled and lighted a large calabash pipe, and passed a box of cigars to the detective. "Throw that stump away and take another," said I. "I owe you more than a cigar or two." He stared at me, took what I offered, and his face relaxed into a grin. "It is pleasant to see that you are a man of humour, Mr. Dawson," I observed, when we were again seated comfortably on opposite sides of the fire. "In my day I have played many parts, but I cannot somehow recall the incident of unsoldering a sardine tin, inserting a paper packed in a mess of putty, soldering it up, and despatching the incriminating product within a parcel addressed to a late lieutenant of Northumberland Fusiliers. I am not denying the charge; the whole affair is too delightful to be cut short. Let us spin it out delicately like children over plates of sweet pudding."

"You are a queer customer, Mr. Copplestone. I confess that the whole business puzzles me, though you and your friends here seem to find it devilish amusing. When I told the Chief Constable, the manager of the shipyard, and the Admiral Superintendent of Naval Work that you were the guilty party, they all roared. For some reason the Admiral and the shipyard manager kept winking at one another and gurgling till I thought they would have choked. What *is* the joke?"

"If you are good, Dawson, I will tell you some day. This is November, and the *Rampagious*—the ship described on your paper—left for Portsmouth in August. In July—" I broke off hurriedly, lest I should tell my visitor too much. "It has taken our friend who put the paper in the sardine tin three months to find out details of her. I could have done better than that, Dawson."

"That is just what the Admiral said, though he wouldn't explain why."

"The truth is, Dawson, that the Admiral and I both come from Devon, the land of pirates, smugglers, and buccaneers. We are law breakers by instinct and family tradition. When we get an officer of the law on toast, we like to make the most of him. It is a playful little way of ours which I am sure you will understand and pardon."

"You know, of course, that I am justified in arresting you. I have a warrant and handcuffs in my pocket."

"Admirable man!" I cried, with enthusiasm. "You are, Dawson, the perfect detective. As a criminal I should be mightily afraid of you. But, as in my buttonhole I always wear the white flower which proclaims to the world my blameless life, I am thoroughly enjoying this visit and our cosy chat beside the fire. Shall I telephone to my office and say that I shall be unavoidably detained from duty for an indefinite time? 'Detained' would be the strict truth and the *mot juste*. If you would kindly lock me up, say, for three years or the duration of the war I should be your debtor. I have often thought that a prison, provided that one were allowed unlimited paper and the use of a typewriter, would be the most charming of holidays—a perfect rest cure. There are three books in my head which I should like to write. Arrest me, Dawson, I implore you! Put on the handcuffs—I have never been handcuffed—ring up a taxi, and let us be off to jail. You will, I hope, do me the honour of lunching with me first and meeting my wife. She will be immensely gratified to be quit of me. It cannot often have happened in your lurid career, Dawson, to be welcomed with genuine enthusiasm."

"Why did that man say that he prepared the description of the ship for you?"

"That is what we are going to find out, and I will help you all I can. My reputation is like the bloom upon the peach—touch it, and it is gone for ever. There is a faint glimmer of the truth at the back of my mind which may become a clear light. Did he say that he had given it to me personally, into my own hand?"

"No. He said that he was approached by a man whom he had known off and on for years, a man who was employed by you in connection with shipyard inquiries. He was informed that this man was still employed by you for the same purpose now as in the past."

"Your case against me is thinning out, Dawson. At its best it is second-hand; at its worst, the mere conjecture of a rather careless draughtsman. I have two things to do: first to find out the real seducer, who is probably also the despatcher of the parcels to the late lieutenant of Northumberland Fusiliers, and second, to save if I can this poor fool of a shipyard draughtsman from punishment for his folly. I don't doubt that he honestly thought he was dealing with me."

"He will have to be punished. The Admiral will insist upon that."

"We must make the punishment as light as we can. You shall help me with all the discretionary authority with which you are equipped. I can see, Dawson, from the tactful skill with which you have dealt with me that discretion is among your most distinguished characteristics. If you had been a stupid, bull-headed policeman, you would have been up against pretty serious trouble."

"That was quite my own view," replied Dawson drily.

"Who is the man described by our erring draughtsman?"

"He won't say. We have put on every allowable method of pressure, and some that are not in ordinary times permitted. We have had over this spy hunt business to shed most of our tender English regard for suspected persons, and to adopt the French system of fishing inquiries. In France the police try to make a man incriminate himself; in England we try our hardest to prevent him. That may be very right and just in peace time against ordinary law breakers; but war is war, and spies are too dangerous to be treated tenderly. We have cross-examined the man, and bully-ragged him, but he won't give up the name of his accomplice. It may be a relation. One thing seems sure. The man is, or was, a member of your staff, engaged in shipyard inquiries. Can you give me a list of the men who are or have been on this sort of work during the past few years?"

"I will get it for you. But please use it carefully. My present men are precious jewels, the few left to me by zealous military authorities. What I must look for is some one over military age who has left me or been dismissed—probably dismissed. When a British subject, of decent education and once respectable surroundings, gets into the hands of German agents, you may be certain of one thing, Dawson, that he has become a rotter through drink."

"That's it," cried Dawson. "You have hit it. Crime and drink are twin brothers as no one knows better than the police. Look out for the name and address of a man dismissed for drunkenness and we shall have our bird."

"The name I can no doubt give you, but not the address."

"Give us any address where he lived, even if it were ten years ago, and we will track him down in three days. That is just routine police work."

"I never presume to teach an expert his business—and you, Dawson, are a super-expert, a director-general of those of common qualities—but would it not be well to warn all the Post Offices, so that when another parcel is brought in addressed to the lieutenant the bearer may be arrested?"

Dawson sniffed. "Police work; common police work. It was done at once for this city and fifty miles round. No parcel was put in last week. The warning has since been extended to the whole of the United Kingdom. We may get our man this week, or at least a messenger of his, but no news has yet come to me. I will lunch with you, as you so kindly suggest, and afterwards I want you to come with me to see the draughtsman in the lockup. You may be able to shake his confounded obstinacy. Run the pathetic stunt. Say if he keeps silent that you will be arrested, your home broken up, your family driven into the workhouse, and you yourself probably shot. Pitch it strong and rich. He is a bit of a softy from the look of him. That tender-hearted lot are always the most obstinate when asked to give away their pals."

"Do you know, Dawson," I said, as he went upstairs with me to have a lick and a polish, as he put it—"I am inclined to agree with Cary that you are rather an inhuman beast."

My wife, with whom I could exchange no more than a dozen words and a wink or two, gripped the situation and played up to it in the fashion which compels the admiration and terror of mere men. Do they humbug us, their husbands, as they do the rest of the world on our behalf? She met Dawson as if he were an old family friend, heaped hospitality upon him, and chaffed him blandly as if to entertain a police officer with a warrant and handcuffs in his pocket were the best joke in the world. "My husband, Mr. Dawson, needs a holiday very badly, but won't take one. He thinks that the war cannot be pursued successfully unless he looks after it himself. If you would carry him off and keep him quiet for a bit, I should be deeply grateful." She then fell into a discussion with Dawson of the most conveniently situated prisons. Mrs. Copplestone dismissed

Dartmoor and Portland as too bleakly situated, but was pleased to approve of Parkhurst in the Isle of Wight—which I rather fancy is a House of Detention for women. She insisted that the climate of the Island was suited to my health, and wrung a promise from Dawson that I should, if possible, be interned there. Dawson's manners and conversation surprised me. His homespun origin was evident, yet he had developed an easy social style which was neither familiar nor aggressive. We were in his eyes eccentrics, possibly what he would call among his friends "a bit off," and he bore himself towards us accordingly. My small daughter, Jane, to whom he had been presented as a colonel of police—little Jane is deeply versed in military ranks—took to him at once, and his manner towards her confirmed my impression that some vestiges of humanity may still be discovered in him by the patient searcher. She insisted upon sitting next to him and in holding his hand when it was not employed in conveying food to his mouth. She was startled at first by the discussion upon the prisons most suitable for me, but quickly became reconciled to the idea of a temporary separation.

"Colonel Dawson," she asked. "When daddy is in prison, may I come and see him sometimes. Mother and me?" Dawson gripped his hair—we were the maddest crew!—and replied. "Of course you shall, Miss Jane, as often as you like."

"Thank you, Colonel Dawson; you are a nice man. I love you. Now show me the handcuffs in your pocket."

For the second time that day poor Dawson blushed. He must have regretted many times that he had mentioned to me those unfortunate darbies. Now amid much laughter he was compelled to draw forth a pretty shining pair of steel wristlets and permit Jane to put them on. They were much too large for her; she could slip them on and off without unlocking; but as toys they were a delight. "I shouldn't mind being a prisoner," she declared, "if dear Colonel Dawson took me up."

We were sitting upon the fire-guard after luncheon, dallying over our coffee, when Jane demanded to be shown a real arrest. "Show me how you take up a great big man like Daddy."

Then came a surprise, which for a moment had so much in it of bitter realism that it drove the blood from my wife's cheeks. I could not follow Dawson's movements; his hands flickered like those of a conjurer, there came a sharp click, and the handcuffs were upon my wrists! I stared at them speechless, wondering how they got there, and, looking up, met the coldly triumphant eyes of the detective. I realised then exactly how the professional manhunter glares at the prey into whom, after many days, he has set his claws. My wife gasped and clutched at my elbow, little Jane screamed, and for a few seconds even I thought that the game had been played and that serious business was about to begin. Dawson gave us a few seconds of apprehension, and then laughed grimly. From his waistcoat pocket he drew a key, and the fetters were removed almost as quickly as they had been clapped on. "Tit for tat," said he. "You have had your fun with me. Fair play is a jewel."

Little Jane was the first to recover speech. "I knew that dear Colonel Dawson was only playing," she cried. "He only did it to please me. Thank you, Colonel, though you did frighten me just a weeny bit at first." And pulling him down towards her she kissed him heartily upon his prickly cheek. It was a queer scene.

The door bell rang loudly, and we were informed that a policeman stood without who was inquiring for Chief Inspector Dawson. "Show him in here," said I. The constable entered, and his manner of addressing my guest—that of a raw second lieutenant towards a general of division—shed a new light upon Dawson's pre-eminence in his Service. "A telegram for you, sir." Dawson seized it, was about to tear it open, remembered suddenly his hostess, and bowed towards her. "Have I your permission, madam?" he asked. She smiled and nodded; I turned away to conceal a laugh. "Good," cried Dawson, poring over the message. "I think, Mr. Copplestone, that you had better telephone to your office and say that you are unavoidably detained."

"What—what is it?" cried my wife, who had again become white with sudden fear.

"Something which will occupy the attention of your husband and myself to the exclusion of all other duties. This telegram informs me that a parcel has been handed in at Carlisle and the bearer arrested."

"Excellent!" I cried. "My time is at your disposal, Dawson. We shall now get full light."

He sat down and scribbled a reply wire directing the parcel and its bearer to be brought to him with all speed. "They should arrive in two or three hours," said he, "and in the meantime we will tackle the draughtsman who made that plan of the battleship. Good-bye Mrs. Copplestone, and thank you very much for your hospitality. Your husband goes with me." My wife shook hands with Dawson, and politely saw him off the premises. She has said little to me since about his visit, but I do not think that she wishes ever to meet with him again. Little Jane, who kissed him once more at parting, is still attached to the memory of her colonel.

* * * * *

Dawson led me to the private office at the Central Police Station, which was his temporary headquarters, and sent for the dossier of the locked up draughtsman. "I have here full particulars of him," said he, "and a verbatim note of my examination." I examined the photograph attached, which represented a bearded citizen of harmless aspect; over his features had spread a scared, puzzled look, with a suggestion in it of pathetic appeal. He looked like a human rabbit caught in an unexpected and uncomprehended trap. It was a police photograph. Then I began to read the dossier, but got no farther than the first paragraph. In it was set out the man's name, those of his wife and children, his employment, record of service, and so on. What arrested my researches was the maiden name of the wife, which, in accordance with the northern custom, had been entered as a part of her legal description. The name awoke in me a recollection of a painful incident within my experience. I saw before me the puffed, degraded face of one to whom I had given chance after chance of redeeming himself from thraldom to the whisky bottle, one who had promised again and again to amend his ways. At last, wearied, I had cast him out. He had been looking after an important shipbuilding district, had conspicuous ability and knowledge, the support of a faithful wife. But nothing availed to save him from himself. "Give me five minutes alone with your prisoner," I said to Dawson, "and I will give you the spy you seek."

I had asked for five minutes, but two were sufficient for my purpose. The draughtsman had been obstinate with Dawson, seeking loyally to shield his wretched brother-in-law, but when he found that I had the missing thread in my hands, he gave in at once. "What relation is —— to your wife?" I asked. He had risen at my entrance, but the question went through him like a bullet; his pale face flushed, he staggered pitifully, and, sitting down, buried his face in his hands. "You may tell the truth now," I said gently. "We can easily find out what we must know, but the information will come better from you."

"He is my wife's brother," murmured the man.

"You knew that he was no longer in my service?"

"Yes, I knew."

I might fairly have asked why he had used my name, but refrained. One can readily pardon the lapses of an honest man, terrified at finding himself in the coils of the police, clinging to the good name of his wife and her family, clutching at any device to throw the sleuth-hounds of the law off the real scent. He had given his brother-in-law forbidden information from a loyal desire to help him and with no knowledge of the base use to which it would be put. When detected, he had sought at any cost to shield him.

"I will do my best to help you," I said.

His head drooped down till it rested upon his bent arms, and he groaned and panted under the torture of tears. His was not the stuff of which criminals are made.

I found Dawson's chuckling joy rather repulsive. I felt that, being successful, he might at least have had the decency to dissemble his satisfaction. He might also have given me some credit for the rapid clearing up of the problem in detection. But he took the whole thing to himself, and gloated like a child over his own cleverness. I neither obtained from him thanks for my assistance nor apologies for his suspicions. It was Dawson, Dawson, all the time. Yet I found his egotism and unrelieved vanity extraordinarily interesting. As we sat together in his room waiting for the Carlisle train to come in he discoursed freely to me of his triumphs in detection, his wide-spread system of spying upon spies, his long delayed "sport" with some, and his ruthless rapid trapping of others. Men are never so interesting as when they talk shop, and as a talker of shop Dawson was sublime.

"If," said Dawson, as the time approached for the closing scene, "our much-wanted friend has himself handed in the parcel at Carlisle—he would be afraid to trust an accomplice—our job will be done. If not, I will pull a drag net through this place which will bring him up within a day or two. What a fool the man is to think that he could escape the eye of Bill Dawson."

A policeman entered, laid a packet upon the table before us, and announced that the prisoner had been placed in cell No. 2. Dawson sprang up. "We will have a look at him through the peephole, and if it is our man—" One glance was enough. Before me I saw him whom I had expected to see. He and his cargo of whisky bottles had reached the last stage of their long journey; at one end had been peace, reasonable prosperity, and a happy home; at the other was, perhaps, a rope or a bullet.

Dawson began once more to descant upon his own astuteness, but I was too sick at heart to listen. I remembered only the visit years before which that man's wife had paid to me. "Will you not open the parcel?" I interposed. He fell upon it, exposed its contents of bread, chocolate, and sardine tins, and called for a can opener. He shook the tins one by one beside his ear, and then, selecting that which gave out no "flop" of oil, stripped it open, plunged his fingers inside, and pulled forth a clammy mess of putty and sawdust. In a moment he had come upon a paper which after reading he handed to me. It bore the words in English, "Informant arrested: dare not send more."

"What a fool!" cried Dawson. "As if the evidence against him were not sufficient already he must give us this."

"You will let that poor devil of a draughtsman down easily?" I murmured.

"We want him as a witness," replied Dawson. "Tit for tat. If he helps us, we will help him. And now we will cut along to the Admiral. He is eager for news."

We broke in upon the Admiral in his office near the shipyards, and he greeted me with cheerful badinage. "So you are in the hands of the police at last, Copplestone. I always told you what would be the end of your naval inquisitiveness."

Dawson told his story, and the naval officer's keen kindly face grew stern and hard. "Germans I can respect," said he, "even those that pretend to be our friends. But one of our own folk—to sell us like this—ugh! Take the vermin away; Dawson, and stamp upon it."

We stood talking for a few moments, and then Dawson broke in with a question. "I have never understood, Admiral, why you were so very confident that Mr. Copplestone here had no hand in this business. The case against him looked pretty ugly, yet you laughed at it all the time. Why were you so sure?"

The Admiral surveyed Dawson as if he were some strange creature from an unknown world. "Mr. Copplestone is a friend of mine," said he drily.

"Very likely," snapped the detective. "But is a man a white angel because he has the honour to be your friend?"

"A fair retort," commented the Admiral. It happens that I had other and better reasons. For in July I myself showed Mr. Copplestone over the new battleship *Rampagious*, and after our inspection we both lunched with the builders and discussed her design and armament in every detail. So as Mr. Copplestone knew all about her in July, he was not likely to suborn a draughtsman in November. See?"

"You should have told me this before. It was your duty."

"My good Dawson," said the Admiral gently, "you are an excellent officer of police, but even you have a few things yet to learn. I had in my mind to give you a lesson, especially as I owed you some punishment for your impertinence in opening my friend Copplestone's private letters. You have had the lesson; profit by it."

Dawson flushed angrily. "Punishment! Impertinence! This to me!"

"Yes," returned the Admiral stiffly, "beastly impertinence."

CHAPTER IV

SABOTAGE

Dawson showed no malice towards the Admiral or myself for our treatment of him. I do not think that he felt any; he was too fully occupied in collecting the spoils of victory to trouble his head about what a Scribbler or a Salt Horse might think of him. He gathered to himself every scrap of credit which the affair could be induced to yield, and received—I admit quite deservedly—the most handsome encomiums from his superiors in office. During the two weeks he passed in my city after the capture—weeks occupied in tracing out the threads connecting his wretch of a prisoner with the German agents upon what Dawson called his "little list"—he paid several visits both to my house and my office. His happiness demanded that he should read to me the many letters which poured in from high officials of the C.I.D., from the Chief Commissioner, and on one day—a day of days in the chronicles of Dawson—from the Home Secretary himself. To me it seemed that all these astute potentates knew their Dawson very thoroughly, and lubricated, as it were, with judicious flattery the machinery of his energies. I could not but admire Dawson's truly royal faculty for absorbing butter. The stomachs of most men, really good at their business, would have revolted at the diet which his superiors shovelled into Dawson, but he visibly expanded and blossomed. Yes, Scotland Yard knew its Dawson, and exactly how to stimulate the best that was in him. He never bored me; I enjoyed him too thoroughly.

One day in my club I chanced upon the Admiral.

"Have you met our friend Dawson lately?" I asked.

"Met him?" shouted he, with a roar of laughter. "Met him? He is in my office every day—he almost lives with me; goodness knows when he does his work. He has a pocket full of letters which he has read to me till I know them by heart. If I did not know that he was a first-class man I should set him down as a colossal ass. Yet, I rather wish that the Admiralty would sometimes write to me as the severe but very human Scotland Yard does to Dawson."

"Does he ever come to you in disguise?" I asked.

"Not that I know of. I see vast numbers of people; some of them may be Dawson in his various incarnations, but he has not given himself away."

Then I explained to my naval friend my own experience. "He tried," I said, "to play the disguise game on me, and clean bowled me the first time. While he was laughing over my discomfiture I studied his face more closely than a lover does that of his mistress. I tried to penetrate his methods. He never wears a wig or false hair; he is too wise for that folly. Yet he seems able to change his hair from light to dark, to make it lank or curly, short or long. He does it; how I don't know. He alters the shape of his nose, his cheeks, and his chin. I suppose that he pads them out with little rubber insets. He alters his voice, and his figure, and even his height. He can be stiff and upright like a drilled soldier, or loose-jointed and shambling like a tramp. He is a finished artist, and employs the very simplest means. He could, I truly believe, deceive his wife or his mother, but he will never again deceive me. I am not a specially observant man; still one can make a shot at most things when driven to it, and I object to being the subject of Dawson's ribaldry. If you will take my tip, you will be able to spot him as readily as I do now."

"Good. I should love to score off Dawson. He is an aggravating beast."

"Study his ears," said I. "He cannot alter their chief characters. The lobes of his ears are not loose, like yours or mine or those of most men and women; his are attached to the back of his cheekbones. My mother had lobes like those, so had the real Roger Tichborne; I noticed Dawson's at once. Also at the top fold of his ears he has rather a pronounced blob of flesh. This blob, more prominent in some men than in others, is, I believe, a surviving relic of the sharp point which adorned the ears of our animal ancestors. Dawson's ancestor must have been a wolf or a bloodhound. Whenever now I have a strange caller who is not far too tall or far too short to be

Dawson, if a stranger stops me in the street to ask for a direction, if a porter at a station dashes up to help me with my bag, I go for his ears. If the lobes are attached to the cheekbones and there is a pronounced blob in the fold at the top, I address the man instantly as Dawson, however impossibly unlike Dawson he may be. I have spotted him twice now since he bowled me out, and he is frightfully savage—especially as I won't tell him how the trick is done. He says that it is my duty to tell him, and that he will compel me under some of his beloved Defence of the Realm Regulations. But the rack could not force me to give away my precious secret. Cherish it and use it. You will not tell, for you love to mystify the ruffian as much as I do."

"I will watch for his ears when he next calls, which, I expect, will be to-morrow. Thank you very much. I won't sneak."

"Remember that nothing else in the way of identification is of any use, for I doubt if either of us has ever seen the real, undisguised Dawson as he is known to God. We know a man whom we think is the genuine article—but is he? Cary's description of him is most unlike the man whom we see here. I expect that he has a different identity for every place which he visits. If he told me that at any moment he was wholly undisguised, I should be quite sure that he was lying. The man wallows in deception for the very sport of the thing. But he can't change his ears. Study them, and you will be safe."

Our club was the only place in which we could be sure that Dawson did not penetrate, though I should not have been surprised to learn that one or two of the waitresses were in his pay. Dawson is an ardent feminist; he says that as secret agents women beat men to a frazzle.

Shortly before Dawson left for his headquarters on the north-east coast he dropped in upon me. He had finished his researches, and revealed the results to me with immense satisfaction.

"I have fixed up Menteith," he began, "and know exactly how he came into communication with the German Secret Service." The contemptuous emphasis which he laid on the word "Secret" would have annoyed the Central Office at Potsdam. I have given the detected British spy the name of Menteith after that of the most famous traitor in Scottish history; if I called him, say, Campbell or Macdonald, nothing could save me from the righteous vengeance of the outraged Clans.

"It was all very simple," he went on, "like most things in my business when one gets to the bottom of them. He was seduced by a man whom the local police have had on their string for a long time, but who will now be put securely away. Menteith was a frequenter of a certain public house down the river, where he posed as an authority on the Navy, and hinted darkly at his stores of hidden information. Our German agent made friends with him, gave him small sums for drinks, and flattered his vanity. It is strange how easily some men are deceived by flattery. The agent got from Menteith one or two bits of news by pretending a disbelief in his sources of intelligence, and then, when the fool had committed himself, threatened to denounce him to the police unless he took service with him altogether. Money, of course, passed, but not very much. The Germans who employ spies so extensively pay them extraordinarily little. They treat them like scurvy dogs, for whom any old bone is good enough, and I'm not sure they are not right. They go on the principle that the white trash who will sell their country need only to be paid with kicks and coppers. Menteith swears that he did not receive more than four pounds for the plans and description of the *Rampagious*. Fancy selling one's country and risking one's neck for four measly pounds sterling! If he had got four thousand, I should have had some respect for him. His home is in a wretched state, and his wife—a pretty woman, though almost a skeleton, and a very nicely mannered, honest woman—says that her husband unexpectedly gave her four pounds a month ago. He had kept none of the blood money for drink! Curious, isn't it?"

"It shows that the man had some good in him. It shows that he was ashamed to use the money upon himself. We must do something for the poor wife, Dawson."

"She will easily get work, and she will be far better without her sot of a husband. She did not cry when I told her everything. 'I ought to have left him long ago,' she said, 'but I tried to save him. Thank God we have no children,' That seemed to be her most insistent thought, for she repeated it over and over again. 'Thank God that we have no children.'"

"I hope that you were gentle with her, Dawson," said I, deeply moved. Long ago the wife had come to me and pleaded for her husband. She had shed no tear; she had admitted the justice, the necessity, of my sentence. "Can you not give him another chance?" she had asked. "No," I had answered sadly. "He has exhausted all the chances." When she had risen to go and I had pressed her hand, she had said, still dry-eyed, "You are right, sir, it is no use, no use at all. Thank God that we have no children."

"I hope that you were gentle with her, Dawson," I repeated.

He astonished me by the suddenness of his explosion. "Damn," roared he—"damn and blast! Do you think that I am a brute. Gentle! It was as much as I could do not to kiss the woman, as your little daughter kissed me, and to promise that I would get her husband off somehow. But I should not be a friend to her if I tried to save that man."

So Dawson had soft spots in his armour of callousness, and little Jane's instinct was far surer than mine. She had taken to him at sight. When I tried to get from her why, why he had so marked an attraction for her, her replies baffled me more than the central fact. "I love Colonel Dawson. He is a nice man. He has a little girl like me. Her name is Clara. Her birthday is next month. I shall save up my pocket money and send Clara a present. I like Colonel Dawson better even than dear Bailey." I tore my hair, for "Bailey" is a wholly imaginary friend of little Jane, whom I invented one evening at her bedside and who has grown gradually into a personage of clearly defined attributes—like the "Putois" of Anatole France. Dawson and "Bailey"; they are both "nice men" and little Jane's friends; she is sure of them, and I expect that she is right. Children always are right.

Dawson, after his outburst, glowered at me for a moment and then laughed. "I am a man," said he, "though you may not think it, and I have my weaknesses. But I never give way to them when they interfere with business. Menteith is in my grip, and he won't get out of it. But he is a poor creature. He handed over the description of the *Rampagious*, saw it hidden in the sardine tin, and was ordered to take the food parcel to the Post Office. The German agent who used him had no notion of risking his own skin. Then followed the discovery and the arrest of the draughtsman who had drawn the plan. Those who had seduced Menteith forbade him to come near them. They slipped away into hiding—which profited them little since all of them were on our string—after threatening Menteith that he would be murdered if he gave himself up to the police, as in his terror he seemed to want to do. When nothing happened for two weeks, the vermin came out of their holes, made up the last parcel, and forced Menteith to go to Carlisle in order to post it. All through he has been the most abject of tools, and received nothing except the four pounds and various small sums spent in drinks."

"You have the principal all right?"

"Yes, I have him tight. The others associated with him I shall leave free; they will be most useful in future. They don't know that we know them; when they do know, their number will go up, for they will be then of no further use to us. It is a beautiful system, Mr. Copplestone, and you have had the unusual privilege of seeing it at work."

"What will your prisoners get by way of punishment?"

"I am not sure, but I can guess pretty closely. The principal will go out suddenly early some morning. He is a Jew of uncertain Central European origin, Pole or Czech, a natural born British subject, a shining light of a local anti-German society, an 'indispensable' in his job and exempted from military service. He will give no more trouble. Menteith will spend anything from seven to ten years in p.s., learn to do without his daily whisky bottle, and possibly come out a decent citizen. The draughtsman, I expect, will be let off with eighteen months of the Jug. We are just, but not harsh. My birds don't interest me much once they have been caught; it is the catching that I enjoy. Down in the south, where I have a home of my own—which I haven't seen during the past year except occasionally for an hour or two—I used to grow big show chrysanthemums. All through the processes of rooting the cuttings, repotting, taking the buds, feeding up the plants, I never could endure any one to touch them. But once the flowers were fully developed, my wife could cut them as much as she pleased and fill the house with them. My job was done when I had got the flowers perfect. It is just the same with my business. I cultivate the little dears I am after, and hate any one to interfere with me; I humour them and water them and feed them with opportunities till they are ripe, and then I stick out my hand and grab them. After that the law can do what it likes with them; they ain't my concern any more."

By this time it had become apparent even to my slow intelligence why Dawson told me so much about himself and his methods. He had formed the central figure in a real story in print, and the glory of it possessed him. He had tasted of the rich sweet wine of fame, and he thirsted for more of the same vintage. He never in so many words asked me to write this book, but his eagerness to play Dr. Johnson to my Boswell appeared in all our relations. He was communicative far beyond the limits of official discretion. If I now disclosed half, or a quarter, of what he told me of the inner working of the Secret Service, Scotland Yard, which admires and loves him, would cast him out, lock him up securely in gaol, and prepare for me a safe harbourage in a contiguous cell. So for both our sakes I must be very, very careful.

"You have been most helpful to me," he said handsomely at parting, "and if anything good turns up on the North-East coast, I will let you know. Could you come if I sent for you?"

"I would contrive to manage it," said I.

Dawson went away, and the pressure of daily work and interests thrust him from my mind. For a month I heard nothing of him or of Cary, and then one morning came a letter and a telegram. The letter was from Richard Cary, and read as follows: "A queer thing has happened here. A cruiser which had come in for repair was due to go out this morning. She was ready for sea the night before, the officers and crew had all come back from short leave, and the working parties had cleared out. Then in the middle watch, when the torpedo lieutenant was testing the circuits, it was discovered that all the cables leading to the guns had been cut. Dawson has been called in, and bids me say that, if you can come down, now is the chance of your life. I will put you up."

The telegram was from Dawson himself. It ran: "They say I'm beaten. But I'm not. Come and see."

"The deuce," said I. "Sabotage! I am off."

CHAPTER V

BAFFLED

When at last I arrived at Cary's flat it was very late, and I was exceedingly tired and out of temper. A squadron of Zeppelins had been reported from the sea, the air-defence control at Newcastle had sent out the preliminary warning "F.M.W.," and the speed of my train had been reduced to about fifteen miles an hour. I had expected to get in to dinner, but it was eleven o'clock before I reached my destination. I had not even the satisfaction of seeing a raid, for the Zepps, made cautious by recent heavy losses, had turned back before crossing the line of the coast. Cary and his wife fell upon my neck, for we were old friends, condoled with me, fed me, and prescribed a tall glass of mulled port flavoured with cloves. My stern views upon the need for Prohibition in time of war became lamentably weakened.

By midnight I had recovered my philosophic outlook upon life, and Cary began to enlighten me upon the details of the grave problem which had brought me eagerly curious to his city.

"I expect that Dawson will drop in some time to-night," he said. "All hours are the same to him. I told him that you were on the way, and he wants to give you the latest news himself. He is dead set upon you, Copplestone. I can't imagine why."

"Am I then so very unattractive?" I inquired drily. "It seems to me that Dawson is a man of sound judgment."

"I confess that I do not understand why he lavishes so much attention upon you."

"Your remarks, Cary," I observed, "are deficient in tact. You might, at least, pretend to believe that my personal charm has won for me Dawson's affection. As a matter of fact, he cares not a straw for my *beaux yeux*; his motives are crudely selfish. He thinks that it is in my power to contribute to the greater glory of Dawson, and he cultivates me just as he would one of his show chrysanthemums. He has done me the honour to appoint me his biographer extraordinary."

"I am sure you are wrong," cried Cary. "He was most frightfully angry about that story of ours in *Cornhill*. He demanded from me your name and address, and swore that if I ever again disclosed to you official secrets he would proceed against me under the Defence of the Realm Act. He was a perfect terror, I can assure you."

"And yet he always carries that story about with him in his breast-pocket; he has summoned me here to see him at his work; and you have been commanded to tell me everything which you know! My dear Cary, do not be an ass. You are too simple a soul for this rather grubby world. In your eyes every politician is an ardent, disinterested patriot, and every soldier or sailor a knightly hero of romance. Human beings, Cary, are made in streaks, like bacon; we have our fat streaks and our lean ones; we can be big and bold, and also very small and mean. Your great man and your national hero can become very poor worms when, so to speak, they are off duty. But I didn't come here, at great inconvenience, to talk this sort of stuff at midnight. Go ahead; give me the details of this sabotage case which is baffling Dawson and the naval authorities; let me hear about the cutting of those electric wires."

"It is, as I told you, in my note, a queer business. The *Antinous*, a fast light cruiser, came in about a fortnight ago to have some defects made good in her high-speed geared-turbines. There was not much wrong, but her engineer commander recommended a renewal of some of the spur wheels. The officers and crew went on short leave in rotation, a care and maintenance party was put in charge, and the builders placed a working gang on board which was occupied in shifts, by night and by day, in making good the defects. When a ship is under repair in a river basin, it is practically impossible to keep up the beautiful order and discipline of a ship at sea. Men of all kinds are constantly coming and going, life on board is stripped of the most ordinary comforts and conveniences, there is inevitably some falling off in strict supervision. Lack of space, lack of facilities for moving about the ship, lack of any regular routine. You will understand. Just as the expansion in the New Army and the New Navy has made it possible for unknown enemy agents to take service in the Army and the Navy, so the dilution of labour in the shipyards has made it possible for workmen—whose sympathies are with the enemy—to get employment about the warships. The danger is fully recognised, and that is where Dawson's widespread system of counter-espionage comes in. There is not a trade union, among all the eighteen or twenty engaged in shipyard work—riveters, fitters, platers, joiners, and all the rest of them—in which he has not police officers enrolled as skilled tradesmen, members of the unions, working as ordinary hands or as foremen, sometimes even in office as "shop stewards" representing the interest of the unions and acting as their spokesmen in disputes with the employers. Dawson claims that there has never yet been a secret Strike Committee, since the war began, upon which at least one of his own men was not serving. He is a wonderful man. I don't like him; he is too unscrupulous and merciless for my simple tastes; but his value to the country is beyond payment."

"But where in the world does he raise these men? One can't turn a policeman into a skilled worker at a moment's notice. How is it done?"

"He begins at the other end. All his skilled workmen are the best he can pick out of their various trades. They have served their full time as apprentices and journeymen. They are recommended to him by their employers after careful testing and sounding. Most of them, I believe, come from the Government dockyards and ordnance factories. They are given a course of police training at Scotland Yard, and then dropped down wherever they may be wanted. Dawson, and inspectors like him, have these men everywhere—in shipyards, in shell shops, in gun factories, in aeroplane sheds, everywhere. They take a leading part in the councils of the unions wherever they go, for they add to their skill as workmen a pronounced, even blatant parade of loyalty to the interests of trade unions and a tasty flavour of socialist principles. Dawson is perfectly cynically outspoken to me over the business which, I confess, appals me. In his female agents—of which he has many—he favours what he calls a 'judicious frailty'; in his male agents he favours a subtle skill in the verbal technique of anarchism. And this man Dawson is by religion a Peculiar Baptist, in private life a faithful husband and a loving father, and in politics a strict Liberal of the Manchester School! As a man he is good, honest, and rather narrow; as a professional detective he is base and mean, utterly without scruple, and a Jesuit of Jesuits. With him the end justifies the means, whatever the means may be."

"And yet you admit that his value to the country is beyond payment. Dawson—our remarkable Dawson of the double life in the two compartments, professional and private, which never are allowed to overlap—Dawson is an instrument of war. We do not like using gas or liquid fire, but we are compelled to use them. We do not like espionage, but we must employ it. As one who loves this fair land of England beyond everything in the world, and as one who would do anything, risk anything, and suffer anything to shield her from the filthy Germans, I rejoice that she has in her service such supremely efficient guardians as this most wickedly unscrupulous Dawson. There is, at any rate, not a trace of our English muddle about him."

"Ours is a righteous cause," cried poor Cary desperately. "We are fighting for right against wrong, for defence against aggression, for civilisation against utter barbarism. We are by instinct clean fighters. If in the stress of conflict we stoop to foul methods, can we ever wash away the filth of them from our souls? We shall stand before the world nakedly confessed as the nation of hypocrites we have always been declared to be."

"Cary," I said, "you make me tired. We cannot be too thankful that we possess Dawsons to counterplot against the Germans, and that personally we are in no way responsible for the morality of their methods. Come off the roof and get back to this most interesting affair of the *Antinous*. I presume one of Dawson's men was working, unknown to his fellows, with the care and maintenance party, and another, equally unknown, with the engineers who were busy upon the gearing of the turbines. Many of the regular ship's officers and men would also have been on board. Had our remarkable friend his agents among them too? Everything is possible with Dawson; I should not be surprised to hear that he had police officers in the Fleet flagship."

"You are almost right. One of his men, a temporary petty officer of R.N.V.R., was certainly on board, and he tells me that down in the engine room was another—a civilian fitter. They were both first-class men. The electric wires, as you know, are carried about the ship under the deck beams, where they are accessible for examination and repairs. They are coiled in cables from which wires are led to the switch room, and thence to all parts of the ship. There are thousands of wires, and no one who did not know intimately their purpose and disposition could venture to tamper with them, for great numbers are always in use. If any one cut the lighting wires, for instance, the defects would be obvious at once; so with the heating or telephone wires. Nothing was touched except the lines to the guns, of which there are eight disposed upon the deck. From the guns connections run to the switch room, the conning tower, the gunnery control platform aloft, and to the gunnery officer's bridge. It was the main cable between the switch room and the conning tower which was cut, and it was one cable laid alongside a dozen others. Now who could know that this was the gun cable, and the only one in which damage might escape detection while the ship was in harbour? At sea there is constant gun drill, during which the electrical controls and the firing-tubes are always tested, but in harbour the guns are lying idle most of the time. It was evidently the intention of the enemy, who cut these wires, that the *Antinous* should go to sea before the defect was discovered, and that her fire control should be out of action till the wiring system could be repaired. That very serious disaster was prevented by the preliminary testing during the night before sailing, but the enemy has been successful in delaying the departure of an invaluable light cruiser for two days. In these days, when the war of observation is more important even than the war of fighting, the services of light cruisers cannot be dispensed with for an hour without grave inconvenience and risk. Yet here was one delayed for forty-eight hours after her ordinary repairs had been completed. The naval authorities are in a frightful stew. For what has happened to the *Antinous* may happen to other cruisers, even to battleships. If there is sabotage among the workmen in the shipyards, it must be discovered and stamped out without a moment's delay. This time it is the cutting of a wire cable; at another time it may be some wilful injury far more serious. A warship is a mass of delicate machinery to which a highly skilled enemy agent might do almost infinite damage. Dawson has been run off his feet during the past two days; I don't know what he has discovered; but if he does not get to the bottom of the business in double-quick time we shall have the whole Board of Admiralty, Scotland Yard, and possibly the War Cabinet down upon us. Think, too, of the disgrace to this shipbuilding city of which we are all so proud."

"We shall know something soon," I said, "for, if I mistake not, here comes Dawson." The electric bell at the front door had buzzed, and Cary, slipping from the room, presently returned with a man who to me, at the first glance, was a complete stranger. I sprang up, moved round to a position whence I could see clearly the visitor's ears, and gasped. It was Dawson beyond a doubt, but it was not the Dawson whom I had known in the north. So what I had vaguely surmised was true—Cary's Dawson and Copplestone's Dawson were utterly unlike. Dawson winked at me, glanced towards Cary, and shook his head; from which I gathered that he did not desire his appearance to be the subject of comment. I therefore greeted him without remark, and, as he sat down under the electric lights, examined him in detail. This Dawson was ten years older than the man whom I had known and fenced with. The hair of this one was lank and grey, while that of mine was brown and curly; the face of this one was white and thin, while the face of mine was rather full and ruddy. The teeth were different—I found out afterwards that Dawson, who had few teeth of his own, possessed several artificial sets of varied patterns—the shape of the mouth was different, the nose was different. I could never have recognised the man before me had I not possessed that clue to identity furnished by his unchanging ears.

"So, Dawson," said I slowly, "we meet again. Permit me to say that I congratulate you. It is very well done."

He grinned and glanced at the unconscious Cary. "You are learning. Bill Dawson takes a bit of knowing."

"Have you any news, Mr. Dawson?" asked Cary eagerly.

"Not much. The wires of the *Antinous* have all been renewed—the Admiralty won't allow cables to be patched except at sea—but I haven't found out who played hanky-panky with them. It could not have been any one in the engine-room party, as none of them went near the place where the wires were cut. Besides, they were engineers, not electricians, and could have known nothing of the arrangements and disposition of the ship's wires. My man who worked with them is positive that they are a sound, good lot without a sea-lawyer or a pacifist among them; a gang of plain, honest tykes. So we are thrown back on the maintenance party, included in which were all sorts of ratings. Some of them are skilled in the electrical fittings—my own man with them is, for one—but we get the best accounts of all of them. They are long service men, cast for sea owing to various medical reasons, but perfectly efficient for harbour work. Among the officers of the ship is a R.N.R. lieutenant with a German name. I jumped to him, but the captain laughed. The man's father and grandfather were in the English merchant service, and though his people originally came from Saxony, he is no more German than we are ourselves. Besides, my experience is that an Englishman with an inherited German name is the very last man to have any truck with the enemy. He is too much ashamed of his forbears for one thing; and for another he is too dead set on living down his beastly name. So we will rule out the Lieutenant R.N.R. My own man, who is a petty officer R.N.V.R., and has worked on a lot of ships which have come in for repairs, says that the temper among the workmen in the yards is good now. It was ugly when dilution of labour first came in, but the wages are so high that all that trouble has settled down. I have had what you call sabotage in the shell and gun shops, but never yet in the King's ships. We have had every possible cutter of the wires on the mat before the Captain and me. We have looked into all their records, had their homes visited and their people questioned, inquired of their habits—Mr. Copplestone, here, knows what comes of drink—and found out how they spend their wages. Yet we have discovered nothing. It is the worst puzzle that I've struck. When and how the gun cable was cut I can't tell you, but whoever did it is much too clever to be about. He must have been exactly informed of the lie and use of the cables, had with him the proper tools, and used them in some fraction of a minute when he wasn't under the eye of my own man whose business it was to watch everybody and suspect everybody. I thought that I had schemed out a pretty thorough system; up to now it has worked fine. Whenever we have had the slightest reason to suspect any man, we have had him kept off the ship and watched. We have run down a lot of footling spies, too stupid to give us a minute's anxiety, but this man who cut the *Antinous*'s wires is of a different calibre altogether. He is A1, and when I catch him, as I certainly shall, I will take off my hat to him."

"You say that the *Antinous* is all right now?" I observed.

"Yes. I saw her towed out of the repair basin an hour ago, and she must be away down the river by this time. It is not of her that I'm thinking, but of the other ships which are constantly in and out for repairs. There are always a dozen here of various craft, usually small stuff. While the man who cut those wires is unknown I shall be in a perfect fever, and so will the Admiral-Superintendent. We'll get the beauty sooner or later, but if it is later, there may be had mischief done. If he can cut wires in one ship, he may do much worse things in some other. The responsibility rests on me, and it is rather crushing."

Dawson spoke with less than his usual cheery confidence. I fancy that the thinness and whiteness of his face were not wholly due to disguise. He had not been to bed since he had been called up in the middle watch of the night before last, and the man was worn out.

"If you take my poor advice, Dawson," I said, "you will cut off now and get some sleep. Even your brain cannot work continuously without rest. The country needs you at your best, and needs you very badly indeed."

His dull, weary eyes lighted as if under the stimulus of champagne, and he turned upon me a look which was almost affectionate. I really began to believe that Dawson likes me, that he sees in me a kindred spirit as patriotically unscrupulous as himself.

He jumped up and gripped my hand. "You are right. I will put in a few hours' sleep and then to work once more. This time I am up against a man who is nearly as smart as I am myself, and I can't afford to carry any handicap."

I led him to the door and put him out, and then turned to Cary with a laugh. "And I, too, will follow Dawson's example. It is past one, and my head is buzzing with queer ideas. Perhaps, after all, the Germans have more imagination than we usually credit them with. I wonder—" But I did not tell to Cary what I wondered.

* * * * *

We were sitting after breakfast in Cary's study, enjoying the first sweet pipe of the day, when the telephone bell rang. Cary took off the earpiece and I listened to a one-sided conversation somewhat as follows:—

"What! Is that you, Mr. Dawson? Yes, Copplestone is here. The *Antigone*? What about her? She is a sister ship of the *Antinous*, and was in with damage to her forefoot, which had been ripped up when she ran down that big German submarine north of the Orkneys—Yes, I know; she was due to go out some time to-day. What do you say? Wires cut? Whose wires have been cut? The *Antigone's*? Oh, the devil! Yes, we will both come down to your office this afternoon. Whenever you like."

Cary hung up the receiver and glared at me. "It has happened again," he groaned. "The *Antigone* this time. She has been in dry dock for the past fortnight and was floated out yesterday. Her full complement joined her last night. Dawson says that he was called up at eight-o'clock by the news that her gun-wires have been cut exactly like those of the *Antinous* and in the same incomprehensible way. He seems, curiously enough, to be quite cheerful about it."

"He has had a few hours sleep. And, besides, he sees that this second case, so exactly like the first, makes the solution of his problem very much more easy. I am glad that he is cheerful, for I feel exuberantly happy myself. I was kept awake half the night by a persistent notion which seemed the more idiotic the more I thought all round it. But now—now, there may be something in it."

"What is your idea? Tell me quick."

"No, thank you, Dr. Watson. We amateur masters of intuition don't work our thrilling effects in that way. We keep our notions to ourselves until they turn out to be right, and then we declare that we saw through the problem from the first. When we have been wrong, we say nothing. So you observe, Cary, that whatever happens our reputations do not suffer."

CHAPTER VI

GUESSWORK

Cary tried to shake my resolution, but I was obdurately silent. While he canvassed the whole position, bringing to bear his really profound knowledge of naval equipment and routine—and incidentally helping me greatly to realise the improbability of my own guesswork solution—I was able to maintain an air of lofty superiority. I must have aggravated him intensely, unpardonably, for I was his guest. He ought to have kicked me out. Yet he bore with me like the sweet-blooded kindly angel that he is, and when at the end it appeared that I was right after all, Cary was the first to pour congratulations and honest admiration upon me. If he reads this book he will know that I am repentant—though I must confess that I should behave in just the same abominable way if the incident were to occur again. There is no great value in repentance such as this.

We reached Dawson's office in the early afternoon, and found his chief assistant there, but no Dawson. "The old man," remarked that officer, a typical, stolid, faithful detective sergeant, "is out on the rampage. He ought by rights to sit here directing the staff and leave the outside investigations to me. He is a high-up man, almost a deputy assistant commissioner, and has no call to be always disguising himself and playing his tricks on everybody. I suppose you know that white-haired old gent down here ain't a bit like Bill Dawson, who's not a day over forty?"

"I have given up wondering where the real Dawson ends and where the disguises begin. The man I met up north wasn't the least bit like the one down here."

"A deal younger, I expect," said the chief assistant, grinning. "He shifts about between thirty and sixty. The old man is no end of a cure, and tries to take us in the same as he does you. There's an inspector at the Yard who was at school with him down Hampshire way, and ought to know what he is really like, but even he has given Dawson up. He says that the old man does not know his own self in the looking-glass; and as for Mrs. Dawson, I expect she has to take any one who comes along claiming to be her husband, for she can't possibly tell t'other from which."

"One might make a good story out of that," I observed to Cary.

"I don't understand," said he. "Mr. Dawson told me once that I knew the real Dawson, but that few other people did."

"If he told you that," calmly observed the assistant, "you may bet your last shirt he was humbugging you. He couldn't tell the truth, not if he tried ever so."

"What is he at now?" I asked.

"I don't know, sir. And if he told me, I shouldn't believe him. I don't take no account of a word that man says. But he's the most successful detective we've got in the whole Force. He's sure to be head of the C.I.D. one day, and then he will have to stay in his office and give us others a chance."

"I don't believe he will," I observed, laughing. "There will be a sham Dawson in the office and the genuine article will be out on the rampage. He is a man who couldn't sit still, not even if you tied him in his chair and sealed the knots."

We spent a pleasant hour pulling Dawson to pieces and leaving to him not a rag of virtue, except intense professional zeal. We exchanged experiences of him, those of the chief assistant being particularly rich and highly flavoured. It appeared that Dawson when off duty loved to occupy the platform at meetings of his religious connection and to hold forth to the elect. The privilege of "sitting under him" had been enjoyed more than once by the assistant, who retailed to us extracts from Dawson's favourite sermon on "Truth." His views upon Truth were unbending as armour plate. "Under no circumstances, not to save oneself from imminent death, not to shield a wife or a child from the penalties for a lapse from virtue, not even to preserve one's country from the attacks of an enemy, was it permissible to a Peculiar Baptist to diverge by the breadth of a hair from the straight path of Truth. Hell yawned on either hand; only along the knife edge of Truth could salvation be reached."

"He made me shiver," said the chief assistant, "and he drove me to thinking of one or two little deceptions of my own. When Dawson preaches, his eyes blaze, his voice breaks, and he will fall on his knees and pray for the souls of those who heed not his words. You can't look at him then and not believe that he means every word he says. Yet it's all humbug."

"No, it is not," said I. "Dawson in the pulpit, or on the tub—or whatever platform he uses—is absolutely genuine. He is the finest example that I have ever met of the dual personality. He is in dead earnest when he preaches on Truth, and he is in just as dead earnest when, stripped of every moral scruple, he pursues a spy or a criminal. In pursuit he is ruthless as a Prussian, but towards the captured victim he can be strangely tender. I should not be surprised to learn that he hates capital punishment and is a strong advocate of gentle methods in prison discipline."

The chief assistant stared, opened a drawer, and pulled forth a slim grey pamphlet. It was marked "For Office Use Only," and was entitled, "Some Notes on Prison Reform," by Chief Inspector William Dawson.

I had begun to read the pamphlet, when a step sounded outside; the assistant snatched it from my hand, flashed it back into its place, and jumped to attention as Dawson entered. He surveyed us with those searching, unwinking eyes of his—for we had the air of conspirators—and said brusquely: "Clear out, Wilson. You talk too much. And don't admit any one except Petty Officer Trehayne."

"The *Antigone*!" cried Cary, who thought only of ships. "The *Antigone*! Is she much damaged?"

"No. Whoever tried to cut her wires was disturbed, or in too great a hurry to do his work well. The main gun-cable was nipped, but not cut through. She will be delayed till to-morrow, not longer. I am not worrying about the *Antigone*, but about the new battleship *Malplaquet*, which was commissioned last month, is nearly filled up with stores, and is expected to leave the river on Saturday. We can't have her delayed by any hanky tricks, not even if we have to put the whole detective force on board of her. Still, I'm not so anxious as I was. This *Antigone* business has cleared things up a lot, and one can sift out the impossible from the possible. To begin with, the *Antinous* was in for repairs to her geared turbines, and the *Antigone* for damage to her forefoot. Engineers were on one job, and platers and riveters on the other. Different trades. So not a workman who was in the *Antinous* was also in the *Antigone*. We can rule out all the workmen. We can also rule out my lieutenant R.N.R. with the German name who has gone to sea in the *Antinous*. The care and maintenance party in the *Antigone* was not the same as the one in the *Antinous*, not a man the same."

"You are sure of that?" cried I, for it seemed that my daring theory had gone to wreck. "You are quite sure."

"Quite. I have all the names and have examined all the men. They were all off the ship by eleven o'clock last night. I hadn't one of my own men among them, but, to make sure, I sent Petty Officer Trehayne on board at eight o'clock to keep a sharp look-out and to see all the harbour party off the vessel. He reported a little after eleven that they were all gone and the ship taken over by her own crew. The damage was discovered at four bells in the morning watch."

"Six o'clock a.m.," interpreted Cary.

"It looks now as if there might be a traitor among her own crew, which is her officers' job, not mine. I wash my hands of the *Antigone*, but it is very much up to me to see that nothing hurtful happens to the *Malplaquet*. The Admiral has orders to support me with all the force under his command; the General of the District has the same orders. But it isn't force we want so much as brains—Dawson's brains. I have been beaten twice, but not the third time. I've told the Yard that if the *Malplaquet* is touched I shall resign, and if they send any one to help me I shall resign. Between to-day, Thursday, and Saturday I am going to catch the wily josser who has a fancy for cutting gun cables or Dawson will say good-bye to the Force. That's a fair stake."

The man swelled with determination and pride. He had no thought of failure, and drew inspiration and joy from the heaviness of the bet which he had made with Fortune. He took the born gambler's delight in a big risk.

"Then you think that the *Antinous* and the *Antigone* were both damaged by the same man, and that he may have designs upon the *Malplaquet*?" said I.

"I don't propose to tell you what I think," replied Dawson stiffly.

"Still," I persisted, passing over the snub, "you have a theory?"

"No, thanks," said Dawson contemptuously. "I have no use for theories. When they are wrong they mislead you, and when they are right they are no help. I believe in facts—facts brought out by constant vigilance. Unsleeping watchfulness and universal suspicion, those are the principles I work on. The theory business makes pretty story books, but the Force does not waste good time over them."

"What are you going to do?"

"This is Thursday afternoon. I am going to join the *Malplaquet* presently, and I'm not going to sleep till she is safely down the river. I'm going to be my own watchman this time."

"How? In what capacity?"

Dawson gave a shrug of impatience, for his nerves were on edge. For a moment he hesitated, and then, recollecting the high post to which I had tacitly been appointed in his household, he replied:

"I am going as one of the Marine sentries."

"It's no use, Dawson," protested I emphatically. "You are a wonder at disguise, and will look, I do not doubt, the very spit of a Marine. But you can't pass among the men for half an hour without discovery. They are a class apart, they talk their own language, cherish their own secret traditions, live in a world to which no stranger ever penetrates. You could pass as a naval officer more easily than you could as a Pongo. It is sheer madness, Dawson."

He gave a short laugh. "Much you know about it. I have served in the Red Corps myself. I was a recruit at Deal, passed two years at Plymouth, and served afloat for three years. I was then drafted into the Naval Police. Afterwards I was recommended for detective work in the dockyards, and at the end of my Marine service joined the Yard. My good man, I was a sergeant before I left the Corps."

"I give up, Dawson," said I. "Nothing about you will ever surprise me again. Not even if you claim to have been a Cabinet Minister."

A queer smile stole over his face. "No, I have not been a minister, but I have attended a meeting of the Cabinet."

Cary interposed at this point. "Yours is a fine idea, Mr. Dawson. As a Marine sentry you can get yourself posted by the Major wherever you please, and the Guard will not talk even though they may wonder that any man should want to do twenty-four hours of duty per day. The Marines are the closest, faith-fullest, and best disciplined force in the wide world. Bluejackets will gossip; Marines never. You will be able to watch more closely than even Trehayne, who, I suppose, will also be on board."

"Yes. He is coming up soon for instructions. It's his last chance, as it is mine. He sees that he must be held responsible for the wire cutting in the *Antinous*, and to some slight extent also in the *Antigone*, and that if anything goes wrong with the *Malplaquet* he will be dismissed. I shall be sorry to lose him, for he is an exceptionally good man, but we can't allow failures in petty officer detectives any more than we can in chief inspectors."

"Where does Trehayne come from? His name sounds Cornish," I asked.

"Falmouth, I believe. He is quite young, but he has had nearly three years in the *Vernon* at Portsmouth and in the torpedo factory at Greenock. A first-class engineer and electrician and a sound detective. He has been with me for some twelve months. You will see him if he calls soon."

I had been thinking hard over the details of Dawson's plans while the talk went on, and then ventured to offer some comments.

"It is fortunate that you have grown a moustache since you were in the north; you could not have been a Marine as a clean-shaven man."

"I often have to shave it," said Dawson, "but I always grow it again between whiles. One can take it off quicker than one can put it on again. False hair is the devil; I have never used it yet and never will. So whenever I have a spell of leisure I grow a moustache against emergencies—like this one."

My next comment was rather difficult to make, for I did not wish either Cary or Dawson to divine its purpose. "If I may make a suggestion to a man of your experience it would be that none of your men here, not even your chief assistant or Trehayne, should know that you are joining the *Malplaquet* as a Marine. Two independent strings are in this case better than a double-jointed string."

"I never tell anything to any one, least of all to Pudden-Headed Wilson. He is loyal, but a stupid ass with a flapping tongue. Trehayne is close as wax, but, on general principles, I keep my movements strictly to myself. He will be in the ship, but he won't know that I am there too. The Commander must know and the Major of Marines, for I shall want a uniform and the free run of the ship, so as to be posted where I like. The Marine Sergeants of the Guard may guess, but, as Mr. Cary says, they won't talk. You two gentlemen are safe," added Dawson pleasantly, "for I've got you tight in my hand and could lock either of you up in a minute if I chose."

A peculiar knock came upon the door, a word passed between Dawson and the police sentry outside, and a young man in the uniform of a naval petty officer entered the room. He was clean-shaven, looked about twenty-five years old, was dark and slim of the Latin type which is not uncommon in Cornwall, and impressed me at once with his air of intelligence and refinement. His voice, too, was rather striking. It was that of the wardroom rather than of the mess deck. I liked the look of Petty Officer Trehayne. Dawson presented him to us and then took him aside for instructions. When he had finished, both men rejoined us, and the conversation became light and general. Trehayne, though clearly suffering from nervous strain after his recent professional failures, talked with the ease and detachment of a highly cultivated man. It appeared that he had been educated at Blundell's School, had lost his parents at about sixteen, had done a course in some electrical engineering shops at Plymouth, and when twenty years old had secured a good berth on the engineering staff of the *Vernon*. He could speak both French and German, which he had learned partly at school and partly on the Continent during leave. Dawson, who was evidently very proud of his young pupil and assistant, paraded his accomplishments before us rather to Trehayne's embarrassment. "Try him with French and German," urged Dawson. "He can chatter them as well as English. But he is as close as wax in all three languages. Some men can't keep their tongues still in one."

I turned to Trehayne and spoke in French: "German I can't abide, but French I love. My vocabulary is extensive, but my accent abominable—incurably British. You can hear it for yourself how it gives me away."

"It is not quite of Paris," replied Trehayne. "Mais vous parlez francais tres bien, tres correctement. Beaucoup mieux que moi."

"Non, non, monsieur," I protested, and then reverted to English.

"Now," said Dawson, when Trehayne had left us, "I must get along, see the Commander of the *Malplaquet*, and draw a uniform and rifle out of the marine stores. It will be quite like old times. You won't see me until Saturday, when I shall be either a triumphant or a broken man. What is the betting, Mr. Copplestone?"

I could not understand the quizzical little smile that Dawson gave me, nor the humorous twitch of his lips. He had contemptuously disclaimed all use of theories, yet there was more moving behind that big forehead of his than he chose to give away. Did his ideas run on parallel lines with mine; did he even suspect that I had formed any idea at all? I could not inquire, for I dislike being laughed at, especially by this man Dawson. I had nothing to go upon, at least so little that was palpable that anything which I might say would be dismissed as the merest guesswork, for which, as Dawson proclaimed, he had no use. Yet, yet—my original guess stuck firmly in my mind, improbable though it might be, and had just been nailed down tightly—I scorn to mystify the reader—by a few simple sentences spoken in French.

CHAPTER VII

THE MARINE SENTRY

We had a whole day to fill in before we could get any news of Dawson's vigil in the *Malplaquet*, and I have never known a day as drearily long. Cary and I were both restless as peas on a hot girdle, and could not settle down to talk or to read or to write. Cary sought vainly to persuade me to read and pass judgment upon his Navy Book. In spite of my interest in the subject my soul revolted at the forbidding pile of manuscript. I promised to read the proofs and criticise them with severity, but as for the M.S.—no, thanks. Poor Cary needed all his sweet patience to put up with me. By eleven o'clock we had become unendurable to one another, and I gladly welcomed his suggestion to adjourn to his club, have lunch there, and try to inveigle the Commander of the *Malplaquet* into our net. "I know him," said Cary. "He is a fine fellow; and though he must be pretty busy, he will be glad to lunch somewhere away from the ship. If we have luck we will go back with him and look over the *Malplaquet* ourselves."

"If you can manage that, Cary, you will have my blessing."

He did manage to work the luncheon part by telephoning to the yard where the *Malplaquet* was fitting out, and we left the rest to our personal charms.

Cary was right. The Commander was a very fine fellow, an English naval officer of the best type. He confirmed the views I had frequently heard expressed by others of his profession that no hatred exists between English and German sailors. They leave that to middle-aged civilians who write for newspapers. The German Navy, in his opinion, was "a jolly fine Service," worthy in high courage and skill to contest with us the supremacy of the seas. He had been through the China troubles as a lieutenant in the *Monmouth*—afterwards sunk by German shot off Coronel—knew von Spee, von Mueller, and other officers of the Pacific Squadron, and spoke of them with enthusiasm. "They sunk some of our ships and we wiped out theirs. That was all in the way of business. We loved them in peace and we loved them in war. They were splendidly loyal to us out in China—von Spee actually transferred some of his ships to the command of our own senior officer so as to avoid any clash of control—and when it came to fighting, they fought like gentlemen. I grant you that their submarine work against merchant ships has been pretty putrid, but I don't believe that was the choice of their Navy. They got their orders from rotten civilians like Kaiser Bill." Imagine if you can the bristling moustache of the Supreme War Lord could he have heard himself described as a civilian!

Our guest had commanded a destroyer in the Jutland battle, and assured us that the handling of the German battle squadrons had been masterly. "They punished us heavily for just so long as they were superior in strength, and then they slipped away before Jellicoe could get his blow in.

They kept fending us off with torpedo attacks until the night came down, and then clean vanished. We got in some return smacks after dark at stragglers, but it was very difficult to say how much damage we did. Not much, I expect. Still it was a good battle, as decisive in its way as Trafalgar. It proved that the whole German Fleet could not fight out an action against our full force and have the smallest hope of success. I am just praying for the chance of a whack at them in the *Malplaquet*. My destroyer was a bonny ship, the best in the flotilla, but the *Malplaquet* is a real peach. You should see her."

"We mean to," said Cary. "This very afternoon. You shall take us back with you."

The Commander opened his eyes at this cool proposal, but we prevailed upon him to seek the permission of the Admiral-Superintendent, who, a good deal to my surprise, proved to be quite pliable. Cary's reputation for discretion must be very high in the little village where he lives if it is able to guarantee so disreputable a scribbler as Bennet Copplestone! The Admiral, fortunately, had not read any of my Works before they had been censored. When printed in *Cornhill* they were comparatively harmless.

I must not describe the *Malplaquet*. Her design was not new to me—I had seen more than one of her type—but as she is now a unit in Beatty's Fleet her existence is not admitted to the world. As we went up and down her many steep narrow ladders, and peered into dark corners, I looked everywhere for a Marine sentry whom I could identify by mark of ear as Dawson. I never saw him, but Trehayne passed me twice, and I found myself again admiring his splendid young manhood. He was not big, being rather slim and wiry than strongly built, but in sheer beauty of face and form he was almost perfectly fashioned. "Do you know that man?" I asked of our commander, indicating Trehayne. "No," said he. "He is one of the shore party. But I should like to have him with me. He is one of the smartest looking petty officers that I have ever seen."

We were shown everything that we desired to see except the transmission room and the upper conning tower—the twin holy of holies in a commissioned ship—and slipped away, escaping the Captain by a bare two minutes. Which was lucky, as he would probably have had us thrown into the "ditch."

The end of the day was as weariful as the beginning, and we were all glad—especially, I expect, Mrs. Cary—to go early to bed. That ill-used lady, to whom we could disclose nothing of our anxieties, must have found us wretched company.

We had finished breakfast the next morning—the Saturday of Dawson's gamble—and were sitting on Cary's big fireguard talking of every subject, except the one which had kept us awake at night, when a servant entered and announced that a soldier was at the door with a message from Mr. Dawson. "Show him in," almost shouted Cary, and I jumped to my feet, stirred for once into a visible display of eagerness.

A Marine came in, dressed in the smart blue sea kit that I love; upon his head the low flat cap of his Corps. He gave us a full swinging salute, and jumped to attention with a click of his heels. He looked about thirty-five, and wore a neatly trimmed dark moustache. His hair, also very dark, was cropped close to his head. Standing there with his hands upon the red seams of his trousers, his chest well filled out, and his face weather tanned, he looked a proper figure of a sea-going soldier. "Mr. Cary, sir," he said, in a flat, monotonous orderly's voice, "Major Boyle's compliments, and could you and your friend come down to the Police Station to meet him and Chief Inspector Dawson. I have a taxi-cab at the door, sir."

"Certainly," cried Cary; "in two minutes we shall be ready."

"Oh, no, we shan't," I remarked calmly, for I had moved to a position of tactical advantage on the Marine's port beam. "We will have the story here, if you don't mind, Dawson."

He stamped pettishly on the floor, whipped off his cap, and spun it across the room. "Confound you, Mr. Copplestone!" he growled. "How the—how the—do you do it?" He could not think of an expletive mild enough for Mrs. Cary's ears. "There's something about me that I can't hide. What is it? If you don't tell, I will get you on the Regulation compelling all British subjects to answer questions addressed to them by a competent naval or military authority."

"You don't happen to be either, Dawson," said I unkindly. "And, beside, there was never yet a law made which could compel a man to speak or a woman to hold her tongue. Some day perhaps, if you are good, I will show you how the trick is done. But not yet. I want to have something to bargain with when you cast me into jail. Out with the story; we are impatient. If I mistake not, you come to us Dawson triumphant. You haven't the air of a broken man."

"I have been successful," he answered gravely, "but I am a long, long way from feeling triumphant. No, thank you, Mrs. Cary, I have had my breakfast, but if I might trouble you for a cup of coffee? Many thanks."

Dawson sat down, and Cary moved about inspecting him from every angle. "No," declared he at last, "I cannot see the smallest resemblance, not the smallest. You were thin; now you are distinctly plump. Your hair was nearly white. Your cheeks had fallen in as if your back teeth were missing. Your lower lip stuck out." Dawson smiled, highly gratified. "I took in all my people at the office this morning," he said. "They all thought, and think still, that I was a messenger from the *Malplaquet*, which, by the way, is well down the river safe and sound. Just wait a minute." He walked into a corner of the room, moved his hands quickly between his side pockets and his face, and then returned. Except for the dark hair and moustache and the brown skin, he had become the Dawson of the Thursday afternoon. "It is as simple for me to change," said the artist, with a nasty look in my direction, "as it seems to be for Mr. Copplestone here to spot me. It will take a day or two to get the dye out of my hair and the tan off my skin. I am going to have a sharp touch of influenza, which is a useful disease when one wants to lie in. Since Sunday I have only been twice to bed."

We filled him up with coffee and flattery—as one fills a motor car with petrol and oil—but asked him no questions until we were safely in Cary's study and Mrs. Cary had gone about her household duties. "Your good lady," remarked Dawson to Cary, "is as little curious as any woman I have met, and we will leave her at that if you don't mind. The best thing about our women is that they don't care tuppence about naval and military details. If they did, and once started prying with that keen scent and indomitable persistence of theirs, we might as well chuck up. Even my own bright team of charmers never know and never ask the meaning of the information that they ferret out for me. Their curiosity is all personal—about men and women, never about things. Women—"

I cut Dawson short. He tended to become tedious.

"Quite so," I observed politely. "And to revert to one big female creature, let us hear something of the *Malplaquet*."

"You at any rate are curious enough for a dozen. It would serve you right to keep you hopping a bit longer. But I have a kindly eye for human weakness, though you might not think it. I joined the ship on Thursday afternoon, slipping in as one of a detachment of fifty R.M.L.I. who had been wired for from Chatham. They were an emergency lot; we hadn't enough in the ship for the double sentry go that I wanted. All my plans were made with the Commander and Major Boyle, and they both did exactly what I told them. It isn't often that a private of Marines has the ordering about of two officers. But Dawson is Dawson; no common man. They did as I told them, and were glad to do it. I had extra light bulbs put on all over the lower decks and every dark corner lit up— except one. Just one. And this one was where the four gun-cables ran out of the switch-room and lay alongside one another before they branched off to the fore and after turrets and to the port and starboard side batteries. That was the most likely spot which any one wanting to cut the gun-wires would mark down, and I meant to watch it pretty closely myself. We had double sentries at the magazines. The *Malplaquet* is an oil-fired ship, so we hadn't any bothering coal bunkers to attract fancy bombs. I was pretty sure that after the *Antinous* and the *Antigone* we had mostly wire-cutting to fear. When a man has done one job successfully, and repeated it almost successfully, he is pretty certain to have a third shot. Besides, if one is out to delay a ship, cutting wires is as good a way as any. I had an idea that my man was not a bomber."

"I thought that you scorned theories," I put in dryly. "When they are wrong they mislead you, and when they are right they are no help."

Dawson frowned. "Shut up, Copplestone," snapped Cary.

"We were in no danger from the lighting, heating, and telephone wires, for any defect would have been visible at once. It was the gun and gunnery control cables that were the weak spots. So I had L.T.O.'s posted in the spotting top, the conning tower, the transmission room, the four turrets, and at the side batteries. Every few minutes they put through tests which would have shown up at once any wires that had been tampered with. After the shore party had cleared out about nine o'clock on the Thursday, no officer or man was allowed to leave the ship without a special permit from the Commander. This was all dead against the sanitary regulations of the harbour, but I had the Admiral's authority to break any rules I pleased. By the way, you two ought never to have been allowed on board yesterday afternoon—I saw you, though you didn't see me; it was contrary to my orders. I spoke to the Admiral pretty sharp last night. 'Who is responsible for the ship?' says I. 'You or me?' 'You,' says he. 'I leave it at that,' says I."

"One moment, Dawson," I put in. "If the shore party had all gone, how was it that I saw Petty Officer Trehayne in the ship?"

"He had orders to stay and keep watch—though he didn't know I was on board myself. Two pairs of police eyes are better than one pair, and fifty times better than all the Navy eyes in the ship. Of all the simple-minded, unsuspicious beggars in the world, give me a pack of naval ratings! I wouldn't have one of them for sentries—that is why the fifty emergency Marines were sent for." Dawson's limitless pride in his old Service, and deep contempt for the mere sailor, had come back in full flood with the uniform of his Corps.

"I started my own sentry duty in the dark corner I told you of as soon as I had seen to the arrangements all over the *Malplaquet*, and I was there, with very few breaks of not more than five minutes each for a bite of food, for twenty-six hours. Two Marine sentries took my place whenever I was away. I had my rifle and bayonet, and stood back in a corner of a bulkhead where I couldn't be seen. The hours were awful long; I stood without hardly moving. All the pins and needles out of Redditch seemed to dance up and down me, but I stuck it out—and I had my reward, I had my reward. I did my duty, but it's a sick and sorry man that I am this day."

"There was nothing else to be done," I said. "What you feel now is a nervous reaction."

"That's about it. I watched and watched, never feeling a bit like sleep though my eyes burned something cruel and my feet—they were lumps of prickly wood, not feet. Dull lumps with every now and then a stab as if a tin tack had been driven into them. Beyond me in the open alley-way the light was strong, and I could see men pass frequently, but no one came into my corner till the end, and no one saw me. I heard six bells go in the first watch ('Eleven p.m.,' whispered Cary) on Friday evening, though there was a good bit of noise of getting ready to go out in the early morning, and I was beginning to think that all my trouble might go for naught, when a man in a Navy cap and overalls stopped just opposite my dark hole between two bulkheads. His face was turned from me, as he looked carefully up and down the lighted way. He stood there quite still for some seconds, and then stepped backwards towards me. I could see him plain against the light beyond. He listened for another minute or so, and, satisfied that no one was near, spun on his heels, whipped a tool from his dungaree overalls, and reached up to the wires which ran under the deck beams overhead. In spite of my aching joints and sore feet I was out in a flash and had my bayonet up against his chest. He didn't move till my point was through his clothes and into his flesh. I just shoved till he gave ground, and so, step by step, I pushed him with the point of my bayonet till he was under the lights. His arms had come down, he dropped the big shears with insulated handles which he had drawn from his pocket, but he didn't speak a word to me and I did not speak to him. I just held him there under the lights, and we looked at one another without a word spoken. There was no sign of surprise or fear in his face, just a queer little smile. Suddenly he moved, made a snatch at the front of his overalls, and put something into his mouth. I guessed what it was, but did not try to stop him; it was the best thing that he could do."

Dawson stopped and pulled savagely at his cigar. He jabbed the end with his knife, though the cigar was drawing perfectly well, and gave forth a deep growl which might have been a curse or a sob.

"Have you ever watched an electric bulb fade away when the current is failing?" he asked. "The film pales down from glowing white to dull red, which gets fainter and fainter, little by little, till nothing but the memory of it lingers on your retina. His eyes went out exactly like that bulb. They faded and faded out of his face, which still kept up that queer, twisted smile. I've seen them ever since; wherever I turn. I shall be glad of that bout of influenza, and shall begin it with a stiff dose of veronal.... When the light had nearly gone out of his eyes and he was rocking on his feet, I spoke for the first time. I spoke loud too. 'Good-bye,' I called out; 'I'm Dawson.' He heard me, for his eyes answered with a last flash; then they faded right out and he fell flat on the steel deck. He had died on his feet; his will kept him upright to the end; that was a Man. He lived a Man's life, doing what he thought his duty, and he died a Man's death.... I blew my whistle twice; up clattered a Sergeant with the Marine Guard and stopped where that figure on the deck barred their way. 'Get a stretcher,' I said, 'and send for the doctor. But it won't be any use. The man's dead.' The Sergeant asked sharply for my report, and sent off a couple of men for a stretcher. 'Excuse me, Sergeant,' I said, in my best detective officer voice, 'I will report direct to your Major and the Commander. I am Chief Inspector Dawson.' He showed no surprise nor doubt of my word—if you want to understand discipline, gentlemen, get the Marines to teach you—he asked no questions. With one word he called the guard to attention, and himself saluted me—me a private! I handed him my rifle—there was an inch of blood at the point of the bayonet—and hobbled off to the nearest ladder. My word, I could scarcely walk, and as for climbing a ship's ladder—I could never have done if some one hadn't given me a boost behind and some one else a hand at the top. The Commander and the Major of Marines were both in the wardroom; I walked in, saluted them as a self-respecting private should do, and told them the whole story."

"It was Petty Officer Trehayne," said I calmly—and waited for a sensation.

"Of course," replied Dawson, greatly to my annoyance. He might have shown some astonishment at my wonderful intuition; but he didn't, not a scrap. Even Cary was at first disappointing, though he warmed up later, and did me full justice. "Trehayne a spy!" cried Cary. "He looked a smart good man."

"I am not saying that he wasn't," snapped Dawson, whose nerves were very badly on edge. "He was obeying the orders of his superiors as we all have to do. He gave his life, and it was for his country's service. Nobody can do more than that. Don't you go for to slander Trehayne. I watched him die—on his feet."

Cary turned to me. "What made you think it was Trehayne?" he asked. This was better. I looked at Dawson, who was brooding in his chair with his thoughts far away. He was still seeing those eyes fading out under the glare of the electrics between the steel decks of the *Malplaquet*!

"It was a sheer guess at first," said I, preserving a decent show of modesty. "When I heard how the enemy plotted and Dawson counter-plotted with all those skilled workmen in his detective service, it occurred to me that an enemy with imagination might counter-counterplot by getting men inside Dawson's defences. I couldn't see how one would work it, but if German agents, say, could manage to become trusted servants of Dawson himself, they would have the time of their lives. So far I was guessing at a possibility, however improbable it might seem. Then when Dawson told us that he had sent Trehayne into the *Antigone* and that he was the one factor common to both vessels—the workmen and the maintenance part were all different—I began to feel that my wild theory might have something in it. I didn't say anything to you, Cary, or to Dawson—he despises theories. Afterwards Trehayne came in and I spoke to him, and he to me, in French. He did not utter a dozen words altogether, but I was absolutely certain that his French had not been learned at an English public school and during short trips on the Continent. I know too much of English school French and of one's opportunities to learn upon Continental trips. It took me three years of hard work to recover from the sort of French which I learned at school, and I am not well yet. The French spoken by Trehayne was the French of the nursery. It was almost, if not quite, his mother tongue, just as his English was. Trehayne's French accent did not fit into Trehayne's history as retailed to us by Dawson. From that moment I plumped for Trehayne as the cutter of gun wires."

Dawson had been listening, though he showed no interest in my speech. When I had quite finished, and was basking in the respectful admiration emanating from dear old Cary, he upset over me a bucket of very cold water.

"Very pretty," said he. "But answer one question. Why did I send

Trehayne to the *Antigone*?"

"Why? How can I tell? You said it was to make sure that the shore party were all off the ship."

"I said! What does it matter what I say! What I do matters a heap, but what I say—pouf! I sent Trehayne to the *Antigone* to test him. I sent him expecting that he would try to cut her wires, and he did. Then when I was sure, though I had no evidence for a law court, I sent him to the *Malplaquet*, and I set my trap there for him to walk into. How did I guess? I don't guess; I watch. The more valuable a man is to me, the more I watch him, for he might be even more valuable to somebody else. Trehayne was an excellent man, but he had not been with me a month before I was watching him as closely as any cat. I hadn't been a Marine and served ashore and afloat without knowing a born gentleman when I see one, and knowing, too, the naval stamp. Trehayne was too much of a gentleman to have become a workman in the *Vernon* and at Greenock without some very good reason. He said that he was an orphan—yes; he said his parents left him penniless, and he had to earn his living the best way he could—yes. Quite good reasons, but they didn't convince me. I was certain sure that somewhere, some time, Trehayne had been a naval officer. I had seen too many during my service to make any mistake about that. So when I stood there waiting in that damned cold corner behind that bulkhead, it was for Trehayne that I was waiting. I meant to take him or to kill him. When he killed himself, I was glad. As I watched his eyes fade out, it was as if my own son was dying on his feet in front of me. But it was better so than to die in front of a firing party. For I—I loved him, and I wished him 'Good-bye,'"

Dawson pitched his cigar into the fire, got up, and walked away to the far side of the room. I had never till that moment completely reverenced the penetrative, infallible judgment of Little Jane.

Dawson came back after a few minutes, picked up another cigar from Cary's box, and sat down. "You see, I have a letter from him. I found it in his quarters where I went straight from the *Malplaquet*."

"May we read it?" I asked gently. "I was greatly taken with Trehayne myself. He was a clean, beautiful boy. He was an enemy officer on Secret Service; there is no dishonour in that. If he were alive, I could shake his hand as the officer of the firing party shook the hand of Lody before he gave the last order."

Dawson took a paper from his pocket, and handed it to me. "Read it out," said he; "I can't."

CHAPTER VIII

TREHAYNE'S LETTER

I took the letter from Dawson and glanced through it. The first sheet and the last had been written very recently—just before the boy had left his quarters for the last time to go on board the *Malplaquet*; the remainder had been set down at various times; and the whole had been connected up, put together, and paged after the completion of the last sheet. Trehayne wrote a pretty hand, firm and clear, the writing of an artist who was also a trained engineer. There was no trace in the script of nervousness or of hesitation. He had carried out his Orders, he saw clearly that the path which he had trod was leading him to the end of his journey, but he made no complaint. He was a Latin, and to the last possessed that loftiness of spirit wedded to sombre fatalism which is the heritage of the Latins. He was at war with his kindred of Italy and France, and with the English among whom he had been brought up, and whom he loved. He was their enemy by accident of birth, but though he might and did love his foes better than his German friends of Austria and

Prussia, yet he had taken the oath of faithful service, and kept it to the end. I could understand why Dawson—that strange human bloodhound, in whom the ruthless will continually struggled with and kept under the very tender heart—would allow no one to slander Trehayne.

Cary was watching me eagerly, waiting for me to read the letter.

Dawson's head was resting on one hand, and his face was turned away, so that I could not see it. He could not wholly conceal his emotion, but he would not let us see more of it than he could help. He did not move once during my reading.

* * * * *

To Chief Inspector William Dawson, C.I.D.

SIR,

Will you be surprised, my friend, when you read this that I have left for you, to learn that I, your right-hand man in the unending spy hunt, I whom you have called your bright jewel of a pupil, Petty Officer John Trehayne, R.N.V.R., am at this moment upon the books of the Austrian Navy as a sub-lieutenant, seconded for Secret Service? Have you ever been surprised by anything? I don't know. You have said often in my hearing that you suspect every one. Have you suspected me? Sometimes when I have caught that sidelong squint of yours, that studied accidental glance which sees so much, I have felt almost sure that you were far from satisfied that Trehayne was the man he gave himself out to be. I have been useful to you. I have eaten your salt, and have served you as faithfully as was consistent with the supreme Orders by which I direct my action. With you I have run down and captured German agents, wretched lumps of dirt, whom I loathe as much as you do. Those who have sworn fidelity to this fair country of England, and have accepted of her citizenship —things which I have never done—and then in fancied security have spied upon their adopted Mother, I loathe and spit upon. I have taken the police oath of obedience to my superiors, and I have kept it, but I have never sworn allegiance to His Majesty your King, whom I pray that God may preserve though I am his enemy. To your blunt English mind, untrained in logic, my sentiments and actions may lack consistency. But no. Those agents whom we have run down, you and I, were traitors—traitors to England. Of all traitors for whom Hell is hungry the German-born traitor is the most devilish. I would not have you think, my friend, that I am at one with them. Never while I have been in your pay and service have I had any communication direct or indirect with any of the naturalised- British Prussian scum, who have betrayed your noble generosity. I have taken my Orders from Vienna, I have communicated always direct with Vienna. I am an Austrian naval officer. I am no traitor to England.

* * * * *

I spring from an old Italian family which has long been settled in Trieste. For many generations we have served in the Austrian Navy. With modern Italy, with the Italy above all which has thrown the Holy Father into captivity and stripped the Holy See of the dominions bestowed upon it by God, we have no part or lot. Yet when I have met Italian officers, and those too of France, as I have frequently done during my cruises afloat, I have felt with them a harmony of spirit which I have never experienced in association with German-Austrians and with Prussians. I do not wish to speak evil of our Allies, the Prussians, but to one of my blood they are the most detestable people whom God ever had the ill-judgment to create.

* * * * *

I was born in Trieste, and lived there with my parents until I was eight years old. In our private life we always spoke Italian or French, German was our official language. I know that language well, of course, but it is not my mother tongue. Italian or French, and afterwards English —I speak and write all three equally well; which of the three I shall use when I come to die and one reverts to the speech of the nursery and schoolroom, I cannot say; it will depend upon whom those are that stand about my deathbed.

When I was eight years old, my father, Captain —— (no, I will not tell you my name; it is not

Trehayne though somewhat similar in sound), was appointed Austrian Consul at Plymouth, and we all moved to that great Devonshire seaport. I was young enough to absorb the rich English atmosphere, nowhere so rich as in that county which is the home and breeding-ground of your most splendid Navy. I was born again, a young Elizabethan Englishman. My story to you of my origin was true in one particular—I really was educated at Blundell's School at Tiverton. Whenever —and it has happened more than once—I have met as Trehayne old schoolfellows of Blundell's they have accepted without comment or inquiry my tale that I had become an Englishman, and had anglicised my name. Among the peoples which exist on earth to-day, you English are the most nobly generous and unsuspicious. The Prussians laugh at you; I, an Austrian-Italian, love and respect you.

* * * * *

When I was sixteen, after I had spent eight years in Devon, and four of those years at an English public school, I was in speech and almost in the inner fibres of my mind an Englishman. Your naval authorities at Plymouth and Devonport, as serenely trustful and heedless of espionage as the mass of your kindly people, allowed my father—whom I often accompanied—to see the dockyards, the engine shops, the training schools, and the barracks. They knew that he was an Austrian naval officer, and they took him to their hearts as a brother, of the common universal brotherhood of the sea. I think that your Navy holds those of a foreign naval service as more nearly of kin to themselves than civilians of their own blood. The bond of a common profession is more close than the bond of a common nationality. I do not doubt that my father sent much information to our Embassy in London—it was what he was employed to do—but I am sure that he did not basely betray the wonderful confidence of his hosts. Our countries were at peace. My father is no Prussian; he is a chivalrous gentleman. I am sure that he did not send more than his English naval friends were content at the time that he should send. For in those years your newspapers and your books upon the Royal Navy of England concealed little from the world. I have visited Dartmouth; I have dined in the Naval College there with bright sailor boys of my own age. It was then my one dream, had I remained in England, to have become an Englishman, and to have myself served in your Navy. It was a vain dream, but I knew no better. Fate and my birth made me afterwards your enemy. I would have fought you gladly face to face on land or sea, but never, never, would I have stabbed the meanest of Englishmen in the back.

When I was sixteen years old I left England with my parents and returned to Triest. I was a good mathematician with a keen taste for mechanics. I spent two years in the naval engineering shops at Pola, and I was gazetted as a sub-lieutenant in the engineering branch of the Austrian Navy. My next two years were spent afloat. Although I did not know it, I had already been marked out by my superiors for the Secret Service. My perfect acquaintance with English, my education at Blundell's, my knowledge of your thoughts and your queer ways, and twists of mind, had equipped me conspicuously for Secret Service work in your midst.

As a youth of twenty, in the first flush of manhood, I was seconded for service here, and I returned to England. That was five years ago.

* * * * *

[I paused, for my throat was dry, and looked up. Cary was leaning forward intent upon every word. Dawson's face was still turned away; he had not moved. It seemed to me that to our party of three had been added a fourth, the spirit of Trehayne, and that he anxiously waited there yonder in the shadows for the deliverance of our judgment. Had he, an English public school boy, played the game according to the immemorial English rules? I went on.]

* * * * *

It was extraordinarily easy for me to obtain employment in the heart of your naval mysteries. Few questions were asked; you admitted me as one of yourselves. I took the broad open path of full acceptance of your conditions. I first obtained employment in a marine engineering shop at Southampton, joined a trade union, attended Socialist meetings—I, a member of one of the oldest families in Trieste. Though a Catholic, I bent my knee in the English Church, and this was not difficult, for I had always attended service in the chapel at Blundell's. To you, my friend, I can say this, for you are of some strange sect which consigns to the lowest Hell both Catholics and Anglicans alike. Your Heaven will be a small place. From Southampton I went to the torpedo training-ship *Vernon*. Again I had no difficulty. I was a workman of skill and intelligence. I was there for more than two years, learning all your secrets, and storing them in my mind for the benefit of my own Service at home.

It was at Portsmouth that there came to me the great temptation of my life, for I fell in love, not as you colder people do, but as a Latin of the warm South. She was an English girl of good, if undistinguished, family. Though in my hours of duty I belonged to that you call the 'working classes,' I was well off, and lived in private the life of my own class. I had double the pay of my rank, an allowance from my father, and my wages, which were not small. There were many English families in Portsmouth and Southsea who were graciously pleased to recognise that John Trehayne, trade unionist, and weekly wage-earning workman, was a gentleman by birth and breeding. In any foreign port I should have been under police supervision as a person eminently to be suspected; in Portsmouth I was accepted without question for what I gave myself out to be—a gentleman who wished to learn his business from the bottom upwards. I will say nothing of the lady of my heart except that I loved her passionately, and should have married her—aye, and become an Englishman in fact, casting off my own, country—if War had not blown my ignoble plans to shatters. There was nothing ignoble in my love, for she was a queen among women, but in myself for permitting the hot blood of youth to blind my eyes to the duty claimed of me by my country. When war became imminent, I was not recalled, as I had hoped to be, since I wished to fight afloat as became my rank and family. I was ordered to take such steps as most effectively aided me to observe the English plans and preparations, and to report when possible to Vienna. In other words, I was ordered to act in your midst as a special intelligence officer—what you would call a Spy. It was an honourable and dangerous service which I had no choice but to accept. My dreams of love had gone to wreck. I could have deceived the woman whom I loved, for she would have trusted me and believed any story of me that I had chosen to tell. But could I, an officer, a gentleman by birth and I hope by practice, a secret enemy of England and a spy upon her in the hour of her sorest trial, could I remain the lover of an English girl without telling her fully and frankly exactly what I was? Could I have committed this frightful treason to love and remained other than an object of scorn and loathing to honest men? I could not. In soul and heart she was mine; I was her man, and she was my woman. With her there were no reserves in love. She was mine, yet I fled from her with never a word, even of good-bye. I made my plans, obtained certificates of my proficiency in the *Vernon*, kissed my dear love quietly, almost coldly, without a trace of the passion that I felt, and fled. It was the one thing left me to do. My friend, that was two years ago. She knows not whether I am alive or am dead; I know not whether she is alive or is dead. Yet during every hour of the long days, and during every hour of the still longer nights, she has been with me. I have done my duty, but I do not think that I wish to live very much longer. If death comes to me quickly—and to those in my present trade it comes quickly—will you, my friend, of your bountiful kindness write to [here followed a name and address] and repeat exactly what I now say. Do not tell what I was or how I died, but just write, "He loved you to the last." There is a portrait in a locket round my neck and a ring on my finger. Send her those, my good friend, and she will know that your words are true.

* * * * *

I fled as far from Portsmouth, where my dear love dwelt, as I could go; I fled to Greenock, that dreadful sodden corner of earth where the rain never ceases to fall, and the sun never shines. At Greenock one measures the rainfall not by inches, but by yards. Sometimes, not often, a pale orb struggles through the clouds and glimmers faintly upon the grimy town—some poor relation of the sun, maybe, but not the godlike creature himself. For six months, in this cold desolate spot, among a people strangely unlike the English of Devon, though they are of kindred race, I laboured for six months in the Torpedo Factory. I lived meanly in one room, for my Austrian pay and allowance had stopped when War cut the channels of communication. I could, had I chosen, have drawn money from German agencies in London, but I scorned to hold truck with them. They were traitors to the England which trusted and protected them, and of which they were citizens. I lived upon my wages and preserved jealously all that I had saved during my years of comparative affluence at Portsmouth. It was duty which made me a Spy, not gold.

One day I was called into the office of the Superintendent, and it was hinted to me, diplomatically, not unskilfully, that I was desired to take service with the English secret police. I feigned reluctance, made difficulties, professed diffidence, until pressure was put upon me, and I was forced to accept a position which I could never by any scheming have achieved. Those whom the gods seek to destroy, they first drive mad—you are a very trustful unsuspicious folk, all except you to whom I write. But even you did not, I am sure, suspect me at the beginning. I was sent to Scotland Yard in London to be trained in my new duties. You saw me there, and claimed me for your staff, and I came to this centre of shipbuilding and worked here with you. I was clothed in the uniform of the Royal Naval Volunteer Reserve.

There are two matters closely affecting my personal honour which will seem of small moment to you—you who display always a sublime patriotic scorn of every moral scruple; but to me they are great. I am of the old chivalry of Italy, and I have been taught at school in England always to play the game. Though I wore the uniform of the R.N.V.R., it was as a disguise and cloak of my police office; I was never attested. I have never, never, never sworn allegiance to England. I have always kept troth with my own country; I have never broken troth with England. Had the English naval oath been proffered to me, I should have refused it at any hazard to my personal safety. My honour is unstained.

You have paid me for my work, I have taken your pay, but I have not spent it upon myself. Every penny of it for the last twelve months will be found at my quarters. I have lived upon what I saved at Portsmouth—lived sometimes very scantily. My funds are running low. What I shall do when they are exhausted I cannot tell. Perhaps, who knows, they will last my time. As for the rest, that packet of Treasury Notes which has been my police pay, unexpended, will you take it, my friend, and pay it to the fund for assisting the English sailors interned in Holland? I should feel happier if they would accept it, for I have, as you will presently learn, taken some of their names in vain. I have not broken any oath, and I have not used your pay; my honour is unstained.

* * * * *

[Again I paused and glanced at Dawson. He had not even winced—at least not visibly—when Trehayne had held him free from every moral scruple. He must, I think, have read the letter many times before he had handed it to me. Cary looked troubled and uneasy. To him a spy had been just a spy—he had never envisaged in his simple honest mind such a super-spy as Trehayne. I went on.]

* * * * *

Now nothing was hidden from me; I had within my hands all the secrets of England's Navy. My one difficulty—and it was not so great a one as you may think—was communication with my country. Never for one moment did it fail. Years before it had been thought out and prepared. I varied my methods. At Portsmouth, during the early weeks of the War, I had employed one means, at Greenock another, here yet another. The basis of all was the same. It was much more difficult for me to receive orders from my official superiors in Austria, but even those came through once or twice. Never, during the whole of the past year, have I failed to send every detail of the warships building and completed here, of the ships damaged and repaired, of the movements of the Fleets in so far as I could learn them. My country and her Allies have seen the English at work here as clearly as if this river had been within their own borders. John Trehayne has been their Eye—an unsleeping, ever-watching Eye. Shall I tell you how I got my information through? It was very simple, and was done under your own keen nose. One of the R.N.V.R. who went with your Mr. Churchill to Antwerp, and was interned in Holland, was a friend of mine at Greenock, well known to me, I wrote to him constantly, though he never received and was never meant to receive my letters. They were all addressed to the care of a house in Haarlem where lived one of our Austrian agents who was placed under my orders. All letters addressed by me to my friend were received by him and forwarded post haste to Vienna. Do you grasp the simplicity and subtlety of the device? My friend was on the lists of those interned in Holland, no one here knew where he lodged, the address used by me was as probable as any other; what more natural and commendable than that I should write to cheer him up a bit in exile, and that I should send him books and illustrated magazines? If it had been noticed by the postal authorities in Holland that my friend did not live at the address which I used, it would have been supposed that I had made a mistake, and no suspicion would have been attracted to me. But how did my letters, books, and magazines containing information, the most secret and urgent, pass through the censorship unchecked? That again was simple. My letters were those which a friend in freedom in England would write to his friend who was a captive in Holland. They were personal, sympathetic, no more. The books and magazines were just those which such a man as my friend would desire to have to lighten the burden of idleness. Between the lines of my letters, and on the white margins of the books and papers, I wrote the vital information which my country desired to have, and I desired to give. The ink which I used for this purpose left no trace and could not be made visible by any one who had not its complementary secret. It is the special ink of the Austrian Secret Service; you do not know it, your Censors do not know it, your chemists might experiment for months and years and not discover it. I used it always, and you never read what I wrote. Now you will understand why I wish the small stock of money, my police pay, which I could not myself have used without dishonour, to go to the interned sailors in Holland. I feel that I owe to my friend some little reparation for the crooked use to which I have put his name.

There is little more to tell. Three weeks ago I received by post from London a copy of *Punch*. It had been despatched to me unordered, from the office of the paper in an office wrapper. You know that English papers may not now be sent abroad to neutral countries except direct from the publishing offices of the newspapers themselves. It is a precaution of the censorship, childish and laughable, for what is easier than to imitate official wrappers? I guessed at once, when I saw this unordered copy of *Punch*, that the wrapper was a faked one, and that it had come to me bearing orders from my superiors. I applied my chemical tests to the margins of the pages and upon the advertisement of a brand of whisky appeared the orders which I had expected. I read what was written, and I have not suffered greater pain—no, not upon that day when I fled from Portsmouth without a word of good-bye to the woman who possessed my heart. For I learned then that my country, the proud, clean-fighting Austria, had given up its soul into the keeping of the filthy Prussian assassins. I was directed to damage or delay every warship upon which I worked, to employ any means, to blow up unsuspecting English seamen—not in the hot blood of battle, but secretly as an assassin. A step in rank was promised for every battleship destroyed. Had these foul Orders admitted of no loophole through which my honour might with difficulty wriggle, I should have taken the only course possible to me. I should have instantly resigned my commission in the Austrian Navy, and taken my own life. But it happened that I had an alternative. I was ordered to damage or delay warships. I would not treacherously slay the English sailors among whom I worked, but I would, if I could, delay the ships. My experience taught me that the simplest and most effective way was to cut the electric wires, and I decided to do it whenever opportunity offered. I could not do this for long. I was certain to be discovered. You are not a man who fails before a definite problem in detection. But before I was discovered I could do something to carry out my Orders.

I cut the gun-wires of the *Antinous*. It was easy. I was the last to leave of the shore party. Then you sent me on board the *Antigone*. She was closely watched, the task was very difficult, and dangerous; I was within the fraction of a second of discovery, but I took one chop of my big shears. The job was ill done, but I could do no better.

You warned me fairly, that if injury came to the *Malplaquet*, while under my charge, that I should be dismissed. She was my last chance as she was your own. But what to me were risks? I had lost my love, and my country had dishonoured herself in my eyes. I was nameless, loveless, countryless. All had gone, and life might go too.

* * * * *

I am completing this letter before going on board the *Malplaquet* and placing it where you will readily find it. I know you, my friend, more intimately than you know yourself. I am certain that even now you are in the ship, that you are preparing snares into which I shall in all probability fall.

Your snares are well set. If I fail, it will be through you; if I am caught, it will be through you. But be sure of this—if we meet in the *Malplaquet*, the fowler and the bird, it will be for the last time. You may catch me, but you will not take me. For a long time past I have provided against just such an outcome as this. Upon my uniform tunics, upon my overalls, I have fixed buttons, hollowed out, each of which contains enough of cyanide of potassium to kill three men. If I were court-martialled and shot, there would be no disgrace to me, an officer on secret service, but a whisper of it might steal to Portsmouth and give deep pain to one there. No one will learn of the petty officer of R.N.V.R. who died far away in the north. The locket with the portrait is round my neck, the ring is upon my finger. Both are ready waiting for you who will do what I ask and will keep my secret from her.

I have the honour to be, sir,
Your obedient servant,

JOHN TREHAYNE.

* * * * *

I folded up the papers and returned them to Dawson, who carefully placed them in his pocket. In the shadows the spirit of Trehayne still seemed to be waiting. I thought for a few minutes, and then rose to my feet. "He was an officer on secret service," said I slowly. "An enemy, but a gallant and generous enemy. In love and in war he played the game, Requiescat in pace."

"Amen," said Cary.

Dawson rose and gripped our hands. "I have the locket and the ring, and I will write as he wished. It is the least that I can do."

They buried Trehayne with naval honours as an enemy officer who had died among us. England does not war with the dead. Though he had fallen by his own hand, the Roman Church did not withhold from an erring son the beautiful consolation of her ritual. Cary and I openly attended the funeral. Dawson was officially in bed, suffering from his much-desired attack of influenza. But in the firing party of Red Marines, whose volleys rang through the wintry air over the body of Trehayne, I espied one whom I was glad to see present.

PART II

MADAME GILBERT

CHAPTER IX

THE WOMAN AND THE MAN

If one believed Dawson's own accounts of his exploits—I can conceive no greater exercise in folly—one would conclude that he never failed, that he always held the strings by which his puppets were constrained to dance, and that he could pluck them from their games and shut them within his black box whenever he grew wearied of their fruitless sport. He trumpets his successes, but he never speaks of his failures—he buries them so deeply that he forgets them himself. He veils his plans, movements, and personal appearance in a fog of mystery. None, not even his closest associates, know what he would be at until a job is completely finished, and finished successfully. Thus when he succeeds, his own small world is deeply impressed—even nauseated—by the compelling spectacle of a Dawson triumphant; when he fails, very few know or hear of the failure. He loves the jealousy of his equals and inferiors even more than the admiration of his superiors. Thoroughly to enjoy life he must be surrounded by both in the amplest measure.

What I now have to tell is the story of a failure—a failure due to his refusal ever to allow his right hand to know what his left hand sought to do. He never told me himself one word concerning this story. I obtained the details partly from Captain Rust, partly from Dawson's Deputy, but chiefly from the lady who filled the star role. Dawson himself foolishly introduced me to her nearly two years later; he did not anticipate that we should become friendly, confidential, that we should discuss him and his little ways over cups of tea, made the sweeter by the clandestine nature of our frequent meetings. He had not allowed for the fascinations of the lady—fascinations so alluring that even I, a middle-aged Father of a Family and Justice of the Peace, was instantly reduced by them to the softest moral pulp; and he had not allowed for the Puckish glee with which I welcomed the tale, rolled it round in my wicked fancy, and bent its ramifications into an orderly narrative.

* * * * *

I very vividly remember my first meeting with the lady. She came one day, a fortnight after I had returned from Cary's flat to my neglected duties, heralded by a short note from Dawson. "I shall be greatly obliged if you will give Madame Gilbert all assistance in your power. She is one of my team." That was all, but my curiosity was piqued. I had heard much of Dawson's team of feminine assistants—rudely called by rivals his "harem"—and I was eager to meet one of them. I ordered Madame Gilbert to be admitted to my presence. She came, I saw, she conquered. When I assert that in two minutes she had plucked me from my chair of dignity, flung me upon the Turkey carpet, and jumped upon me with her daintily shod feet, I do not exaggerate.

She was not very young—I put her at two or three years over thirty. She was, or gave herself out to be, a widow. She was a female detective; I was a modest gentleman of rigid English respectability, not without some matrimonial experience in the ways of Woman. There was nothing in the purpose of her visit to have caused her to come upon me as a Venus, fully armed, and to have forced me to an abject surrender. From the feathers of her black picture hat to the tips of her black velvety shoes she was French-clad, the French of Paris, and wore her clothes like a Frenchwoman. She was dressed—*bien habillée, bien gantée, bien coiffée*. Her hair was red copper, her skin—the "glad neck" of her dress showed a lot of it—had the colour and bloom, the cream and roses, of Devon. Her eyes were very large and of a deep violet All these charms of dress and face and colour I could have gallantly withstood, but the voice of her settled my business at once. Its rich, full tone, its soft, appealing inflection, the pretty foreign accent with which she then chose to speak English—I can hear them now. I have always been sensitive to beautiful voices, and Madame Gilbert's voice is beyond comparison the most beautiful voice in the wide world.

Madame Gilbert made one or two small requests to which I gave an immediate assent, and then she asked me to do something within my power but much against my uncontrolled will. "Madame," said I shamelessly, "as you are strong be merciful; let me off as lightly as you can." She laughed, and eyed me with interest. My defeat had been with her, of course, a certainty, but perhaps it took place more rapidly than she had expected. "I have not asked for much," said she.

"It is not what you have asked that I fear, but what you may ask before I get you out of my room," said I.

She laughed again and let me down very gently. I did not tell her more than three secrets which I was pledged never to reveal. "That's all," said Madame Gilbert. "Thank Heaven," said I.

On the following afternoon, about four o'clock, Madame Gilbert called again upon me. When her card was brought in I trembled, and for a moment had in mind to deny myself to her. But I thrust away the cowardly thought. Be brave, said I to myself, advance boldly, attack the terrible delightful siren, say "no" to her once, and you will be saved! She entered, and though my knees shuddered as I rose to greet her, my mien was bold and warlike. She warmly squeezed my hand, and I returned the attention with *empressement*. For a few minutes we exchanged polite compliments, and then she sprung upon me in her tender confident tones, a request so preposterous that my rapidly flitting courage was stimulated to return. Be brave, I murmured to myself, attack boldly, say "No," and you will be saved for ever.

"I deeply regret, madame," said I coldly, "that it is not possible for me to accede to your wishes." It was done, and I breathed more freely though the sweat broke out on my forehead.

Her eyes opened upon me with the pained surprised look of a deeply disappointed child. "Oh, Mr. Copplestone," she moaned, "and I thought that you were my friend."

I clutched tightly at the arms of my faithful chair and held to my programme of heroic boldness.

"You shouldn't have asked me such a question. You really shouldn't—you know you shouldn't."

Her eyelids flickered, and the violet pools which they uncovered glittered with a moisture which was not of tears, and she laughed, laughed, and continued to laugh with the deepest enjoyment.

"I wanted to see how much you would stand," said she at last.

From that moment her spell over me was broken, and we became friends. I admired her as much as ever, but she was no longer the all-devouring siren. I could say "no" to her as easily as to the most dowdy and unbeautiful of female axe-grinders.

"Will you permit me to offer you a cup of tea so as to wash from your mouth the unpleasant taste of my brutal refusal?"

"I will," said Madame Gilbert graciously.

We issued from my office and betook ourselves to a pleasant shop where we could drink tea and nibble cakes, and talk without being overheard. Madame Gilbert, I observed, had a healthy appetite.

We talked of ourselves and exchanged delicious confidences. "You have asked me many questions," I said. "May I ask one of you? What are you? You are not English, and you are not, I think, French."

"Shall I also learn a lesson from you in unkindness and say 'No'?" she inquired. "But it would be cruel, for you have really been quite nice to me. I will reveal the secret of my birth." She put up one hand and began to tick off the countries which had been privileged to play a part in her origin and education. "My father was a Swede—one; my mother was an Irishwoman—two. I was born at Cork in Ireland, but remember nothing about it, for my father died when I was three years old, and my Irish mother removed instantly to Paris—three. By the way, I have observed that the Irish and the Scotch always run away from their own countries at the first possible opportunity. Why is this?"

"It is much pleasanter," I remarked sententiously "to sentimentalise over the fringes of the United Kingdom from a safe distance, than to live in them."

"Oh! Let me see, I had got as far as Paris. When I was old enough I went to a convent school there. I speak French rather better than I do the Irish-English which my mother taught me."

"You speak English most charmingly. There is about it now a delicate suggestion, no more, of Ireland. When you first came to me your accent was distinctly foreign, French or Italian. I am afraid that you are a wicked woman, a deceiver, and that the fascinating accent was put on for my subduing. It was a very pretty accent."

"I have found it most effective," said she brazenly.

"When I was eighteen I was married—to an Italian (Guilberti)—four. I should have become a Catholic, my husband's faith, but for my mother's Protestant-Irish prejudices. She was of the Irish Church, my husband of the Roman, so I compromised. I joined the Church of England, the High Branch."

"Your religion is almost as complicated as your nationality."

"Yes, isn't it?" said she. Her hand was still uplifted; she had paused at the fourth finger. "We lived in Italy and in France. Two years ago my husband died, and shortly after the war began my mother died. I had a little money, I was known to the Embassy in Paris as one who could pass indifferently as English, or French, or Italian. I wanted to strike a blow for all my countries, and I was recommended to Mr. Dawson for"—she looked round carefully, bent her head close to mine, and whispered—"the Secret Service. So I came for the first time that I remember to England—five."

"But what are you?" I asked, with knitted brows; "I am not an international lawyer."

"Mr. Dawson says"—I found that she has a childlike confidence in the redoubtable Dawson—"that by birth I am a British subject. My Swedish father doesn't count, as I never adopted Sweden when I came of age. My domicile before marriage was France, but by marriage I became an Italian. It is no matter; I am of the Entente, and I do my bit. It is not a bad bit sometimes."

That was the first of many agreeable tea-drinkings which Madame Gilbert and I took together.

Madame Gilbert believes herself to be, as she puts it, a woman of "surprising virtue," and I am by no means sure that she is not right. For the doing of her bit has led her into situations from which nothing but the coolest of hearts and the quickest of wits could have brought her out untarnished. She has played her part gallantly, serenely, in the service of the Alliance; I should be a poor creature if I judged her by British provincial standards. Among other stories she told me the tale which I will repeat to the reader. Here and there were gaps which I have sought diligently to fill up until the whole has been made complete. Madame Gilbert told to me the most intimate details without a blush, and if in my telling I startle the blood to the cheek of the very oldest of readers, the fault will rest with me.

* * * * *

"I have a notion, Madame Gilbert, which I should like you to follow up," said Dawson. He was at that time (the Spring of 1915) in his office in London—he had not yet been despatched on his spacious pilgrimage to the northern shipyards—and Madame Gilbert sat opposite to him in an attitude deliberately provocative. She sat back in a comfortable chair facing the light, her legs were crossed, and she displayed a great deal more of beautifully rounded calf and perfectly fitting silk stockings than is usual even in the best society. Although she did not look at Dawson, she was fully conscious of the frowning glare which he threw at the audacious leg.

"Please give me your attention—if you can. I have been out at the Front lately, at General Headquarters, to advise upon the means of stopping the flow of information from our lines to the enemy. All the obvious channels have been stopped—the telephones hidden in French cellars, the signals given by the hands of clocks, the German spies dressed in uniforms stripped from our dead, and so on. Lots of them, all obvious and simple. One can deal with that sort of thing by a careful system of unremitting watchfulness. We must have caught up with most of the arrangements made by the Germans before the war, but they still get much more information than is good for them to have, and for us to lose. I am convinced—and G.H.Q. agrees—that there are many officers, especially in the French and Belgian armies, who were planted there years before the war for the precise purpose to which they are now put. Even in our own Army, which is expanding so rapidly, the same thing is possible, even probable. An infantry officer spy can do little—he knows nothing of the Staff plans, and cannot get into communication with the enemy at all readily, without arousing suspicion. I went into the whole thing at the Front, and I put my finger, as I always do, upon the danger spot—the Flying Corps. Those who fly constantly over our own and the enemy's lines have complete information as to distribution and movements, and, if they choose, can drop dummy bombs containing news for the enemy to pick up. A French, Belgian, or English aeroplane 'observer' in the enemy's secret service could convey information to him at pleasure and without the possibility of detection. I don't suspect our own Flying Corps, except on the general principle of suspecting everybody and everything, but I do that of the French and the Belgians. France and Belgium were salted through and through by the Germans in anticipation of war. There in the Flying Corps we have a very grave danger which—But I see that you are not attending, madame," he broke off angrily.

Her eyes withdrew from the offending leg for an instant, and flashed at Dawson with a penetrative power which even he felt.

"Shall I repeat what you have said, word for word?" asked Madame
Gilbert coldly.

"I am not now dealing with facts, but with conjecture;" went on Dawson, after begging her pardon. "I have nothing to go upon, but the Germans have far more of imagination and ingenuity than we always credit to them. They must see that with the great advance in the Flying Corps of the Allied armies, and the opportunities which flying men have for collecting and conveying information, one flying spy would be worth a hundred spies on foot. For them to perceive is to act. I therefore conclude positively that they have agents in the flying squadrons of France and Belgium, and possibly even in our own. So I told the C. in C., and he agreed with me. He was good enough to say that he would never have thought of this had I not suggested it to him. Soldiers are not detectives, madame, and very few detectives are William Dawsons. If the War Office knew its business, every Assistant Provost-Marshal would be, not a soldier, but a man from the Yard, and I should be the P.M. in Chief on the Headquarters Staff. I should wear a general's uniform and hat."

"You would look sweet," said Madame politely.

Dawson, the ex-private of Red Marines, swelled out his chest and felt himself to be a Major-General at the least.

"They will do their best to follow up my idea at the Front, and I shall start a campaign here. For I become more and more convinced that the head centre of the German secret service is here in London. Paris, even before the war, was too watchful, and now is as hot as Hell. London reeked with spies, and though we locked up the worst of them when war broke out, lots still remain. If you only knew how many we laid by the heels and keep shut up without any trial, or nonsense of that sort, you would be surprised. It is only since the Defence of the Realm Act was passed that England has become a free country. We keep a drag-net going continually, we have hundreds of agents in all suspected quarters, but this wilderness of bricks and mortar is too big even for us. Once an enemy agent has got himself into an English or Allied uniform, he is horribly difficult to run down. That is where you, and those like you, come in. Are you sure, my dear madame, that you can pass without detection as a Frenchwoman or a French-Belgian?"

Madame Gilbert put up her left hand, and began to tick off her qualifications. "My father was a Swede, my mother was Irish, I was educated in France from the age of three to eighteen, I married an Italian. Brussels I know almost as well as dear Paris. I can be Parisienne or Bruxelloise—whichever you wish, Mr. Dawson."

"Good," said Dawson. "What I want of you is this. Whenever here in London you see a French or Belgian officer wearing the badges of the Flying Corps, mark him down. Make his acquaintance somehow; you will know how. Entertain him, fascinate him, let him entertain you; fool him as you would fool me if I let you; worm out his secrets, if he has any. If you get upon a promising track, go strong; let the man make love to you—he will, whoever he is, if you give him half a chance—intoxicate him with those confounded eyes of yours. If you can find only one who is in the enemy's service, you will be fully repaid for all your trouble."

"It is a largish contract," murmured Madame thoughtfully.

"There are not so very many flying officers," said Dawson, "and they are all young. You will work through them pretty quickly. Most of them will be the genuine article upon whom you need not waste much time. But the others, those whom I suspect, you must grab hold of and never let go, whatever happens."

"I hope," said Madame primly, "that you do not expect me to do anything—improper."

Dawson stared at her in wonder. Her big eyes, shining with the lovely innocence of childhood, met his without a flicker. "Bless my immortal soul," he muttered, "she is getting at me again." Then aloud, and gravely—"My assistants are always expected to conduct themselves with the strictest propriety."

Madame laughed softly. "I have known many men in my time, Mr. Dawson, but I have never enjoyed any man so much as I do you."

"I appear to have rather a roaming commission," Madame Gilbert went on, after a thoughtful pause. "Can you not give me any guidance?"

"Not at present. I am testing an idea, that is all. You must be guided by your own wit and judgment, in which I have the utmost confidence. Don't waste your time or fascinations on the wrong people. Find out if among the French or Belgian flying officers, who from time to time visit London, there are any whose connections and movements will repay close watching here and at the Front. Sift them out. When you get upon a track which seems promising, follow it up, and do not be—what shall I say?—do not be too squeamish. Money is no object. Behind us is the whole British Treasury, and you can have whatever you want. Will you take on the contract, madame?"

"I will do my best," she replied soberly, "and I will not be—too squeamish. I can look after myself, my friend."

In another room of the great building upon the Thames Embankment sat Deputy Chief Inspector Henri Froissart, a French detective officer who had been "lent" to the English service. Opposite him was sitting a young handsome man in the uniform of a captain in the British Army. Froissart was frowning and speaking in savage disrespect of Dawson, his immediate chief. "This English Dawson, with whom it is my misfortune to work, is of all men the most impossible. He is clever, as the Devil, but secretive—my faith! He tells me nothing. He lives in disguise of body and mind. There are twenty men in his face, his figure, and his dress. He comes to me as a police officer, a doctor, a soldier, a priest, even as an old hag who cleans the stairs. He deceives me continually, and laughs, laughs. He is a reproach and an insult. I have it in my mind to score off him; what do you say, mon ami?"

Froissart spoke in French, and the English officer replied in the same language. "With pleasure, in the way of business. I have been placed at your orders, not at old man Dawson's. Go ahead, what is the game?"

Froissart nodded approval. "I think that you can pass as a French officer or a French-speaking Belgian. Is it not so?"

"You should be able to certify that better than I can myself," replied the officer modestly. "As a boy I was brought up at Dinard in Normandy. I served two years in the French Army as a volunteer, a gunner. Then I went to St. Cyr, but England, the home of my father, claimed me, and I was given a commission in the Artillery. That was two years ago. I volunteered for the Flying Corps, served in it at the outbreak of war, but was invalided after that confounded accident which spoilt my nerve. I fell two hundred feet into the sea, and passed thirty hours in the bitter water before a destroyer picked me up. Thirty hours, my friend. My nerve went, and I was besides crippled by rheumatism of the heart. Then I was for a few weeks liaison officer on the Yser at the point where the English and Belgian lines met. The wet, the cold, were too great for me, and again I was invalided. I was a temporary captain without a job until you met me and asked for me to be attached to you for secret service. Yes, M. Froissart, I can pass as a French or a Belgian officer. It needs but the uniform."

"Good," cried Froissart. "You are English of the English, and French of the French. You have served under the Tricolor and under the Union Jack. You are an embodiment of L'Entente Cordiale. You almost reconcile me to that detestable Dawson, but not quite. He is of the provincial English, what you call a Nonconformist—bah! He is clever, but bourgeois. He grates upon me; for I, his subordinate in this service, am *aristocrat*, a Count of *l'ancien regime, catholique, presque royaliste*. His blood is that of muddy peasants, yet he is my chief! Peste, I spit upon the sacred name of Dawson!"

"You don't seem to be a very loyal subordinate," observed the officer, smiling.

"Me, not loyal!" cried Froissart astonished. "I surely am of all men most loyal to l'Entente.

Have I not proved my loyalty? I have left my beautiful France and come here to this foggy London to aid this flat-footed *homme de bout*, Dawson, in his researches. Yet he tells me nothing. He disguises himself before me, and laughs, laughs, when I fail to recognize his filthy, obscene countenance. But I am loyal, of a true loyalty unapproachable."

"I believe you, though you have a queer way of showing it. What is now the game that you want to play off on the old man as a proof of your unapproachable loyalty?"

"He is clever, my faith, clever as the Devil. He discerns the German plans before they are made. He has their agents within a wire net which closes whenever he wishes. He has swept London clean of the foul brood which festered here before the war. I have great, limitless confidence in this Dawson whom I detest, but to whom I am of all his assistants the most loyal. He now suspects that contained within the Flying Corps of us, the Belgians, and the English are observers in the pay of Germany. It is an idea most splendid. For if it is true, what greater opportunity could be given to any spies! To fly over our lines, to learn of everything, and then to convey the news to the enemy by way of the air! If he had told me of this most perspicuous of theories, I would have aided him with all the wealth of my genius. But no, he tells to me nothing. He comes and goes, he spins his web like a great fat female spider, but he tells me nothing. It is my belief that he despises me because I am French, *aristocrat*, and *catholique*. But I will show him; I will, as you call it, score most bitterly off him; I will do in my way successfully what he vainly seeks to do in his way. *Conspuez* Dawson!"

"This is quite like the old times of the Dreyfus case," said the Englishman.

"Dreyfus! But I will speak not of that. It is buried. We French are one people now, one and indivisible. Though of traitors, the villain Dreyfus was of the most horrible. Let us speak of *cet homme tres sale*, Dawson. I do not know his plans. They will be shrewd, but without imagination, without flair. He will watch, with his eyes of a cat, the French and Belgian flying officers who come to London, but he will not discover their secrets. For he does not understand, this cold English Dawson, that secrets which endanger the neck are told only to women."

"Yet I have heard that he has a team of women—his harem, as it is called. I have never seen one of them."

"Bah! Englishwomen, of the large feet and the so protruding teeth! Who would tell of his precious secrets to them!"

"Oh, come, M. Froissart. We have as many pretty women in London as you have in Paris."

"It is possible, my friend. All things, the most improbable, are possible. But they conceal themselves most assiduously. I have not seen them, these so pretty Englishwomen."

"Well, well. You are a bit out of date as regards our women. But I don't want to argue. What is the game?"

Froissart leaned forward and spoke solemnly, forcibly.

"If the man Dawson is right, and there are German spies in the French and Belgian flying services, they will come to London to get their orders. And they will get them from women, depend upon it, my friend. From women who are of French education, who appear to be French, yet who are the deadly, the most dangerous, enemies of France. Let Dawson watch the men themselves; but watch you such women as I indicate—women who appear to be French and yet are not French. I will speak to the Chief, not to Dawson, but to the Great Chief of us all. You shall be dressed in the tenue of a French flying officer; you shall avoid French or Belgian officers who might ask questions the most embarrassing. You shall make the acquaintance of women who appear to be French, yet who are not French. Grip on to these, my friend, entertain them, make yourself of the most fascinating and agreeable, give to them attentions and love of the warmest. And when after two or three glasses of champagne you repose at ease with your arm about their waists, get you at their secrets. You are young, handsome, and your eye is bold. I give you a pleasant task—the deception of deceiving women. In my younger days what joy would I not have taken in it."

Captain Rust became very gloomy during this speech for, though French in education, he was by instinct an Englishman.

"I don't like the business at all. It sounds mean and grubby, ugh! Not quite what one would ask of a gentleman."

Froissart was genuinely surprised. "What do you say, not for a gentleman? Am I not a gentleman, I, who speak, a Froissart, a Count of *l'ancien regime*, a Royalist almost? I offer you a task which combines business and pleasure in the most delicious of proportions. And you call my offer mean and grubby, *meprisable et crotte*! I do not ask you to consort with those of the *demi-monde*. The women who are of most danger to our countries are not *courtisanes*; they are of the *monde*, fashionable. They meet officers in society; they humour and flatter them; they display a melting softness of sympathy and interest. I do not ask you, my friend, to endanger your English virtue."

The tone of wondering contempt with which he ended brought a smile to Rust's lips.

"I am not so very virtuous, monsieur. But I am English, and I try, vainly perhaps, to be a gentleman. It seems to me a dirty business to make up to women in order to wheedle out their secrets."

"We have to do worse than that in defence of our country. We have to plot and counterplot, to lie and deceive. But we do these things, and you must do them too, if you would be of the Secret Service. Content yourself. Think always that it is for *la belle France* or for *le bel Angleterre*, for *la grande Alliance*. You have qualifications unusual; you are young, handsome, and French in manner and speech. You are a soldier; it is for me to command, and for you to obey. Besides, think you; if success comes to us, picture to yourself the desolation of Dawson!"

"Desolating Dawson is more your fun than mine. I have no grudge to work off on the old man. Since you command, I will obey. I will do my best, but, to be quite frank, I do not like the job."

"But you will do it. I think that you English, slow to move, do best those things which you like least. You despise the Secret Service, what you call dirty spying, yet you do it to admiration—with a courage and *sang froid* most wonderful. You hate to begin a war, and yet when you fight you are, of all people, the most unwilling to stop. When we French and the Russians yonder have supped of this war to the dregs, you English will just have begun to find your appetites. Stop? you will cry. Make peace? Be content? Why, we have just got our second wind! It will be the same with you, my friend. You begin reluctantly, but when the chase becomes hot, you will be on fire with zest. You will not trouble then that *vous vous faites crottes*."

"I will do my best; I cannot say more than that."

CHAPTER X

A PROGRESSIVE FRIENDSHIP

Neither Madame Gilbert nor Captain Rust are very communicative concerning their adventures, until they begin to speak of that day when first they met one another in the courtyard of the Savoy Hotel. They both then become voluble. I rather gather—though I did not cross-examine them at all closely—that they had been a good deal bored. Their instructions were so very vague, and the best method of carrying them out so far from clear to their ingenious minds, that they wandered aimlessly about the resorts most affected by officers on leave, spent much money, made a good many pleasant acquaintances, but progressed not at all in their researches. Madame did not meet with any French or Belgian flying officers who seemed likely to be German agents, and Captain Rust failed to discover a siren who appeared to be French and yet was not French, and who aroused any plausible suspicion that she dwelt in the central web of German intrigue. Madame began to think that for once the impeccable Dawson had despatched her upon a wild goose chase, and Rust became convinced that Froissart's vivid longing to score off the detested Dawson had misled him in the selection of the means to bring about this much-desired consummation. They told me little of these wanderings, but when I asked for details of their first meeting, the one with the other, and their subsequent rather startling proceedings, they broke into eager speech. It was not until my keen and curious eye began to penetrate the delicate mysteries surrounding their surprising week-end visit to Brighton that Rust again became tongue-tied. He reprehensibly slurred over the most entertaining details. Madame Gilbert, on the other hand, revealed everything with that plain-spoken frankness which, in any other woman, would appear to be brazen. Madame is thirty-two; Captain Rust no more than twenty-six. He is a modest young man in spite of his French training; she, I am afraid, is a hussy. But I would not have her other than she is.

Madame Gilbert was taking tea alone in the courtyard of the Savoy. She occupied one place at a table laid for four. It was a fine afternoon in late spring, motors and taxis ran in and out unceasingly, the open-air restaurant began to fill up, but none ventured to approach any one of three empty places at Madame's table. She was, as usual, perfectly dressed—though she assures me that her clothes cost next to nothing. "It is the wearing of them, my friend, not the cost which counts." I fancy that her unshakable temper and her gay humour, like her beauty, are really based, as she says, upon her complete freedom from ailments. She loves life, and this, perhaps, is why life loves her.

Madame Gilbert, though to the unobservant eye intent upon her tea and cakes, saw every one who came and went. Many officers were in the restaurant, but one only attracted her special notice. He was a young handsome man in the field-service kit of the French Army, and upon his sleeves and cap were the wings of the Flying Corps. This young man was looking for a table, but could not find one that was empty. She waited until he paused not far from her, and then, sweeping her eyes slowly over the crowded tables, brought them to rest upon his face. He was quite an attractive-looking young man. There was an appeal in his dark eyes as they met hers; he was imploring her of her gracious kindness to permit him to occupy one of her superfluous seats, and she telegraphed to him an encouraging reply. The French officer approached, saluted, and bowed: "Is it permitted, madame, to inconvenience you?" he asked humbly. "The tables are very full, or I would not venture to intrude." He spoke in careful, accurate English, and with an accent markedly French.

"Please favour me by sitting down at once," replied Madame. "I feel
myself to be very selfish with my four places and one small person."
She spoke in careful, accurate English, and with an accent markedly
French.

"Ah!" he exclaimed, seating himself opposite to her, and breaking into
French. "Madame is of my country, is it not so?"

"But certainly," said Madame in the same language, which was to her a second mother-tongue. "I am of Paris. If you had not been French I should not have dared to hint to you that a place at this table might be taken."

For a few minutes they talked together in the ceremonious style for which the French language is the perfect medium, and then dropped into more easy friendly speech. Madame, when she likes the look of a man, becomes intimate at the shortest notice, and Rust, like every man born of woman, succumbed helplessly, instantly, to the wiles of Madame. Though she had finished tea, she urged Rust not to be hurried; there was plenty of time, and one did not often have the happiness to meet a French officer in this dreary London. She enveloped him in her meshes of kindliness, and he responded by thinking to himself that she was the loveliest, most friendly creature whom he had ever met. Madame knows a great deal more of military details than most male civilians, but when she talked to Captain Rust at the Savoy, her ignorance of the Flying Corps was absolute. She asked questions, quite intelligent questions, and he bubbled over with eagerness to answer them. Poor Rust; I can picture the humbling scene. He made an ass of himself, of course, but not a greater ass than I always make of myself—and I am not far from double his age—whenever Madame gets to work upon me.

Within ten minutes she had wheedled out of him an account of his accident. "I was out on patrol duty," he explained, "spotting for submarines between the Straits and Zeebrugge. When the weather is fine we can see deep down into the water, a hundred feet or so, and quite easily make out a submerged U boat. I was testing a new plane fitted with a 90 h.p. R.A.F. engine—" He paused and quickly glanced at her, for he realised his blunder the instant the slip had been made. Madame was all eager attention—what did she know of the marques of aeroplane engines!—"It was a day of rotten luck for me. I spotted nothing, and late in the afternoon my engine began to overheat and miss fire. I did my utmost to struggle towards Do——, Dunkirk, but the beastly thing gave out altogether, and down I dropped into the sea. I had an ordinary land plane without floats, and was obliged to cut myself clear and keep up as best I could with my air belt. It was a weary time, waiting to be picked up, all that night and all the next day; the cold of the water struck right through me, and I was senseless, like a dead man, when at last, thirty hours afterwards, one of our destroyers found me floating there, picked me up, and carried me into Dover. I was in hospital for six weeks, crippled with rheumatic fever, and my heart went wrong. It is much better now, and I hope soon to get back to flying again. I am still on sick leave."

"Poor heart," sighed Madame, and smiled to herself.... "He looked at me," she explained long afterwards, "as if there was still life in his poor strained heart. It was a real kindness to give it some gentle exercise."

"And when you are well you will again fly for France?" she inquired.

"Ah, yes. I yearn for the day when the obdurate doctors will permit me to fly again—for France.... And you, madame, who are so kind to a poor crippled soldier, is it permitted to ask—"

"I am, alas, a widow." She paused, and though demurely looking at her empty tea cup, saw his eyes light up. ["The silly boy was pleased that I was a widow," she explained. "As if that mattered."] "My poor husband fell for France—at Le Grand Couronne. That was eight months ago, and I am still inconsolable. I love to meet the brother officers of my dear lost husband. He was killed by a shell, close beside his general, and I do not even know where he was buried." She delicately wiped her eyes, and Rust murmured broken words of the deepest sympathy. Yet he was not sorry to hear that his new friend was a widow. It must have been a most pathetic scene.

Madame recovered from her sudden rush of grief—brought on by thoughts of that unknown grave upon Le Grand Couronne!—and began to pull on her gloves. "And you, my friend?" she asked gently.

"No one lives who will grieve for me," he replied sadly.

"You are young, my friend, and your heart will—recover itself. I am old, made old by illness and sorrow." She was a picture of glowing health! "May I ask the name by which I may remember you?"

He was clean bowled, for he, foolishly, had not prepared a plausible name. "I am called," stammered he, "Captain Rouille." It was the best that he could do on the instant—the translation of his uncommon English name into French.

"A strange name," she murmured, "though the sound of it is beautiful. Rouille! It signifies, for the moment, the decay of hopes, a mould of rust obscuring ambition. But in a little while the steel of your courage will shine bright once more. I am Madame Gilbert; my husband was of the Territorial Army—a Captain also." She had thought to have made him a Colonel on General Castelnau's staff, but refrained from so risky a flight of imagination. An obscure Captain of Territorials might well be called Guilbert, and pass unidentified.

As they pressed hands at parting, Rust hesitated. "May one hope, madame, to meet you again. Your kindness has been great, and I feel that I have made a new friend."

"And I also," sighed Madame. "I often come here to drink the English tea. It is a pleasing custom of London."

"To-morrow?" he inquired anxiously. "It is possible," replied Madame, very graciously.

* * * * *

"Well," said I, when Madame had told me of this meeting, "I hope that you had the grace to feel ashamed of yourself. To deceive an invalided flying officer with your tale of the Captain of Territorials, blown up by a shell beside his general upon Le Grand Couronne. It was abominable."

"It was the unknown grave which fetched him," said Madame cheerfully.

"Worse and worse. Why could you not have told him the truth?"

"Because, my stupid friend, the Captain Rouille interested me, and I was on duty. What was a captain in the French Flying Corps doing with an aeroplane driven by a 90 h.p. Royal Aircraft Factory engine (R.A.F.)? Why should he speak of 'our' destroyers, referring to those of the British, when he ought to have said the 'English' destroyers as a French officer would have done? Why again should he hesitate over his name, and then give so impossible a one as Rouille? No, I had discerned plainly that M. le Capitaine Rouille, whatever he might be, was not the man he pretended that he was. He spoke French perfectly, but he was not in the French flying service. He was English. I recollected my instructions from the great Dawson—to stick to any one who excited my suspicions, to let him make love to me if need be, and to discover his secrets. I am, my friend, a martyr to duty. Besides, le Capitaine Rouille was a handsome young man, very attractive. I was not grieved at the thought that he might pursue me with his attentions."

"Why," I asked in turn of Rust, "did you begin by telling lies to the charming Madame Gilbert?"

"I was in French uniform," said he, "and I had to play my part."

"And a nice mess you made of it," said I rudely.

"I am afraid that I did. That slip about the R.A.F. engine was unpardonable. But then how was I to know that the dear woman knew as much about aeroplanes as I did myself? She was like Desdemona at the feet of Othello, and, of course, I lost my head. You are as crazy about her as I am, with less excuse. Besides, I was on duty. Before Madame had spoken to me for five minutes, I was certain that she was not French. She spoke perfectly, but there was a little accent, a delightful accent, that told me she was Irish. That soupcon of a brogue which gives so delicate a spice to her English appears also in her French. My mother was an Irish woman, though I have never lived in Ireland. You know that all the Irish, especially those of America or of France, are watched most carefully by the police. Many of them hate the English, and spy upon us. When, therefore, I perceived that Madame, though she appeared to be French was by birth Irish, I recollected my instructions from Froissart. It was my duty to stick to her, to study her. If necessary to make love to her. It did not seem wholly disagreeable to me," he added dryly, "to make love to Madame Gilbert."

"I forgive you," said I, "though, from what I learn, you somewhat exceeded your instructions."

* * * * *

If I were not a most serious writer, this veracious history of Madame Gilbert and Captain Rust would tend to degenerate into comedy, possibly to reach the depths of farce. But, to one of my grave bent of mind, wasted deception, wasted energies, and, above all, wasted national money, excite rather to tears than to laughter. What a spectacle was this which I place before the reader! Here were two trusted members of the English Secret Service pitting against one another those treasures of intelligence, wit, and sensibility which they were employed—and paid—to exercise in the defence of their countries. It may be conceded that one of them was more or less honest. Rust, I am convinced, had persuaded himself—he has no marked ability or attractions of any kind that I can discern—that his duty impelled him to watch Madame with exceeding closeness of attention. That his strong inclinations marched with his duty may be allowed him as a privilege; the plea of duty was not, I believe, merely an excuse. But what can one say in defence of Madame, one who has stored within her little copper-covered head enough brains to furnish a brigade, say, of the Women's Emergency Corps? She had perceived that Rust was an English officer masquerading as a Frenchman, yet she could not have thought that he was a German spy. Why did she not ask him point blank what he was doing in that galley. She has never supplied me with a credible explanation, She pleads, with obvious insincerity, the instructions of Dawson, which in the most reprehensible way granted to her the vaguest of roving commissions. She parades her duty before me in the most tattered of rags.

Upon the following afternoon, when Madame Gilbert drove up to the Savoy in a taxi-cab at half-past four, a young man, in the uniform of a French officer, opened the door and handed her out. It was, of course, Captain Rust, who had waited palpitating upon the curb for some three-quarters of an hour. He led her to a small table which he had reserved for another charming duet of tea, cakes, and conversation.

At this second meeting, Madame bent herself to the deft cross-examination of Rust "Had the Captain Rouille joined St. Cyr as a cadet officer, or had he served in the ranks of the French Army?" He had served in the ranks, and broke into details of his training and garrison service which convinced her that he really had served. She became thoughtful. Rust, eager to show off his accomplishments, explained that he had been recommended for a commission and had joined St. Cyr. More details followed, all of a verisimilitude wholly convincing. Madame, who knew France and the French Army up and down, became more thoughtful and more puzzled. It was plain that Rust had really served in the ranks of the Army, and had been at St. Cyr. Yet he was an Englishman and an officer of the English Flying Corps! She asked further questions, innocent, flattering questions, seeking to discover what had happened to him after his course at St. Cyr. He did his best, but he was of inconsiderable agility of mind and deficient in imagination. He had been, he said, with Maunoury's Sixth Army, which, emerging from Paris in red taxis, had fallen upon the exposed right wing of von Kluck. His description was accurate enough, but the lavish details of former narratives were lacking. He had been *officier de liaison* on the Aisne; again the little intimate touches were lacking. He had joined the flying corps, but omitted to explain how he had learned to fly. It had been at Farnborough, but he could hardly admit this, and was, unhappily, quite ignorant of the French flying grounds.

Madame's quick mind began to see daylight. "How came it, my friend, that you were flying upon the coast when you suffered that accident, so terrible, and paralysed that poor brave heart of yours?" Madame asked the question in the most natural, sympathetic way. It was a facer for Rust, who regretted that he had been so communicative at that first meeting "I was lent to the Naval Wing," he explained, and avoided to particularise. By this time Madame had sorted out his service. She was quite sure that he had not been with Maunoury or upon the Aisne, but that in some manner, as yet not clear, he had left St. Cyr to pass into the English Army.

When in his turn Rust sought diffidently to penetrate the mystery surrounding Madame Gilbert, she overflowed with untruthful particulars. She resembles her master Dawson in this—it is unwise to believe one word which she wishes you to believe. Of her early life in Paris she spoke with emotion. She was the beloved only child of a French doctor—ah, the most learned and pious of men! He died early smitten by disease contracted during his gratuitous practice amongst the friendless poor. A most noble parent! Her mother, too, a saint and angel, had gone aloft shortly after seeing her daughter, Madame, happily married to a maker of caloriferes (anthracite stoves). "I am unworthy of those so noble parents," wailed Madame in broken tones. It was not until they were about to separate that Madame Gilbert herself threw him a bone of truth designed to test his appetite for curiosity. "I must fly," exclaimed she; "I am a woman *tres occupee*. I work, oh, so very hard, for my belle France and to avenge the death of my glorious husband." The blown-up stove maker did not seem to Rust to be a figure of glory, yet he forced himself again to express the deepest sympathy. "Yes," went on Madame, "I would avenge him. I work,"—she glanced round cautiously, and then whispered—"I work for the *gouvernement anglais*. I am an *agent de police*."

"Were you not rather rash," I asked of Madame Gilbert, "to give yourself away so completely? He might not have been so thorough an ass as you thought."

"My friend," said Madame calmly, "I had taken tea with him twice, and had satisfied myself that he was not, what you call, very bright. A dear fellow, handsome, a gentleman of the English pattern, but not bright. If I had not helped him to get a move on, I might have lunched with him, had tea, dined with him, attended theatres, traversed in motors your pleasant countryside, flirted, until I had become a very old woman, and there would have been nothing to show for all my exertions. I remembered the instructions of Mr. Dawson, I recalled to myself my duty, I was compelled to discover who and what was this Capitaine Rouille, and I could only succeed by forcing him to reveal himself—to give himself away. When I said that I was an agent of the English police, he did not believe me; but he was curious—he watched me. I gave him much to watch and to imagine that he had discovered. Then one began to get forward."

* * * * *

I am ignorant of the diplomatic pourparlers which led up to the week-end trip to Brighton, that remarkable trip which ended *l'affaire* Rust. It must have been planned by Madame; it bears the unmistakable imprint of her impish wit; it was, too, a bold development of her designs for the effective speeding up of Rust. He would have dallied all through the summer, looking feebly for an opportunity to ravish a despatch-case which always accompanied Madame and which had become the inseparable and ostentatious "gooseberry" at their meetings. Madame declared that it was stuffed with papers the most secret. "The English Government would be desolated if they passed for one moment out of my hands." This despatch-case played parts quite human. It was perpetually provocative of Rust's curiosity, and a reminder that the agreeable pastime of making love to Madame was not an end in itself, but a means whereby he might discharge his official duties. It was, moreover, a visible sign that Madame was a woman, *tres occupee*, and a self-styled *agent de police*; it rested always silent at her side as a protector of innocence. Rust becomes uneasy when that case is mentioned, but Madame bubbles over at the thoughts of her *petite chere portefeuille, cette idee de genie*. She brags of her genius, of her notion *si lumineuse*, of her *guet-apens si adorable*.

While Madame must have planned the Brighton trip, she contrived that the suggestion should come timidly, deprecatingly, from Rust. She would have scorned so crude an advance, one, too, falling so far short of her high standard of womanly virtue, as a direct hint that she was willing to pass three days in a seaside hotel with a young man! *Mais, non. Ce serait une betise incroyable*! I can imagine her hints, increasing in strength as she beat against the obtuse heaviness of Rust's intellect. But I cannot imagine how any one, least of all the brilliant Froissart, should have conceived that lumpish soldier to be capable of the finesse needful for the Secret Service. He has since been returned empty, and I do not wonder at it.

Madame must have lamented the stuffiness of London during the bright days of early June, and painted, in her enthusiastic French fashion, a picture of southern England and the glittering Channel. "*Ma foi, mon ami*, what would I not give for one hour of peace and rest, away from this swarming hive of men and women? It is as yet too cold to swim in that sea which washes the shores of my beautiful France—and bears the so gallant English soldiers to her help—but I would love to sit upon the sands and gaze, gaze across the waters towards my poor bleeding land. But, alas, I am a woman *tres occupee*." After a great deal of this sort of thing, Rust was spurred up to suggest that he also was weary, and that nothing could be more delightful than to sit beside Madame upon those sands and to bewail with her the woes of their common country. The idiot did not reflect that a woman of Madame's taste in dress does not usually mess up her Paris frocks with nasty sea sand. Madame sighed. It was a charming picture, but, alas, quite impossible. Rust still further spurred by Madame—"Le Capitaine Rouille is not very bright"—at last broke into a proposal delivered with many hesitations and many apologies. Why should not they travel to Brighton on the Friday evening and draw solace for their weary souls from a Saturday, Sunday, and possibly Monday, at Brighton? Madame became a frozen statue of offended womanhood! What, *mon Dieu*, had she done that he should conceive her to be a light woman? She, the never-to-be-comforted widow of the incomparably gallant hero of anthracite stoves and le Grand Couronne. She had been too unsuspicious, too trustful; their pleasant acquaintance must end upon the instant; the too-gross insult which he had put upon her could never be pardoned. Rust was borne away and overwhelmed in the flow of her sad reproaches. Abjectly he grovelled: He regard the ineffable Madame Guilbert as a light woman! Perish the thought! He, to whom she had been an angel of kindness and discretion! He cast a slur upon the shining brightness of her reputation! Rust had never in his life been so eloquent. Madame listened with satisfaction. She might in time, after long years, forgive him, but not yet. The insult, however unintended, was too fresh and her heart was desolated! She scorched and scarified Rust during two whole days, for their meetings continued unbroken, and at last, as an undeserved concession and as evidence of her soft forgiving heart, she consented to go to Brighton on the Friday. "We must regard closely *les convenances*. You men, so rash and so stupid, you do not understand how infinitely precious to us poor women is the spotless bloom of our reputation." Rust protested that the bloom upon the unplucked peach was not, in his eyes, more stainless than the reputation of Madame. How she must have grinned! He made plans, rude, coarse plans, for the shielding of the so precious reputation of dear Madame Guilbert, but she gently put them aside. "In my hands," she declared grandly, "le Capitaine Guilbert has left his honour, and I will guard it with my life. Alas, what is my life when my heart is buried in that lonely grave upon le Grand Couronne in which I pray rests his much-blown-up body. I myself will devise the means by which I can grant you a mark of my condescending forgiveness and preserve *sans reproche* the honour of a Guilbert."

I confess that I have drawn upon my imagination for most of this touching scene, but, knowing Madame as I do, I am sure that I have given the hang of it.

CHAPTER XI

AT BRIGHTON

Madame Gilbert and Captain Rust travelled to Brighton on the Friday evening in the Pullman train. They occupied different carriages. Their hotel, one of those facing the sea which washed the far-off shores of their beloved, bleeding France, had been selected by Madame—"I desire a hotel, my friend, not a *caravanserai*!" Madame arrived ten minutes before Rust, and had disappeared within her own *appartement* when his cab drove up to the doors. Rust then booked his room, one upon the second floor. He took that which was offered, and did not observe that Madame's room was also *au seconde*. But he did notice—he could not help it—that the imposing lady in charge of the hotel office was French. "Ah, monsieur le capitaine," said she, beaming caresses upon him, "with what joy do I perceive the *tenue de campagne* of my own Army. I will gladly grant to you one of the rooms of the very best and at the price of the lowest. The patron, he also is French, and would be furious if I did not give the most cordial welcome to an *officier francais*." Rust thanked the lady of the bureau, and heartily approved Madame's choice of an hotel.

"One moment, if you please," said I to Madame, who supplied me with these details. "I perceive that both the rooms, yours and Rust's, were upon the second floor. Is it in this way, you shameless woman, that you preserved from reproach the honour of the late imaginary stove man?"

Madame sighed, and turned upon me the look which, in my mind, I have labelled "Innocence unjustly traduced." One of these days, with German thoroughness, I shall prepare a numbered and annotated catalogue of Madame Gilbert's looks and tones. Though it cannot teach her sex anything which the youngest member does not already know, it will be full of valuable instruction and warning for the innocent male.

"Am I responsible," wailed Madame, "for the allotment of rooms by *hoteliers*?"

"Most certainly," I said severely. "I do not know your methods. It is not given to man to penetrate the unfathomable duplicity of woman. But I am convinced that had you wished it, you would have been placed *an premier*, and Rust consigned to the uttermost cock-loft in the roof."

Madame and Rust dined that first evening at separate tables, but discovered in one another old friends when they accidentally met afterwards in the lounge.... "What happiness, can it indeed be le Capitaine Rouille, the friend closer than a brother of my poor slain husband?" ... "Madame Guilbert! Can it be you whom I meet thus unexpectedly? You whom I have not seen since that dreadful never-to-be-forgotten day upon which I broke to you the news, the terrible news—" Rust's voice failed; even Madame, who thinks little of his ability, admits that he performed on this occasion to admiration. The rencontre was a most affecting one, conducted in voluble French in the full blaze of publicity in a crowded hotel lounge. The English audience was impressed and honestly sympathetic; our insular reserve has been melted in the fires of war. "It is a French lady, poor thing, who has lost her husband," they whispered, the one to another, "and that handsome fellow in ordinary evening-dress is her man's brother officer, who was with him at the last, and who brought the sad news to her. How sweet she looks, and how tenderly sympathetic he is!" The eyes of the men had already been drawn to Madame's royal beauty and those of the women to her dress, a masterpiece of Paquin. Now that she had met Rust the men were sorrowful, regretting a vanished opportunity of making her acquaintance, and the women were relieved. She was too formidable a rival to be at large, alone and unattended, but now she would be monopolised naturally and properly by her good-looking compatriot. So when Madame and Rust slipped away to a corner of the lounge, kindly eyes followed them, and the voices of the censorious had no excuse to be raised. "You are a wonder, madame," whispered Rust. "And you, my friend, did not so badly," replied Madame in frank approval.

They separated early that evening, for Madame, who knew not what it was to feel really tired, shammed fatigue as a reason for retiring betimes. To her came Marie, a little dark French *femme de chambre* of the second floor, imploring to be allowed to assist at the night toilet of a desolate widow of France. While Marie brushed out the long, rich, copper hair the two chattered unceasingly of France and the Army of steel-hearted poilus which held the frontiers of civilisation away yonder in Picardy, Artois, Champagne, and the Vosges. Marie herself had a man out there of whose welfare she had heard nothing since the war began. She had received no letters, and the French publish no casualty lists. "*Mon cher petit homme est mort, madame. C'est certain, mais j'espere toujours.*" There are many, many Frenchwomen to whom the death of their loved ones is certain, though they hope always. "I felt rather a pig talking fibs to the poor girl," confessed Madame.

Madame Gilbert had made her plans with thoughtful care, and proposed to carry them out with hardihood. She had determined to work so adroitly on the Saturday upon the curiosity and "poor strained heart" of Rust that he would be speeded up to run big risks. He did not know that, however judiciously frail her conduct might be, she was a very dragon of virtue in defence of her honour. "I gave my heart," said she to me quite seriously, "to the Signor Guilberti, one far, far different from *le mari imaginaire* of le Grand Couronne. Until, if ever, I give my heart again no man shall possess me. I play, I kiss, I philander—as you call it—but what are these trifles? *Des bagatelles, rien de tout!*" He did not realise her serene indifference to the small change of love and her respect for its true gold. But I do not think that Rust, when Madame consented to be his companion at Brighton, seriously misjudged her motives. He did not know, of course, or in the last degree suspect that she designed his capture as a professional victim.

Again and again she had told him that she was an agent of the English police, and again and again, as she intended, he had disbelieved her. She was so incomparably his intellectual superior that she could make him believe or disbelieve precisely as she chose. She made him think that she had come to Brighton for companionship, and as a proof of her kindly forgiveness of a grave indiscretion. He believed; for never was Rust, even Rust, so idiotic as to suppose that she had succumbed before his charms and had come to throw herself into his arms.

But for the machinations of Madame the visit would, I am sure, have passed without incident. Rust would not have lost his turnip of a head. He would, out of loyalty to his orders from Froissart, have tried to grab the despatch-case and ravish its secrets. But he would not have done what he did, at the risk of compromising the bloom of her so precious reputation, if she had not deliberately worked him up to do it. Therefore, while I acquit Rust of evil intention, my reproofs, my grave reproofs—at which she laughs and snaps her fingers—are reserved for that unscrupulous Madame.

At breakfast Madame Gilbert and Captain Rust found that a private table, a table of the best in a bay window facing the sea, had been reserved for them by orders of the patron. The news of their pitiful rencontre in the lounge had sped to his ears; he had wept copiously before his sympathetic staff, and declared that the bereaved widow and the so gallant captain should lack for nothing in his hotel. "If it were not that I feared to offend their delicacy I would refrain from presenting to them *l'addition*. Make, I pray you, *mademoiselle du bureau*, their charges of the lowest." He was a most noble patron.

The path of the wicked was thus made smooth. By the English guests, by the entire staff, it was considered inevitable, indeed highly becoming, that Madame and Rust should devote themselves wholly to one another. Had they embraced in public, and wept many times a day upon one another's necks, the staff—half of which was French—would have deemed the exhibition most seemly and fitting, and the English, though embarrassed, would not have been censorious. By so much has war brought to us an understanding of the simple honest hearts of our closest Allies. In ceasing to be insular we are ceasing to worship our wooden conventional gods.

Madame, who, as I have before remarked, says the most frightful things in her soft, musical voice, regarding one the while with frank, steady eyes, commented thus upon the attitude of *le patron* and his assistants towards them. "They wrapped us about so thoroughly in their tender sympathy that nothing which we had chosen to do in mutual consolation could have shocked them."

I do not propose to weary the reader by detailing at length the progress of Madame's Saturday campaign. Her methods of offence will, by now, have become clear. To the "suffocating gas" of her smiles, and the "liquid fire" of her eyes she had added the devastating "Tank"—her despatch-case. She worked its mysteries unceasingly. When it was not under her own hand it reposed—during meal times, for example—in the steel safe of *le patron*. All except one paper, of the most thrilling importance, which never left her person. This small, unobtrusive paper, upon which, according to Madame, the destinies of nations depended, was hidden always—happy paper—in the bosom of her corset.

Did she not, inquired Rust, greatly daring, find it rather hard and scratchy? To him its resting-place seemed too delicate a spot to be used as a general store. Madame frowned at the allusion to so intimate a topic, and Rust, terrified, implored her pardon, which was graciously vouchsafed.

"You should not, *mon ami*, speak to me as if I were that which you once thought me—a light woman." She reduced him nearly to tears, and then, in kindly consolation, permitted him to hold her hand. Both as a pretended French officer, and as an English agent of the Secret Service, Rust was the most derisory of frauds.

During the day the pair of plotters were inseparable, and Madame played continually with unfailing deftness upon the two strings of Rust's poor heart and of his intense curiosity, which she clearly perceived though she did not know it to be professional. When the heart swelled with stimulated emotion, and Rust began to show inconvenient fondness, Madame would frown reproof and lead the despatch-box into action. Very often she would carry her hand to that pleasant spot where nestled the paper of so great international importance, and she would speak of it and of the terrible responsibilities which rested upon her as a secret *agent de police*. "When I carry a document such as this," she would say, "one *pour faire les Boches se crever*, it never leaves my bosom all the day and rests under my pillow by night. Under my pillow, *mon ami*." She dwelt upon that pillow, and raised in the mind of Rust a charming vision of a white lace-edged surface upon which was spread out a lovely disorder of red copper hair. She so worked upon him that his emotions and his duties became inextricably mixed. Somehow he must secure that paper and solve the baffling problem of the wonderful widow who appeared to be French, and yet was not French. His brain by itself could not have conceived of a means, but Madame assisted to stimulate its imagination as she had done the beating of his heart. "It was wrong of you, *mon ami*" she said, in gentle reproof, "to select a room upon the same floor as mine, it was a proceeding bold and not a little indelicate, which might have compromised my precious reputation had I not been secure in the honour of my poor lost Captain Guilbert." Rust protested that he had left the choice of rooms entirely to the lady of the bureau, but Madame's smile showed that she was wholly sceptical. "I speak frankly to you," said she, "so that there may be no longer in your mind any thought that I am a woman of light conduct. I have come here, driven by your sad pleadings, to give you of my companionship, and my heart would be desolated if I thought that you still misjudged me." The beautiful voice shook, and I do not doubt that the violet eyes, glistening with pumped-up tears, were raised to Rust's face. I, her friend, know that she can feel deeply, and I can distinguish that which she simulates from that which moves her, but the poor creature Rust was in her hands the most helpless and deluded of victims.

So the day passed. They lunched together and dined together. In the intervals they walked upon the sunny front, for the weather was perfect and the sun shone as it only shines at Brighton. Madame, I am quite sure, did not sit upon the sand. It appears also that they visited a succession of picture houses. Madame declares that she is fascinated by this form of entertainment; the variety and rapid movement delight her—as I admit they do my dull self—and she deeply enjoys the blatant crudity of cinematic drama. "It is so entirely unlike life that it transports one to another world," says she. "Here in this strange visionary world of the pictures one lives in a maelstrom of emotions. Boys and girls meet, embrace, and marry all within the space of a few minutes upon the screen and of an hour or two of dramatic action. Children are conceived and born by some lightning process which it would be a happiness for the human kind to learn. Heroes die while strong men bare their heads in grief, and ten minutes later the corpse is capering joyously in a new piece. By attending three or four houses in one afternoon one sups upon emotions and feeds without restraint upon rich, satisfying laughter. Yes, *mon ami*, I love the cinema. Rust did not, I think, greatly interest himself in the pictures, but was happy in the darkness—holding my hand."

She laughed as I broke into growls. "Is it not, *mon cher*" she went on, "that the cinemas will always be most popular—however dull may be the pictures—so long as boys and girls, men and women, who love, desire to fondle one another's hands in the dark?"

"You and Rust did not love one another," I grunted.

"No. We were not the real thing, but we made ourselves into quite a plausible imitation."

Madame pursued her programme with indefatigable ardour and patience. She impressed again and again upon Rust's imagination a picture of herself sleeping unprotected, in a room not far distant from his own, while beneath her pillow reposed a paper precious and mysterious beyond words to describe. She even hinted that a dread of fire, from which she always suffered when sleeping at hotels, forbade the locking of her door. "I am not afraid to die," said she, "for what have I to bind me to life now that I can never visit the spot where repose the shattered fragments of my beloved Capitaine Guilbert? But to be burned, helpless, while rescue was cut off from me by a locked door! I shrink from so terrible a fate." Subtlety, she had discovered, was thrown away upon the obtuseness of Rust. She was compelled to be brutally plain, and so she drove into his thick head the tempting fact that nothing interposed during the hours of darkness between his eager hands and the paper which she had taught him to covet. If she awoke and mistook his motives—if she thought that he had ventured into her room with designs upon her honour—Rust felt sure that her kind heart would forgive him, by breakfast-time, though she would certainly dismiss him from her bedside with the most haughty of reproaches. If he could not find some other way before they separated for the night, he had almost decided to essay the venture. She slept very soundly, said Madame; she had not awakened in her *appartement* in Paris upon one night when a bomb from a Prussian aeroplane had exploded within two hundred yards of her house. Another way was still possible, and Rust, while he was dressing for dinner, determined to try it; it was a way, too, which thrilled him with pleasurable anticipation.

At dinner Madame declined champagne, which she said was a poor, feeble drink. Let them for once share a bottle of sparkling Burgundy, a royal wine, the Wine of Courage. The patron brought them the bottle himself, and lamented that they would not indulge themselves in a second. Madame had no desire that Rust should, under its influence, become too enterprising. The evening was warm, and afterwards they moved into the pleasant garden behind the hotel and sat together in a quiet corner. Other guests were in the garden, but it had become tacitly agreed among them that Madame and Rust—the "dear French things"—should be permitted to console one another in seclusion. No one could perceive that the black-sleeved arm of Rust had found a happy resting-place around Madame's black-covered waist, or that her glowing head was not far from his shoulder. Her Paris evening frock was cut low, though never by the fraction of an inch would Madame permit her *couturier* to exceed the limits of perfect taste. Looking down over her shoulder

Rust could see, protruding from the white lace below her bodice, the corner of a paper. She talked little. It seemed to give her pleasure to lean against his shoulder and dreamily, half asleep, to rest there reposefully like a tired child. "But, *mon ami*" said Madame to me in relating these tender details with the greatest satisfaction, "I was very wide awake indeed."

Rust eyed that corner of paper and waited without speaking until his companion should become almost unconscious of his movements. Then gently he moved his right arm from her waist and placed it over her shoulder. She moved slightly, but it was only to nestle more closely against him. His dangling fingers moved little by little towards the opening of her corsage, they descended, and with his thumb and forefinger he gripped the paper. Madame did not move her body nor, to Rust, did she seem to suspect his intentions. But her right arm lifted slowly up, she gently grasped his hand in hers, pressed it kindly for a moment, and then, still holding it, removed his arm from her shoulder to her waist. "Your coat sleeve scratches my shoulder," she murmured. Rust, who had instantly released the paper when Madame took his hand, never again got an opportunity of touching it, for she kept her arm pressed over his during the whole time that they sat together. "I gave him the chance," explained Madame to me, "and it worked beautifully. But once was enough. From that moment I became really suspicious of Rust. Before I had only been puzzled. What he was I could not guess, but I was dead set on finding out before the night was over. Till then I had allowed only little freedoms, but when I rose to go into the hotel and he bent over me I let him kiss me on my lips. It was a severe disappointment, that kiss," added Madame contemplatively.

"Spare me the loathsome details," said I crossly.

When at last Madame Gilbert went to her room she was smiling gaily and showing no signs of fatigue at the tiresome exercises of the day. Though it was approaching midnight the faithful Marie was waiting to assist her toilet. "Ah, madame," sighed Marie in her frank Parisienne fashion, "le Capitaine is so beautiful and devoted. He regards you as one who would devour. I marvel that you have the heart to separate from him."

"Marie," said Madame, laughing, "you are a naughty girl, a corrupter of my youthful morals. I am afraid that *le bon Capitaine* must go hungry. For—" and then she pranced off upon that wearisome old story about the blown-up Territorial bore of *le Grand Couronne*. Fidelity to the scattered corpse of a husband—*un mari assommant, mon Dieu, pas un amant joyeux!*—seemed to Marie the most wasted of emotions. She, in common with all the other Frenchmen and women in the hotel, was an ardent partisan of Captain Rouille.

"If my bell rings in the night, come quickly, Marie," said Madame, as she dismissed the girl. "I shall need you *a la grande vitesse*."

Madame slipped the seductive paper and something else under her pillow, saw that the electric and the light switch were close to her hand upon the bedside table, and snuggled down contentedly. "The trap is set and baited," she murmured; "I hope that the bird will not keep me waiting."

An hour passed slowly. Rust has told me little of his feelings, but admitted that he was in the "devil of a funk." He had determined to make a daring shot at the paper and the solution of Madame's identity, but he shivered at the prospect of her wrath should she awake and catch him in the act. "She would have thought the worst of me, and, like you, Copplestone, I cherish her beautiful friendship as the most precious of privileges. On my honour I was only after the paper." Madame found the waiting time very tedious, but I am sure that her pulse did not quicken by a beat. She has a wonderful nerve.

At one o'clock, when the hotel was very quiet, and the boot-cleaner had made his round of collection, Madame heard the handle of her door move and the door itself push slowly open. Through her partly closed eyes she saw the momentary flash of an electric torch with which Rust took his bearings, and then she felt, rather than saw or heard, a figure draw gently towards her bed. Her right hand was under the pillow grasping that something, not the paper, which she had laid there in readiness. Rust approached, bent over her, and his fingers felt for the pillow. They touched her hair, and she knew that the moment for action had come. Out stretched her arm, holding the pistol well clear of his body, for she was loath to hurt him, and a sharp report within a couple of feet of his side frightened Rust more thoroughly than had the hottest of "crumps" in Flanders. He sprang away, and darted for the door; but in an instant the lights went up, and a loud, commanding voice—utterly unlike Madame's soft musical social tones—called to him to halt. "Halt!" cried Madame in English. "Right about turn! 'Shun!" The familiar words of command brought him round in prompt obedience, and there before him he saw Madame Gilbert sitting up in her bed, pointing a most business-like automatic pistol straight for his heart. Her hand held it true, without a quiver, and along the sights glittered an eye remorseless as blue steel. This was a woman wholly different from that kindly yielding creature whom he had embraced and kissed a couple of hours earlier!

"You will please stand quite still," said Madame, speaking the slightly tinged Irish-English of her birth, "for if I shoot, le Capitaine Rouille will be no more. See! Upon my dressing-table behind you is a small vase supporting a rose. I will cut off its stem," She quickly moved the pistol, and fired. "You may turn round." He obeyed, and saw that the vase was unbroken, but that the rose, cut off at the stem, lay upon the dressing-table. Behind it appeared a bullet-hole in the plaster of the wall.

Madame flicked the spent cartridge off her counterpane, where it had fallen upon ejection, and resumed. "I have rung the bell, and in a moment there will be a most interested audience. You will then please explain what brings you to my bedroom."

He had faced round towards her again, and his poor mind was a blank. The situation was too big for him. He had fallen into a trap, but why it had been set he could not guess. Who was this calmly capable, straight-shooting widow who, with the copper hair falling over her shoulders and streaming down the front of her dainty nightdress, appeared in action even more lovely than in repose?

The first to arrive was Marie, then followed another *femme de chambre*, then came the night porter, then the boot-collector, last, with eyes opened wide at the surprising spectacle of a beautiful young woman receiving her lover at the point of a pistol, appeared *monsieur le patron* himself. They clustered in a group by the door. "I think," said Madame serenely, "that we have enough. Marie, the house is full; shut the door and lock it." The order was obeyed. "Now," went on the commanding voice from the bed, using French for the effective shutting out of the English boot-cleaner and night porter, "if you men will turn your backs, and Marie will hand me my dressing-gown, I will prepare myself for the examination of Monsieur le Capitaine Rouille. It is not seemly that a court of inquiry should be conducted in a nightdress."

The men turned round, or were pushed round. Marie—gasping with wonder at the whole incredible business, so unlike that which she had suggested—brought the silk dressing-gown and robed Madame, who skipped out of bed for the purpose. Then the fair *juge d'instruction,* wrapped to the neck in blue silk, and looking prettier than ever, propped herself upon the pillows and opened the court.

"Captain Rouille," ordered she in French, "please tell these others why you came to my bedroom."

I regret to record that Marie and the other girl looked towards one another and sniggered. The patron lifted up his hands in amazement. *Mon Dieu*, what a question! The two English servants did not understand French.

Rust said nothing. Madame, who had observed the excusable misunderstanding of her French audience, condescended to explain. "I am sure," she said, "that Captain Rouille will not suggest that his visit was designed to attack my honour."

"*Quelle dame extraordinaire!*" moaned the patron. "*C'est incroyable la sangfroid de celle-la.*"

"Of course not," cried Rust, speaking for the first time. "Never would I have dared to think of such a thing. Madame Gilbert is a lady of the highest virtue. It was not to compromise her that I entered her room."

"The man," groaned the patron, "is no less extraordinary than the woman. Why in God's name this pistol, this scene so public! They are lovers, beyond doubt, yet they spring upon my hotel this scene of the most scandalous. It is not the way of France; I do not understand such goings on."

Madame drew a paper from her bed, and held it up. "Was it for this that you came?"

"Yes," said Rust, "for that and that only."

"*Un billet doux*" said the patron, playing without design the part of a bewildered chorus, "Why should not madame have given it to him if she wished to write that which she was too modest to say?"

"Why did you want it?"

"What more natural," cried the patron, "than that the brave captain should be eager to read the sweet confession of your love?" Madame missed not a word which dribbled from the lips of the poor, puzzled patron, who contributed the comic sauce which titillated her humorous palate. The patron to her was a sheer joy.

"Why did you want it?" repeated Madame sternly.

"Because," said Rust, "you said that it contained the most important of secrets."

"What have you to do with secrets which concern the fate of nations at war?"

"Nations! War!" muttered the patron. "What words are these to find upon the lips of lovers? By now they should, had they not both been quite mad, have forgotten war in their mutual embraces."

Rust was silent, considering what he should say. He had not the wit to invent a plausible story, and to such men there is only one safe rule—when in doubt, tell the truth. He told the truth.

"I wanted that paper because I am a member of the Secret Service."

"Of Germany?" snapped Madame, flashing violet lightning from her eyes. Sensation! The two French women broke into screams of rage, dreadful to hear; the patron raised his clenched hands, and roared like a furious beast. Rust, a brave man, shrank for a long, startled moment. His flesh quivered, as if it felt fierce French nails fasten into it. He saw the blood-lust flame in the eyes which searched his face. He trembled, but spoke up firmly.

"No. The Secret Service of England."

"Liar!" roared the patron. "*Menteur! Espion*! Foul seducer of a desolate *veuve de France*! Die, traitor! Madame, raise your pistol; shoot—shoot instantly for the honour of France!" The man, a fat, comfortable bourgeois, was transfigured with frightful, murderous rage. He had become a figure almost heroic.

But Madame did not shoot. In ten seconds her swift brain had recalled the whole series of incidents during her commerce with Rust; she penetrated to the heart of the mystery, and immediately became convinced that he spoke the truth.

"No," said she. "*Monsieur le patron* and you, *mes demoiselles*, cease your cries. You do the brave Capitaine Rouille a very grave injustice for which you must pray his forgiveness *sur le champ*. He is a soldier of France, and of our noble Allies, the English. He is an officer of the English Secret Service. The mistake was mine, for which, *mon capitaine*, I implore your pardon."

She lay back in her bed, and the laughter poured out of her in one unbroken flood. She laughed until she became weak as a baby, for the idiotic comedy which they two had played—at the expense of the British Treasury—was beyond any other means of expression. Rust, who began to grasp something of the truth, also broke into a laugh, and the amusement of the principals brought instant conviction to the audience. The repentance of those who had thirsted for Rust's blood a moment since was very pleasant to witness. The women begged permission to kiss his brave hands, which had slain the foul Boches, and the patron cast his burly person upon Rust's pyjama-clad bosom and saluted him on both cheeks. He had a stiff, hard beard!

"And now," cried the patron, "this scene, so deplorable and scandalous, is happily ended. Our beautiful Madame and the brave captain, their mistakes and misunderstandings removed, are again lovers of the fondest. Let us go, my friends, and leave them to forgive one another as they will desire to do in decent privacy. *Allons, allons, vite*!"

He drove away the boot-collector and the night porter, who had not understood one word of the quick French which had been spoken. They explained the scene satisfactorily to themselves by the one word, "French." The women would also have gone if Madame, who was still laughing, had not hastily recalled Marie.

"Marie," she whispered, spluttering with cheerful impropriety, "lead that captain away and lock him into his room or my reputation is gone for ever. Take Rouille away, and then leave me, for I want to laugh and then to sleep."

But Rust, blushing deeply at the preposterous closing of the scene, had sneaked quietly out of the room.

* * * * *

They met at breakfast without embarrassment. At least Madame was perfectly tranquil; I cannot answer so surely for Rust. In the eyes of the little world of the hotel nothing had been changed. They retained their assumed characters as a Widow and Soldier of France, who consorted with the freedom of old friends.

"So," said Madame, when all had been explained, "you were put on by our dear, fiery Froissart, and I by the dear, secretive Dawson. We blundered up against one another, and the rest followed naturally. You were such an one as I looked for, and I was of the kind pictured by the imaginative Froissart. It has all been most amusing, especially when one reflects that the English Government has paid for all our delightful lunches, teas, dinners, and motor runs. I doubt, though, whether we can with easy consciences send in the bill for this week-end."

"No. We will divide the cost between ourselves, for I am sure that you will refuse to be my guest. All I ask is that you do not cut our holiday the shorter on account of what has passed."

"Not by an hour," replied Madame heartily. "I like you, Captain Rust; we will enjoy ourselves to-day as colleagues *en vacance*, and to-morrow we will report at headquarters. We will leave Dawson and Froissart to sort out the responsibility for the whole comedy. It has been a most pleasing experience. Never shall I forget that scene of last night and the bewilderment of the poor patron. His comments were a delight, and the conclusion was so purely French in its artless conception that I felt for your innocent blushes."

"The patron was the limit," muttered Rust, flushing deeply.

"He was. And yet no one could convince him that the reconciliation so desired by him was not the most natural and decorous for us. I am still sore with excessive laughter. Again and again in the night I woke up and simply bellowed."

The Sunday was again a very fine day, and Rust speaks of it still with enthusiasm. Madame revealed herself to him, no longer as the seductive siren, but as a true-hearted colleague and helper. He saw her not only as a beautiful and most compelling fascinator, before whom he had grovelled, but as a big-brained and big-souled friend. "She is the only woman whom I have ever met with whom I would go tiger-shooting," said Rust to me. I will accept that one sentence as his considered verdict; no greater tribute could be paid by a man to a woman.

At first he did not fully grasp that the Madame of that Sunday, the real Madame, was wholly different from the one he had known before. As they sat together upon the cliffs towards Rottingdean, he slipped his arm about her waist. Gently, but very decidedly, she removed it. "No, *mon ami*," said she. "All that has passed with the necessity for its exercise. I do not play with my friends."

"Thank you," replied he—it was the brightest speech which Madame has recorded of him. There is hope that Rust will, with years and experience, develop in intelligence.

When Madame returned to London on the Monday, she sought an audience of Chief Inspector Dawson, and told the whole story. He was not pleased, but handsomely conceded that she had carried out her duties with skill and enterprise. "The farce was not your fault," said he; "it was entirely due to that French ass Froissart, who has no right to play games of his own without consulting me. I will make a protest to the Chief."

"Don't do that," urged Madame. "Froissart is rather a dear, and you know that the fault was partly yours, for not taking him into your confidence. I have determined to cultivate Froissart, and shall endeavour to persuade him that your feminine assistants are not all of microscopic intelligence and of repulsive appearance."

"You will succeed," said Dawson handsomely.

Froissart, to whom Rust reported, gleaned some consolation from the failure of his agent.

"This wonder of a woman, of whom I must instantly make the honourable acquaintance, has saved the detested Dawson from the deeps of humiliation. But we have scored off him most surely. He has shown himself to be a blundering, conceited English pig, and I will protest to the Chief that never again must he keep me in ignorance of his projects. I shall laugh at him; all our people here will laugh. I shall be revenged. *Conspuez* Dawson!"

"Don't be too hard on Dawson," urged Rust. "Madame Gilbert thinks a lot of him, and would be pained if he suffered discredit through any fault of hers."

"Fault!" shouted the gallant Froissart. "*La belle Madame* is *sans faute*, peerless, a prodigy of skill and discretion! She is superb. If she implores me to spare the man Dawson, then I will consent, though my heart is rent in fragments. As for you, *mon ami*, I fear that in her hands you were not a figure of admiration. She twisted you about her pretty fingers like a skein of wool. I do not think that you are, what you call, cut out for the Secret Service."

"That is quite my own opinion," assented he gloomily.

PART III

TO SEE IS TO BELIEVE

CHAPTER XII

DAWSON PRESCRIBES

The mind of Dawson has the queerest limitations. He is entirely free from any sense of proportion. If I wrote of those incidents which he pressed upon me, this book would be intolerably dull. He sees no interest in any episode which is not Dawson, Dawson, all the time. The emotion which was aroused in the hearts of Cary and myself by Trehayne's letter caused Dawson no small anxiety. He feared lest in rendering this episode I should turn the limelight upon Trehayne and leave the private of Marines in the shadows. Which is precisely what I have done. From his "sick bed" he sent me a letter explaining that his own honourable weakness of sympathy with an enemy spy was physical, not moral—reprehensible failing induced by lack of sleep. He laboured to convince me that the spirit of Dawson in the full flush of health was of a frightfulness wholly Prussian in its logical completeness. But I smiled, went my own way, and Dawson, when he comes to read this book, can swear as loudly as he pleases.

If I had depended only upon Dawson, I should never have secured the details of the story which I am about to write. It was Froissart who first put me upon the track of it during one of those visits which I paid to him when I was investigating *l'affaire* Rust. Froissart, in imaginative insight, is as much superior to Dawson as the average Frenchman is to the average Englishman. But in execution he admits sorrowfully that he cannot hold a candle to his brutal secretive English chief. "I have genius," exclaimed Froissart, "of which the sacred dog Dawson has not a particle. I know not whence come his ideas, the most penetrative. It cannot be from *son Esprit* of which he has none; his brain reposes, without doubt, in his stomach. Yet, *ma foi*, that man whom I detest and to whom I am a colleague most loyal, is of a practical ingenuity most wonderful. Did you ever learn how he hid the great cruisers *Intrepid* and *Terrific* from the watching eyes of the Boche, and won, here in England, a glorious victory for the English Navy, eight thousand miles away? I was with him, and at the end, falling upon his bosom in generous admiration, I kissed him on both cheeks. And what was my reward? It was to receive a short-arm blow upon the diaphragm. That man of mud took my wind, as he called it, and I was laid gasping upon the floor. It was in this fashion that he repulsed me—me a Count of *l'ancien régime*. I could have his blood."

I soothed Froissart, and extracted enough from him in rapid French spasms—his idiomatic staccato French is often beyond my understanding—to give me a general idea of what Dawson had done. Thereafter I pursued my inquiries, pumping Dawson himself—who, for some reason, did not greatly value the affair—tackling others who knew more than they were always willing to tell, even to me their friend. Yet in many ways, of which it were well not to be particular, I arrived at the full story which I now tell. To my mind it shows Dawson at his best, and Dawson's best is very good indeed.

* * * * *

It was early in November, three months after war had begun. Dawson, to whom had been committed the general supervision of all known enemy spies in London, and who had already put in force that combination of tight net and loose string which I have described, received a summons from his Chief the moment he arrived at his office at the Yard. "You are wanted at the Admiralty," said the Commissioner—"and wanted badly. You are to report at once in the First Lord's private room."

"What is the game?" inquired Dawson. "I have lots to do here which I cannot well leave."

"I don't know. But I have orders to send you, and to relieve you from all other duties. If you want help, you can take Froissart, that French detective who has just been sent to us from Paris as a sort of liaison officer. He is strongly recommended as a first-class man."

"Hum," said Dawson, between whom and his Chief was a very close friendship. "I suppose I must toddle round and see what the little man wants this time. Last month he had secret wireless installations on the brain."

Dawson found the First Lord striding up and down his big room. All round the walls were set great maps bristling with pins to which were attached numbered labels. Each pin represented a ship, and each ship was obedient to an order flashed from the big aerials overhead. Here was the Holy of Holies, the nerve ganglion of the English Navy, and here, striding up and down, the man who could jab the nerve-centre with his finger whenever he pleased. He often pleased. Then he would gloat over the pins as they skipped about the maps.

Chief Inspector Dawson was announced, and stood to attention.

"Ha!" cried the First Lord, "so you are Dawson, the Master of Spies. We need you, Dawson; the country needs you; I need you. You have a great chance this day to show your quality, Dawson. Those of whom I approve, I advance. They become great men. Am I to approve of you?"

Dawson observed that he could not well say until he learned what was wanted of him.

"Ha!" cried the First Lord again, "you are a man of few words. I like those with me who do not talk. When there is talking to be done—well, I can do a little in that line myself. Among my instruments I demand silence."

Dawson said nothing. The First Lord struck a bell; a servant in blue uniform appeared. "Will you please tell his lordship that Chief Inspector Dawson is here, and that I await his presence."

The man retired and presently returned. "His lordship is in his room making out the orders for the Fleet. He bids me say that he is quite at your service."

The First Lord flushed, and glanced hurriedly at Dawson, who stood at attention, stolid, silent, immovable. It would seem that he read nothing in the message.

"The Mountain is old and stiff in his joints," remarked the First Lord playfully. "When he settles into his chair, it would take a bomb to lift him out. We are young and active; we must consider the infirmities of age. Mahomet will go to the Mountain, and you will please to follow."

Mahomet, swinging his long coat-tails, strode out of the room and down a passage, whence they emerged into another room also set about with pin-studded maps.

"Ha!" said the First Lord, "as you would not come to us, we have unbent our dignity and come to you. This is Chief Inspector Dawson."

"So I supposed," growled the grizzled old man, who sat at a big desk upon which was piled many flimsies. It was the great Lord Jacquetot, who for all his French name was English of the English.

"Will you explain to Mr. Dawson what we want of him or shall I?" inquired the First Lord. Lord Jacquetot rose from his chair, showing nothing of the infirmities of age. He approached Dawson, looked over him keenly, and said, "You don't look like a civilian policeman. Where have you served?"

Dawson explained that he had in former days been a Red Marine.

"I thought as much," said Jacquetot. "There is no mistaking the back and shoulders of them. Once a Pongo, always a Pongo." He held out his hand, which Dawson shook diffidently. An ex-private of Marines does not often shake the hand of a First Sea Lord.

Lord Jacquetot walked over to one of the maps and beckoned to Dawson to follow. The First Lord hovered in the background, ready to put in a word at the first opportunity.

"There has been a serious naval disaster in the South Seas," said Jacquetot, "and we must clean up the mess, pretty damn quick. The news came yesterday. Orders were wired at once that two battle-cruisers, the *Intrepid* and *Terrific*, should be sent at full speed from Scotland to Devonport to dock, coal, and complete with stores. To keep them outside the enemy's observation, and to avoid any risk of mines or submarines in the Irish Channel, they have been sent far out round the west coast of Ireland. Here they are; we get messages from them every hour." He indicated two pins. Just then a messenger entered and handed to the First Sea Lord a wireless flimsy. Jacquetot read it, slipped a scale along the map, took out the two pins, and shifted them further south. "They are going well," said he; "doing twenty-five knots. They should be off Plymouth Sound by to-morrow evening."

"It is a long way," put in Dawson, deeply interested. "Fifteen hundred miles."

"There or thereabouts. The coast lights are all out, so that they will steer a bit wide. They should do it in sixty hours."

"I gave the order within thirty minutes of getting the news of the disaster," remarked the First Lord, smacking his lips.

Jacquetot made no reply, though his eyes hardened and his mouth drew into a stiff line. It was his province to give Orders to the Fleet.

"Those battle-cruisers," went on Lord Jacquetot, addressing Dawson, "will go into dock at Devonport as soon as they arrive. They will be there forty-eight hours at least. They must be clean ships before they go through the hot tropical water if their speed is to be kept up. They have gun power, but power without speed is useless for the work which they have to do. After leaving England it will be a month before the Squadron, of which they are to form the chief part, will be concentrated in the South Seas. For two days at Devonport, and for four weeks while at sea, there must be the completest secrecy if our plans are to succeed. Without absolute secrecy we shall fail. The Board of Admiralty is responsible for the sea, but not for the land. We can make certain that no news of the despatch of these two cruisers gets out at sea; can you, Mr. Chief Inspector Dawson, undertake that no news gets out on land—that no whisper of their sailing reaches the enemy by means of his spies on land?"

"It is a large order," said Dawson thoughtfully.

"It is a very large order," asserted Lord Jacquetot, frowning.

"But large or small, the thing must be done," broke in the First Lord. "If this news gets out, and we fail to come up with the German Squadron down south, the effect upon the public will be horrible. The English people may even lose their perfect, their sublime, faith in ME."

"They may lose their faith in the Navy," muttered Jacquetot.

"It is the same thing," said the First Lord.

"Can you let me know more details, my lord?" asked Dawson. "What is the programme? I don't see at present how the arrival, docking, and sailing of the battle-cruisers can possibly be kept secret, but there may be a way if one could only think of it."

"If the *Intrepid* and *Terrific* arrive according to programme," said Jacquetot, "they will not come up the Sound till after dark. Then in the small hours they will slip into dock, and no one but the regular dockyard hands will know that they are there. We will haul them out also in the middle of the night, and they will be clear away by daybreak, forty-eight hours after arrival. Coal and other stores are on the spot in plenty, and the shells and cordite for the twelve-inch guns can soon be got down from the Plymouth magazines. The secrecy of the operation seems to me to turn on whether we can trust the dockyard hands."

Dawson shook his head. "I wouldn't plump on that, my lord. There have been enemy agents working in every dockyard in the kingdom for years past, and we haven't spotted all of them. Still, we have our own men working alongside of them—Scotland Yard men engaged from among the shipbuilding trades unions—accounting for every one, so that no man can be away from his post without our knowing and shadowing him. It is not easy to get any information out of the country nowadays. The secret wireless stories are all humbug. Wireless gives itself away at once. If one wants to get news to the enemy, one has to carry it oneself, or hire some one else to carry it. Most of that which goes we allow to go for our own purposes. I am pretty sure that no dockyard hand could get anything away to Holland without our knowledge, so that it doesn't matter whether they are trustworthy or not so long as we're not fools enough to trust them. You may not know it, but I have my own Yard men among your messengers here in this building, and among your clerks too."

"What!" cried the First Lord. "You don't even trust the Admiralty!"

"Least of all," said Dawson grimly. "If I was head of the German Secret Service, I would have my own man as your private secretary."

The First Lord sat down gasping. Jacquetot nodded kindly to Dawson, and laughed in his grim old way. "You are the man we want," said he.

"I am not thinking much of the dockyard hands," went on Dawson; "I can look after them. They're all provided for. The danger is in the gossip of a seaport town. I have lived in Portsmouth for years, and Plymouth is just like it. You may take my word for it that the arrival of the *Terrific* and *Intrepid* in dock at Devonport will be known all over the Three Towns half an hour after they get there. Their mission will be discussed in every bar, and it won't be difficult to make a pretty useful guess. Here is a disaster in the South Seas—which will be published all over the country by to-morrow morning—and here are two of our fastest battle-cruisers summoned in hot haste from Scotland to be cleaned and loaded for a long voyage. Any child, let alone a longshoreman, could put the two things together. 'So the *Intrepid* and *Terrific* are off to the South Seas to biff old Fritz in the eye.' That is what they will say in the Three Towns where there must be hundreds of men—British subjects, too, the swine, and many of them natural born—who would take risks to shove the news through to Holland if they could get enough dirty money for it. Our worst spies are not German, you bet; they are Irish and Scotch and Welsh and English. That's where our difficulties come in. I am not afraid of the dockyards, but the gossip of the Three Towns gives me the creeps."

"Then what can we possibly do?" wailed the First Lord, who saw his prospect of a brilliant coup wilt away like a fair mirage. "The secret will get out, our plans will fail, and MY Administration, my beautiful Administration, will have to stand the racket. How shall I defend myself in the House?"

"That won't matter much to the country," put in Jacquetot bluntly. "What matters, is that we should do everything possible to keep the secret in spite of all the inherent difficulties. Sit down, Mr. Dawson, and do some hard thinking."

"I prefer to stand, my lord. When I want to think I do a bit of sentry-go."

"So do I!" exclaimed the First Lord. "All my most famous speeches were composed while I walked up and down my dressing-room before my—" He broke off hastily, but as neither Jacquetot nor Dawson were listening, he might have completed the sentence without revealing the secrets of his looking-glass.

"May I speak my mind, my lords?" asked Dawson.

"It is what you are here for," replied Jacquetot.

"I always work on certain general principles. They apply here. People will talk; that is certain. If one doesn't want them to talk about something really important, one puts up something else conspicuous, harmless, and exciting to occupy their minds. In your politics" —turning to the First Lord with an air of simplicity—"when you've made a thorough mess of governing England, and don't want to be found out, you set the people fighting about Home Rule for Ireland. I don't mean you, sir, but politicians generally."

"Quite so," said the First Lord, blinking.

"Well, see here. We don't want any talk about the *Intrepid* and *Terrific*. So, before they arrive, we must give the people of the Three Towns a real titbit of excitement. Battle-cruisers come to dock in Devonport quite often when they are damaged. Two battle-cruisers which had been mined or submarined, one towing the other, would be a pretty picture in the Sound. It would set all the folk talking for days, and no one would think that two damaged cruisers had anything to do with the South Seas. Everybody would say, 'What cruel luck. If the *Terrific* and *Intrepid* hadn't got blown up they would be just right and handy to send down south. As it is—' And then the German agents would somehow get the news to Holland—we would help them all we could in a quiet way—that the *Intrepid* and *Terrific*, two fast battle-cruisers, had been nearly lost, and were being patched up at Devonport. The Germans, hearing the glorious news, would hug themselves and say that now was the time for the High Seas Fleet to come out and smash Jellicoe. The last thing in their minds would be any concentration in the south against their own Pacific Squadron. That's how I apply my general principles to this case. Meanwhile, of course, the *Terrific* and *Intrepid*, well and sound, would be racing away down to the South Seas and no one in the Three Towns—except the dockyard hands, whom we would look after—and no one at all in Germany, would have a glimmer of the real truth."

While Dawson was thinking aloud in this rather halting, stumbling way, the First Lord and his chief naval colleague were looking hard at one another. The politician, with his quick House-of-Commons wits, jumped to the idea before his slower thinking expert colleague could sort out the two battle-cruisers who were to be mined or submarined from the two which were to speed away south to avenge the recent disaster.

"If the two battle-cruisers are mined or submarined—which God forbid," said Jacquetot, "how can they sail for the south?"

"Need they be the same ships?" inquired Dawson, whose eyes had begun to flash with excitement. "Need they be the same?"

"Don't you see?" interposed the First Lord. "The idea is quite good. I was just about to suggest something of the kind myself when Mr. Dawson anticipated me. That is where the mind with a wide universal training has a great advantage over the narrow intensive intelligence of the professional expert. Even in war. What I propose, what Mr. Dawson here proposes with my full concurrence, is that two severely damaged battle-cruisers, known temporarily as the *Terrific* and *Intrepid*, should be brought into the Sound in broad day and displayed before the eyes of the curious in the Three Towns. The real ships will slip in, be docked and coaled, and slip out again. The two others, upon whom public attention has been concentrated, shall be put aground somewhere in the

Sound to be salved with great and leisurely ostentation. We will keep them well away from the Hoe, and allow no one whatever to approach them. We will, unofficially, allow the news of their sorry state to get out of country and into the Dutch papers. Meanwhile, as Mr. Dawson says, the real *Terrific* and *Intrepid* will be speeding towards the south, and the saving for the nation's service of my invaluable public reputation for accurate judgment and quick decision. Mr. Dawson's suggestion—I should, perhaps, rather say my own suggestion—shall be laid before the Board at once."

Though the stiff mind of Lord Jacquetot was not very quick to take in a new idea, no man alive was better equipped for practically working out a naval scheme. While the First Lord was assuming that sorely damaged battle-cruisers, or vessels which could be passed off in place of them, needed but his summons to spring from the deeps, Jacquetot had pressed a bell and ordered a messenger to request the immediate presence of the Fourth Sea Lord, within whose province was the whole art and mystery of ship construction. Upon the appearance of this officer the plan was gone over anew, and he was asked whence and within what time he could produce two presentable dummies to do duty in the Sound for the entertainment of the population of Plymouth, Devonport, and Stonehouse. There were, said he, two if not three at Portsmouth, constructed out of old cargo tramp hulls for the mystification of the enemy. They had already done duty as newly completed battleships, but with a little alteration to the canvas of their funnels, the lath and plaster of their turrets and conning towers, and the wood of their guns, they might be made into perfect likenesses —at a distance—of the *Intrepid* and *Terrific*. The ships' carpenters, he explained, could make the changes while the dummies were coming round to Plymouth. Seated at the desk of Lord Jacquetot he wrote the necessary orders in code, his Chief signed them, and they were put at once on the wires for Portsmouth. The sea-cocks, said the Fourth Lord, would be opened twenty miles from land so that the "*Intrepid*" might come in sadly down by the bows, and the "*Terrific*" with a list of twenty degrees, pluckily towing her sorely crippled sister. With a chart of Plymouth Sound before them, the two officers settled the precise spot, sufficiently remote, yet well within sight of the Hoe, at which the two unhappy battle-cruisers should come to rest upon the mud. "It will be a most pathetic spectacle," said the Fourth Lord laughing, "and I will bet a month's pay and allowances that at the distance not a man in the Three Towns will have the smallest suspicion that the genuine copper-bottomed *Terrific* and *Intrepid* are not ditched before his blooming eyes." He rose from the table, upon which the chart had been laid, walked over to Dawson and shook him warmly by the hand. "You won't get any credit for the idea," he whispered. "One never does. But it was a damned good notion. What are you going to do now?"

"I am going to Plymouth this afternoon to make sure that the German truth gets over the water to Holland, and that the English truth stays safely behind. If you will all do your part, I will do mine."

CHAPTER XIII

THE SEEN AND THE UNSEEN

"Every man to his trade," said Dawson. "I didn't go into the difficulties of our job to those high folks at the Admiralty, but they are not at all small. You have a head on you, Froissart, though it has the misfortune to be French; set it going on double shifts."

The two men were sitting in a specially reserved first-class compartment in the Paddington-Plymouth express; as companions they were hopelessly uncongenial, yet as colleagues formed a strong combination in which the qualities of the one served to neutralise the defects of the other. Dawson, in spite of his love for the Defence of the Realm Regulations, was still sometimes unconsciously hampered by an ingrained respect for the ordinary law and the rights of civilians; Froissart, like all French detective officers, held the law in contempt, and was by nature and training utterly lawless. The more reputable a suspect, the more remorseless was his pursuit. They were, professionally, a terrible pair who could have been passed through a hair sieve without leaving behind a grain of moral scruple.

Froissart, when he would be at the trouble, understood and spoke English quite well, though with me he used nothing but the raciest of boulevard French. "My friend," said he, "your promise to those Ministers of Marines was rash; for, unless there is the most perfect execution of your scheme and the most sleepless watching of those whom you call dockyard hands—*ceux qui travaillent dans les chantiers, ne c'est pas?*—the sailing of these *grands croiseurs* will be told to Germany. There are too many who will know. We are upon *une folle enterprise*—a chase of the wild goose."

"You do not know my system if you think that," remarked Dawson, frowning.

"And if I do not, of whom is the fault?" inquired Froissart blandly; "for, my faith, you never tell what you would be doing."

"A secret," said Dawson sententiously, "is a secret when known to one only. If two know of it there is grave danger. If three, one might as well shout it from the housetops. Therefore I keep my own counsel."

"That is just what I said," cried Froissart triumphantly. "If the secret of these *grand croiseurs* is known to one hundred, two hundred, *le bon Dieu* knows how many hundreds of dockyard hands, one might as well print it in these dull English *journaux*. You attempt the impossible, *mon ami*."

"They are Englishmen," proclaimed Dawson, who felt compelled to uphold the character of his countrymen in the presence of a foreigner. "They are patriots. Not a man of them would sell his country."

"I would not bank on their patriotism, my friend, when there is much
Boche gold to be won and much beer to be drunk."

"And who said that I did bank upon it?" cried Dawson testily, forgetting his noble, words of two minutes earlier. "I wouldn't trust one of them out of my sight. I have two dozen of my own men working alongside of those dockyard hands, watching them by night and day. We know if a man drinks two glasses of beer when he used to drink one, and takes home to his wife eighteenpence above his ordinary wage. Do you take me for a fool?"

"You'll be a bigger fool than I take you for if you do not play straight this time with me, and tell me your plans in detail. I have to work with you, and I cannot give service blindfold."

"You are not a bad fellow, Froissart," said Dawson thoughtfully—the name in his mouth became Froy-zart—"and I will tell you here and now more of my mind than I have yet shown even to the great Chief of us all. It will take all your brains—for you have some brains—and all of mine to keep the secret of those battle-cruisers."

* * * * *

In the morning the newspapers published the meagre details of the disaster in the South Seas, and the Three Towns were shaken to their foundations. For when naval ships go down, they take with them crews of whom half have their homes in Devon. The disaster meant that eight hundred families in the West mourned a son or a father. Ever since the days of the Great Queen—whose name in the West is not Victoria, but Elizabeth—Devon has paid in the lives of its best men the price of Admiralty. The Three Towns mourned with a grief made more bitter by the realisation that the disaster was one which never should have happened. Bad slow English ships had been sent against good fast German ships, and had been sunk with all hands without hurt to the enemy. The Three Towns know the speed and power of every fighting ship afloat, British or foreign, as you or I before the war knew the public form of every leading golfer or cricketer. In every bar where sailormen met one another, and met, too, the brothers and fathers of sailormen, the Lords of the Admiralty were weighed and condemned. It is a thing most serious when in the cradles of the Navy, Portsmouth and the Three Towns, faith in the wisdom of Whitehall becomes shaken. One may muzzle the Press, but no muzzle yet devised can close the mouths of sailormen and their friends in dockyard towns.

In the afternoon of the same day, while the news of the disaster was still fresh, there came a whisper, which gained in loudness and in precision of detail as it passed from mouth to ear and from ear to mouth, that the worst had not yet been told. There had been not one, but two disasters. Two battle-cruisers, it was declared, had been sunk in the Channel by German mines or submarines. What were their names? inquired the white-faced women. The names were not yet known, but they would soon come. A little later the severity of the rumour became softened. The battle-cruisers had not, it appeared, been sunk, but severely damaged. They were at that moment on their way to the Sound, crippled sorely, yet afloat. Men groaned. Two battle-cruisers blown up in the Channel; what in God's name were two battle-cruisers doing in the mine-strewn Channel when their proper place was in one of the safe eyries overlooking the North Sea? A plausible explanation was offered. The two battle-cruisers had been coming to Plymouth to take in stores that they might speed away south to avenge those other two cruisers sunk by the Germans as had been told in the morning's papers. If this were indeed true, the news was of the worst; England's prestige afloat was gone. She could not spare two other whole battle-cruisers to proceed upon a mission of vengeance to the South Seas while the Germans' Battle Squadrons in the North Sea ports were still undefeated. Meanwhile the Germans far away to the south could do what they pleased; they could sink and burn our merchant steamers at will. The command of the Pacific had passed from England to Germany, and the White Ensign hung draggled and shamed for all the world to sneer at. The Three Towns almost forgot their personal grief for drowned friends in their horror at the disgrace which had come to their own sacred Service.

It was still light, though late in the afternoon, when the anxious watchers upon the Hoe made out, beyond Drake's Island, two big ships coming in round the western end of the breakwater. Though deep in the water they towered above their escort of destroyers and fast patrol boats. The leading ship was listing badly, her tripod mast with its spotting top hung far over to port, and she was towing stern first a sister ship whose bows were almost hidden under water. The Three Towns, which can recognise the outlines of warships afar off, rapidly pronounced judgment. "That's the *Intrepid*" they declared, "and the one she's towing is a battle-cruiser of the same class—the *Terrific* or *Tremendous*. They're both badly holed." "Gawd A'mighty," cried a grizzled longshoreman, who might have sailed with Drake or Hawkins—as no doubt his forbears had done—"look to the list of un! And thicky with her bows down under, being towed by the stern to keep her from swamping entire. If it worn't for them bulk'eads un wouldn't never have made the Sound." It was plain to those who had glasses turned on the damaged ships that they were drawing far too much water to be brought into the Hamoaze and over the sill of the dry dock at Devonport, so that no one felt surprise when the battle-cruisers were seen to pull out of the deep fairway and make towards the shore. The purpose was plain to read. They were to be put aground under Mount Edgcumbe, patched up, and pumped dry, and then would go into dock for repairs. It was a job of weeks, and during all that time the Fleet would be short of two battle-cruisers which might have swept the South Seas clear of the German Ensign. It was cruel luck, and the Three Towns had enough to talk of to keep them occupied for many days. Presently more news came, authentic news, and passed rapidly from mouth to mouth. The vessels were the *Intrepid*, the flagship of Admiral Stocky, and her sister the *Terrific*, a pair of fast Dreadnought cruisers. They had, as was surmised, been speeding down from Scotland to dock at Plymouth on their way to clean up the mess made in the far South. They had come safely through the Irish Sea and round the Land's End, but when near their journey's end off Fowey they had run into a patch of mines laid by German submarines. The *Terrific* had had her bow plates ripped into slivers of ragged steel, and the three fore compartments flooded. The *Intrepid* had picked up the wire of a twin mine, got caught badly on the port side, but had luckily escaped to starboard. She had taken her crippled sister in tow, and brought her in safely. Both ships could easily be repaired, but it would take time. The voyage to the South Seas was off. Nothing could have been more convincing than the story which quickly got about; the ships had been seen and recognised by the Three Towns—there was no concealment and no mystery. For once the Silent Navy appeared to be talkative. The hearts of German agents in the Towns swelled with pride and joy. Here was convincing proof of the kindly hand of the Prussian Gott. If the great news could be carried through to the Kaiser and von Tirpitz, there would be much ringing of church bells in the Fatherland. But these English, since the war began, had become very watchful, very suspicious. The problem was: how to get the glad news through.

* * * * *

It was two o'clock in the morning and very dark. The big dry docks at Devonport were deserted except for a few picked hands, not more than two score at the outside, told off on night shift for special duty. Against all workmen who had not been warned for this duty the big gates would be closed for two whole days. There were important jobs awaiting completion, but they must wait. One hundred and twenty men, working in three eight-hour shifts per day—forty at a time—could do all that was needed to the *Intrepid* and *Terrific*, and not one man was included who had not served at Devonport for at least ten years. Dawson had been very firm, and the Commander-in-Chief had backed him with full authority. "Don't make any mistake," said Dawson. "Among even one hundred and twenty, though picked in this way, there will be some few who would sell us if they could. One would have to go back more than ten years to weed out all those whom the Germans have corrupted. But out of this lot there should not be more than two or three swine, and I can look after them." He did not say that he had already been in touch with the Scotland Yard officer at Devonport, and had arranged that a dozen out of his precious twenty-four counter-spies should be put among the chosen hundred and twenty. Dawson never did allow his left hand to know the wiles of his right.

Under the thick cover of the autumn night two massive silent forms, which had crept with all lights out into the Sound after their long fast voyage from the northern mists, were warped into dock; the supporting shores were fitted, and the water around them run out. Long before the flagship *Intrepid* stood clear and dry on the dock floor, Dawson, in his uniform of a private of Marines—"A Marine can go anywhere and do anything," he would say—had slipped on board and shown the Commander credentials from the Board of Admiralty which made that hardened officer open his eyes. "My word," exclaimed he, "you must be some Marine! Come along quick to the Admiral." So Dawson went, not a little nervous—the moment his foot trod the decks of a King's ship all his assurance dropped off, his old sense of discipline flowed back over him, and an Admiral became a very mighty potentate indeed. Ashore Dawson could face up to the Lord Jacquetot himself; on board ship a two-ring lieutenant was to him a god! He followed the Commander, and was ushered into the Admiral's presence. "What!" cried Stocky, stern in manner always, but very kindly at heart towards those whom he found to be true men. "A private of Marines with plenary powers from the First Lord? Take the papers off him and chuck the damned comedian into the ditch. We have no time here for the First Lord's humour." The Commander drew near and whispered. "What! Authority endorsed by Jacquetot? There is something queer about this. Look here, my fine fellow, who the devil are you? Are you a Marine, or a too clever German spy, or what? Make haste. There is still enough water left over the side to pitch you into without breaking your dirty neck."

Dawson knew his man. He had served in the same ship with Stocky when that officer had been a lieutenant; he had waited upon him in the wardroom. He had felt the rasp of his tongue in old days. He approached, and without saying a word handed the letters given him by the First Lord and Jacquetot, adding his official card. The Admiral read the papers slowly and came at last to the card. Then his frowning brows softened, and he smiled. It was the old smile of Lieutenant Stocky. "Why, it's Dawson who was my servant in the old *Olympus*; now Chief Inspector of Scotland Yard. That explains all. But why the hell, man, do you dress up as a Marine?"

"Once a Marine, always a Marine," replied Dawson, who felt happier now that the Admiral had recognised him. "I can't keep out of the uniform, sir. Besides, it's very useful when I want to be about the docks."

"My orders," said the Admiral, "are to dock, clean, coal, and be off. I am expecting more detailed instructions, but they have not yet come. These letters say that you will explain the programme here, and that you have been charged with full responsibility for keeping our movements secret. I am to give you all possible assistance. All right. Go ahead. What do you want of us?"

Dawson rapidly told how the two dummy battle-cruisers had come stumbling into the Sound in the afternoon, and how the Three Towns believed that the *Intrepid* and *Terrific* were at that moment lying on the shoals out of service for weeks to come. "No one must guess," he concluded, "that the real *Intrepid* and *Terrific* are here safe in dock, that they will go out two days hence in the middle of the night, and dash away south to wipe Fritz's flag off the seas. We have picked the dockyard hands with the greatest care, and have them under watch like mice with cats all about them. If a single one of your officers or men goes out of the dock gates the game will be up and I won't answer for the consequences. Everything rests with you, sir. Will you give orders that no one, no one, not even you yourself, shall leave either of the battle-cruisers while they are in dock—no one, not for a minute."

The Admiral laughed, and the officers in his room respectfully joined in. "So we have been mined and are aground somewhere yonder on the mud surrounded by sorrowing patrols. And the Three Towns are dropping salt tears into their beer. It is a fine game, Dawson. I didn't believe much in Lord Jacquetot's dummies, but they've come in darned useful this time. Are you going to keep Plymouth and Devonport in the dumps for long?"

"Until you've done your work, sir," said Dawson.

"So until then the *Intrepid* and *Terrific* will lie crippled in the Sound for all the world to see and for Fritz to believe. If this very bright scheme is yours, Dawson, we will all drink your health down south as soon as our work has been done. For the credit will be yours rather than ours. I will help you all I can; it is my duty and my very keen desire. A man who can make so brilliant a plan for confounding the enemy's spies is worth a statue of gold. He is even worth the sacrifice of two day's leave while one's ship is in dock. What do you say, gentlemen?"

"I never thought," said the Flag Captain, "that I would willingly spend two days shut up in a smelly dock, but you may count me in, sir. I won't head a mutiny when all leave is refused."

"You shall have your way, Dawson. All leave stopped in both ships. Not a man is to go ashore on any pretence, no matter what the excuse. The mothers of the lower decks may all die—they always do when a ship is in port—but not a man shall leave to bury them. Give the orders in the *Intrepid*, and ask the captain of the *Terrific* to be so good as to come aboard."

* * * * *

"So far, good," exclaimed Dawson when he got back to his hotel and found Froissart sitting up for him. "The ships are in and no one is to be allowed ashore. I shall be in a fever till both of them are away again. We are on very thin ice, Froissart. It is lucky that the dockyard is on the Hamoaze, out of sight even of most of Devonport, and far away from Plymouth and Stonehouse. I have seen all the foremen of the dockyard myself, told them the whole trick which we are playing on the Huns, and put them on their mettle to tackle their men. They will pitch it fine and strong on the honour and patriotism of complete silence, but not neglect to throw in a hint of the Defence of the Realm Act and penal servitude. Never threaten an Englishman, Froissart, but always let him know that behind your fine honourable sentiments there is something devilish nasty. Preach as loud as you can about the beauty of virtue, but don't forget to chuck in a description of the fiery Hell which awaits wrongdoers. I don't depend much either on the sentiments or the hints of punishment. I've got every man of that hundred and twenty on my string, and if one of them asks leave, within the next day or two, to go and bury his mother on the East Coast, he shall go—but I shall go with him, and he shall have a jolly little funeral of his own. Every letter which they write will be read, every telegram copied for me, every message by 'phone taken down. They are on my string, Froissart—every man."

"You do everything, Mr. Dawson," grumbled Froissart. "Where do I come in?"

"You have helped me a lot already," replied Dawson handsomely. "You being a foreigner make me talk very simple and plain, and think out my plans so that I can explain them to you. One sees the weak points of a scheme when one has to make it clear to a foreigner. You don't always twig my meaning, Froissart, and sometimes your remarks are a bit foolish; but you mean well, and, for a Frenchman, are quite intelligent. I will say that for you, Froissart—quite intelligent."

"*Sacre nom d'un chien*—" began Froissart hotly; but Dawson paid no heed. He just went on talking, and Froissart, realising that Dawson could not understand his French, and that he himself could not give words to his feelings in English, relapsed into wrathful silence. Much as I respect and admire Dawson, I should not care to be his subordinate.

"We must keep the cinema show going nice and lively for the Three Towns," went on Dawson. "A big salvage steamer is coming down to-morrow to give an air of verisimilitude to the proceedings. Patrol boats will buzz about the Sound, and the potentates, naval and civil, will gather from all parts. The unfortunate wrecks out at Picklecombe Point will be guarded so that no shore boat can get within half a mile. They won't bear a very close inspection. I hope that none of the guns will break loose and float about the harbour. That would be what you might call a blooming contretemps. I shall be pretty busy all the next two days myself. Though I am a strict teetotaller, I shall get into shore rig and spend my days in the public bars. I must know what the Three Towns are talking about, and whether any suspicion of the truth gets wind. I don't think that it can; at least, for some time. The stage management has been too good. Later on there may be some wonderment because none of the men from the *Intrepid* and *Terrific* are allowed ashore. A lot of wives and families must be around here, especially as the *Intrepid* is a Plymouth ship. Of course it must be given out that they are all needed to help with the salvage operations, and no leave is allowed. You, Froissart, might spend your time reading copies of all telegrams sent out from the Towns. If any German agent wants to get news of the damage to the battle-cruisers over to Holland, he will probably travel up to the East Coast and send a wire on ahead. That is what I hope for. You shall then follow him up, and make smooth the path of crime. Half our trouble will be lost unless we can help the spoof news over to the Kaiser, bless him. The job, at first, will be pretty dull for you, Froissart, and not over lively for me. I hate pubs, yet for two days I must loaf about them, pretending to drink. You can read the telegrams, but you can't understand English well enough to pick up the gossip of the bars. I must do that myself."

"You have stopped all leave on the battle-cruisers—the real ones, I mean—but what about the dockyard men," inquired Froissart. "Are they to be allowed to go to their homes when they come off their shifts?"

"I have thought of that and weighed both sides. It will be safer to let them go home as usual. If we locked them all up in the dockyard till the *Intrepid* and *Terrific* were both safe away, there would be no end of curiosity and gossip. What so very special, people would ask, could be going on in the yard that no one was allowed out for two days. I don't want wives and families and neighbours to come smelling round those dockyard gates. They might see the spotting tops of the cruisers inside. Of course there is a regular forest of masts and gantries showing, and a couple of spotting tops more or less might not be noticed. But my general idea is to concentrate attention on those dear old dummies down at Picklecombe Point. They are the centre of interest, the eye of the picture—the cynosure, as a scholar would say. I am not a bad scholar myself. I passed the seventh standard, and went to school all the time I was in the Red Marines. I was a sergeant, which takes a bit of doing. But see here, Froissart," exclaimed Dawson, looking at his watch, "it is five o'clock, and we must get quick to bed so as to be bright and lively in the morning."

Dawson carried out his programme. Though a strict teetotaller, he passed hours at public houses, especially in the evenings, listening to the talk of the port. It was all about the disaster in the South Seas, the heavy casualties suffered by the Three Towns, and the rotten ill-luck of the avenging battle-cruisers running upon the German mines. Not a whisper could Dawson hear of suspicion that the ships beached under Mount Edgcumbe were other than the genuine article. The salvage steamer with her big arc lights glowing through the darkness had been the last artistic touch which brought complete conviction. Gold-laced officers, including the Commander-in-Chief himself, had been coming and going all day; the acting of the Navy had been perfect. Dawson blessed the four bones of old Jacquetot, who, when he tackles a job, does it very thoroughly indeed. "I should not be surprised," thought he, "if the Mountain, as that young Jackanapes called him, came trotting down here himself just to make the show complete." And sure enough he did, accompanied by the Fourth Sea Lord who had worked out all the convincing details. Dawson was ordered to meet them in the Admiral's quarters of the *Intrepid*. He went, looking a very different person from the private of Marines of some thirty hours earlier, and had the honour of being invited to luncheon. That lunch was the one scene in the comedy upon which he dwelt in telling the story to me. "Lord Jacquetot," he said, "clinked glasses with me and wished me the best of luck and success. It was as much as he could do, he said, to keep the First Lord from coming down and monkeying the whole affair. Luckily there was a debate in Parliament that he wanted to figure in, and so couldn't get away. Lord Jacquetot said that the First Lord had grabbed the whole scheme as his very own, and forgotten that I had any part in it. I don't mind. The Secret Service never gets any credit for anything. If it did, it wouldn't be Secret very long."

"No credit," I remarked, "and not much cash I expect."

"Little enough, sir," replied Dawson. "I suppose we do the job for the love of it. There's no sport like it. Our real work never gets into the papers or the story-books."

"Never?" I asked slily. "What about that story of mine in the *Cornhill Magazine*, which you still carry about next your heart?"

Dawson changed the subject. He never will appreciate chaff.

At midnight of the day of the luncheon party the *Intrepid* and *Terrific*, clean and fully loaded, cleared out of dock and slipped off into the darkness attended by their destroyer escort, whose duty it was to see them safe round Ushant. Eight hours later Dawson came down to breakfast and found that Froissart, satisfied with his *petit dejeuner* of coffee and rolls, had already gone out. Dawson felt satisfied with himself, and was confident now that his work in the Three Towns had been well and truly done. The rest could be left to the Navy, and to his Secret Service agents. He sat down to a hearty meal, but was not destined to finish it. First came a messenger from the Officer in charge of the Dockyard, who handed over a sealed note and took a receipt for it. Dawson broke the seal. "Dear Mr. Dawson," he read, "You will be interested to learn that one of the hands engaged upon the work we know of has asked for three days' leave—that he may bury his mother in Essex. She died, he says, at Burnham. I await your views before granting the leave asked for. The man has been in our service for sixteen years, and bears the best of characters."

"Now what do I know of Burnham?" muttered Dawson. "The name seems familiar." He rang the bell, asked for an atlas, and studied carefully the coast of Essex. Burnham stood upon the river Crouch, which Dawson had heard of as a famous resort for motor-boats. His eyes gleamed, and he threw up his head, which had been bent over the map. "The man shall have his leave," murmured he. "But I don't think it will be his mother who is buried."

Just at that moment in came Froissart, looking, as Dawson at once remarked, merry and bright. "It is no wonder," said he, "for see this telegram of which I have just had a copy. It was spotted at once at the Bureau, and the man who despatched it has been shadowed by a police officer." The telegram read, "Coming to-day by South Western. Meet me this evening at usual place." It was addressed to Burnham-on-Crouch in Essex.

Dawson picked up the note which he had received and passed it to
Froissart, who read it slowly. "The same place!" cried he.

"Yes," said Dawson slowly, "the same place, and a famous resort for motor-boats. We have not finished yet, my friend, with the *Intrepid* and *Terrific*"

CHAPTER XIV

A COFFIN AND AN OWL

Dawson laid the letter and the telegram upon his breakfast-table, and bent his head over them. In a few minutes he had weighed them up, sorted out their relative significance, and spoke. "We have here, Froissart, two distinct people. I am almost sure of that. My man of the dockyard who wants leave to bury his mother in Essex has not yet received permission from his Chief. He would not therefore be telegraphing about his train. He does not know yet whether he will be permitted to go at all. Your man is quite confident that his movements are in no way restricted. As I read between the lines I judge that my man, who knows the actual truth about the docking and sailing of the battle-cruisers, wants to reach the East Coast, whence he has means of transmitting the priceless news to Germany. Your man is of one of the Towns; he has seen the dummy cruisers ashore in the Sound; he believes them to be genuine, and he also wants to transmit the news to his paymasters in Germany, He will be an ordinary German agent. The identity of place whither both wish to go is partly a coincidence, and partly explained by its excellence as a jumping-off place for fast motor-boats, which, during these long autumn nights, could race over to and get back again between sunset and dawn. We have coast watchers always about for the very purpose of stopping such lines of communication. You shall accompany your own man, and make sure that he is allowed to get through. If he does not himself cross, arrest him as soon as his boat has gone. If he does go, watch for his return and arrest him, and his boat and all on board, the moment that they return. In any event the boat and its crew must be seized upon return to Essex. Are you quite clear about what you have to do?"

"Quite," said Froissart. "The spies and their boat must be caught red-handed, but not till after the false news of the mining of the battle-cruisers has been carried to Holland. But how shall we make certain that the sleepless English Navy will not butt in and catch the boat at sea before it gets across to Holland. The Narrow Seas swarm with fast patrols."

"I will provide for that. I will write at once for you a letter to the Inspector of police at Burnham, and enclose copies of my credentials from the Admiralty. I will also wire to Lord Jacquetot in private code. You will find on arrival that the responsible naval authorities of the district will be entirely at your service. That motor-boat with the news of the great spoof shall be shepherded across most craftily, but when it comes to return will find that the way of transgressors is very hard. Get ready and be off, Froissart; we depend upon your skill and discretion. Get a good view of your man—the police will point him out—before he boards the train, and then don't let him out of your sight. Take two plain-clothes officers with you. Run no unnecessary risks of being spotted. You are rather easily recognisable with those shining black eyes and black beard, but no one here has seen you officially, and you should pass unsuspected as a Scotland Yard man. Can I trust you?"

"*Mais certainement*," said Froissart crossly. "This is simple police work, which I have done a thousand times. I could do it on my head."

"Your train leaves at 10.8; the South Western station. I will give you the letters at once, and then you can start."

Within a quarter of an hour Dawson—his breakfast forgotten—had given Froissart his letters, sent a long telegram by special messenger to the Commander-in-Chief for despatch in code to Jacquetot. Not even to Dawson would the Admiralty entrust its private cypher. Then, as soon as Froissart had disappeared, he called up the Chief of the Dockyard on the telephone and arranged to come at once to his office.

"I had given the easy job to Froissart," he explained to me long afterwards. "It was, as he called it, simple police work. He had, without arousing suspicion, to make smooth the path for his spy just as you and I opened the door to the Hook for the late-lamented Hagan, and escorted him across in the mail-boat. We have helped false news over to the Germans scores of times. It is grand sport. My job was something much more tricky. I had to get plain proof that my man was a spy in the dockyard, to keep him playing on my line to the very last minute, but to make dead certain of stopping him at the fifty-fifth second of the eleventh hour."

"Why did you not cut out your difficulties by just stopping him from going to Essex? At a word from you his Chief would have refused leave."

Dawson smiled at me in a fashion which I find intensely aggravating. He has no tact; when he feels superior, he lets one see it plainly.

"The fat would have been in the fire then," exclaimed he. "Suppose he lay low for a day or two, took French leave, and went. I should have been off his track. Shadowing is all very well, but it does not always succeed in a crowded district like the Three Towns. If he had got away without me beside him, the man might have reached Essex and done there what he pleased. Besides, he might have had accomplices unknown to me. No, it was the only possible course to give him leave and follow him up close. Then whatever he did would be under my own eye."

Dawson gulped down a cup of coffee, sadly regarded his rapidly congealing bacon, and skipped off to the dockyard. "Who is this man of yours whose mother has died at so very inconvenient a moment for us? What the deuce is he doing with a mother in Essex at all? He ought to be a Devon man."

"He isn't, anyway. I have been making close inquiries. Though he has been with us for sixteen years, he did come originally from somewhere in the East. The man is one of the best I have—never drinks, keeps good time, and works hard. He makes big wages, and carries them virtuously home to his wife. He has money in the savings bank, and holds Consols, poor chap, on which he must have wasted the good toil of years. I can't imagine any one less likely to take German gold than this man Maynard. Sure you haven't a bee in your bonnet, Dawson? To a police officer every one is a probable criminal, but some of us now and then are passably honest. I will bet my commission that Maynard is honest."

Dawson sniffed. "The honest men, with the excellent characters and the virtuous wives, are always the most dangerous because least likely to arouse suspicion. How do you know that Maynard hasn't a second establishment hidden away somewhere in the Three Towns? The upper and middle classes have no monopoly in illicit love affairs. Their working class betters do a bit that way too."

"All right. Have it your own way. We will assume for the sake of security that Maynard is a spy, that he has no dead mother whom he wants leave to bury, and that he has sold his country for the sake of some bit of fluff in Plymouth. The point is: what am I to do? Shall I grant leave?"

"Yes," said Dawson, "and do it handsomely. Give him four days and run the sympathetic stunt. Offer him a Service pass by the Great Western. Say how grieved you are and all the rest of the tosh. Have him up now, and put me somewhere close so that I can take a good look at the swine when he comes in and when he goes out."

The Chief of the Dockyards shrugged his shoulders, placed Dawson in an adjoining room, and summoned Maynard from the yard. The man, who was dressed in the awful dead black of his class when a funeral is in prospect, came up, and Dawson got a full sight of him. Maynard was about thirty-five, well set up—for he had served in the Territorials—and looked what he was, a first-rate workman of the best type. Even Dawson, who trusted no one, was slightly shaken. "I have never seen a man who looked less like a spy," muttered he; "but then, those always make the most dangerous of spies. Why has he a mother in Essex, and why has she died just now? Real mothers don't do these things; they've more sense."

Maynard received his third-class pass, respectfully thanked his Officer for his kindly expressed sympathy—which in his case was quite genuine—and disappeared. Dawson jumped into the room again to take a word of farewell. "I should know him anywhere," he cried. "I am going by the same train in the same carriage. Good-bye."

Maynard reached the Great Western station in good time, and found a carriage which was not overcrowded. He was carrying a small handbag. At the last moment before the train started a prosperous-looking passenger, with "commercial gentleman" written all over him, stepped into the same compartment and seated himself in a vacant seat opposite the bereaved workman. It was Dawson in one of his favourite roles. "There is nothing less like a detective," he would say, "than a middle-aged commercial traveller. They are such genial, unsuspicious, open-handed folk. This comes of wandering about the country at other people's expense."

The 10.15 fast express from the Three Towns to Paddington is an excellent one, and the journey was not more tedious than five hours spent in a train are bound to be. All through the journey Dawson, from behind his stock of papers and magazines, studied Maynard, and became, not, perhaps shaken in his conviction, but certainly puzzled. "He looked," he explained to me, "like a sick and sorrowful man. One who had really lost a beloved mother far away would look just like that. But so might one who had been unfaithful to a trusting wife and was now risking his neck to pour gold into the greedy lap of a frowsy mistress. One must never judge by appearances. A man may look as sick over backing the wrong horse as at losing an only son in the trenches. Human means of expression are limited."

"It takes time to learn that you are not such a beast as you pretend,"
I observed. Dawson grinned.

At Paddington Maynard took the Tube to Liverpool Street, and did not observe that his fellow passenger of the brown tweed suit and the fat, self-satisfied, rather oily face followed by the same route. Dawson, who was famished, rejoiced to see Maynard make for the refreshment-room. He could not lunch on the train, since the workman, upon whom he attended, had economically fed himself upon sandwiches put up in a "nosebag."

"No breakfast, no lunch," groaned Dawson. "What a day!" He did his best during five minutes in the refreshment-room at Liverpool Street to fill up the howling void in his person, and then watched Maynard enter a train for Burnham-on-Crouch. In two minutes he had opened up communications with a station Inspector of Police, made himself known, and secured the services of a constable to travel in Maynard's carriage. He did not wish to be seen again himself just at present. He yearned, too, for a first-class compartment and an ample tea-basket. Dawson's brain is a martyr to duty, but his stomach continually rises in rebellion. It was a fast train which would not stop until the Essex coast was reached, so that Dawson did not doubt that his quarry would be upon the platform when he himself got out So he was, and so, too, was a girl in deep mourning who had come to meet him. Dawson was staggered; a girl, also in funeral blacks, upset the picture which he had painted to himself. The man and girl talked together for a few minutes, and then walked slowly arm in arm out of the station towards the village. Dawson picked up his police assistant and followed. He gave no explanation of the reasons for his shadowing of the man Maynard, for he was just beginning to feel uneasy. Slowly the party of four threaded through the pretty little place, bright under the pleasant autumn twilight. Maynard and the girl were in front, Dawson and his policeman followed some fifty yards behind. In a side street, at the door of a small cottage—one of a humble row—the pair of mourners stopped, opened the iron gate, and entered. Dawson waited, watching. He could see through the windows into a little parlour where some half a dozen people, all in deep black, were gathered. Presently, as if they had waited only for the arrival of Maynard—which indeed was the fact—the heavy steps of men clumping down wooden stairs resounded from the open door, and there emerged into the street a coffin borne upon the shoulders of six bearers. The moment that the coffin appeared Dawson realised his blunder. Maynard had really lost his mother, and, like a dutiful son, had come all the way from the Three Towns to bury her! Off flew Dawson's hat, and he nudged the policeman hard in the ribs. "Take off your helmet, you chump," he growled savagely. "Don't you see that it's a funeral." The man, rather dazed—he had been plucked away from Liverpool Street at a moment's notice and sent upon what he thought was police service—did what he was told. The group of mourners formed behind the coffin, which was carried to the cemetery not far off. Still following, with their heads bowed, Dawson and the bewildered policeman attended the funeral, heard the beautiful service read, and the last offices completed. Then they turned away and made for the railway station.

"Why, sir," asked the policeman, looking sideways rather fearfully at his superior officer's stern face—"why, sir, did we come to this place?"

"Why? Haven't you seen?" snapped Dawson. "To attend a funeral, of course."
* * * * *

I have never met that policeman. To have conversed with him and to have sought to chop a way through the tangled recesses of his mind would have gratified me hugely. For, if police constables think at all, in what a bewildered whirl of confused speculation must his poor brain have been occupied during the return journey to London! Dawson tossed him into a compartment of the first train which came along, one of extreme slowness, and then dismissed him into cold space without a scrap of remorse. The humble creature, discharging his station duties with the precision of daily habit, had swung into the overpowering orbit of Chief Inspector Dawson, been caught up, dumped without instructions upon an unknown journey in attendance upon an unknown workman. Then when the train had stopped, he had been spewed out upon a strange country platform, led through strange mean streets, and forced with head bared to the autumn chill of evening, to attend the obsequies of a total stranger. At the end, without a word of explanation, still less of apology, he had been returned as an empty rejected package to the platform at Liverpool Street. Yes, I should dearly love to have met and cross-questioned that policeman, and have listened to the bizarre solution which he had to offer to it all. But most probably, in his stolid, faithful way, he never gave the subject any thought at all. To be tossed about at the whims of superiors was an experience which he would take as composedly as he would those exiguous weekly wages which were the derisory compensation.

Dawson went to the small hotel which he had picked out with Froissart as a convenient rendezvous. There he sat for hours doing nothing, for he was far too wise a man to push his head into another man's business, even though that one were a subordinate and a foreigner. He had failed once; he could not afford, by deputy, to fail a second time. Besides, he knew nothing of the movements of Froissart and his quarry. They had not appeared within the visible horizon of Burnham-on-Crouch, though they had had ample time in which to arrive. I am afraid that his temper got the better of him, and as the night drew on, unsolaced by a word from Froissart, and unrelieved by any literature more engrossing than old railway time-tables and hotel advertisements, he consigned to the Bottomless Pit the Chief of the Devonport Dockyard, the disgustingly virtuous and unenterprising Maynard, and even the harmless soul of his lately buried mother. Dawson in a royal rage is no pleasant spectacle.

It had gone half-past eleven before Froissart came, a boisterous, triumphant Froissart, bragging of his skill and his success in the manner of a born Gascon.

"It was tremendous, *mon ami*," roared Froissart, unchecked by Dawson's scowls. "I have done the blooming trick: the boat has gone to Holland, and the filthy spy is in the strong lock-up. My vigilance, my astuteness, my resource unfathomable, my flair, my soul of an artist, my patience inexhaustible, my address so firm and yet so delicate, my mastery of the minds of those others less gifted, my—"

"Oh, stow it!" roared Dawson.

"Unfailing insight, *mon esprit francais*, my genius for the service of police, my unshakable courage and elan, have had their just and inevitable reward. The boat with the message so false has gone to Holland for the German Kaiser to gloat over, and the filthy spy is in the safe lock-up. I took him with my own hands—I, le Comte de Froissart, I bemired my hands by contact with his foul carcase. The boat it flew down the river; *ma foi*, like a flash of the lightning, going they said thirty knots, *presque cinquante kilometres par heure*. The glorious *Marine Anglaise* will see that it reaches les Pays Bas, and then when it is of return your sailors so splendid, with sang-froid so perfect, will gobble it up. Just gobble it up. As I will gobble up this cold beef upon your table. *Peste*, I am of a hunger excruciating. I have not eaten for five, six, ten hours."

Froissart sat down at Dawson's table, where still lay the cold remains of his supper—he had had the decency to reflect that his colleague Froissart might be hungry upon arrival—and fell to eating copiously and loudly. The French are least admirable when they are seen devouring food.

Froissart ate while Dawson writhed. Though his colleague's success would plant laurels upon his own brow—little would he ever say at the Yard of that journey to Burnham and the preposterous funeral—he was jealous, bitterly jealous. I am by special appointment the Boswell of Dawson, yet I do not spare the feelings of my subject. Rather do I go over them with a rake—for the ultimate good of Dawson's variegated soul. He was bitterly jealous, but from natural curiosity yearned to know the details of those feats of which Froissart prated so triumphantly. And all the while, unconscious, heedless of his wrathful exasperated chieftain, Froissart devoured food in immense quantities. It was a disgusting exhibition.

Satisfied at last, Froissart broke away from the table, lit a cigarette, and sat himself down beside Dawson before the fire. It was well past midnight, but to these men regular habits were unknown, and the hours of work and of sleep always indeterminate.

"Now," exclaimed Froissart, "I will tell to you, my friend Dawson, the true *histoire* of my exploits so tremendous and unapproachable. I reached the station at Plymouth at ten hours, my spy was upon the platform. I knew him, for those who had kept him under watch had informed me of him. I had with me two police officers *en bourgeois*, what you call plain clothes, and I distributed them with the acumen of a strategist. It was *un train a couloir*. The spy disposed himself in a compartment. I placed one of my officers in the same compartment with him, the other in the compartment *contiguee* towards the engine, myself in that *a derriere*. He was thus the meat in our sandwich. If he passed into the corridor and walked this way or that he was seen by me or by my man in advance; all his movements while within his own compartment were supervised every moment. So we travelled. He did himself well that spy so atrocious. He partook of his *dejeuner* in the *buffet du train*, and we all three took our *dejeuner* there also. That was the last meal of which I ate before this my supper here. The journey was without incident, but when he arrived at Waterloo the trouble began. He was not taking risks, that spy. He knew not that he was under watch, but he took not risks. He began to perform a voyage designed to throw any man, except one of the vigilance and resource of Froissart, completely off his track. I was not learned in your Metropolitain before this day, but now I know your Tubes as if a map of them were printed in colours upon my hand. At Waterloo that spy, so astute, burrowed into the earth and entered a train of the railway called Bakerloo, in which he journeyed to Golder's Green. Then he crossed a *quai* and returned to the town called Camden. Again he descended, passed through tunnels, and emerging upon another *quai* proceeded to Highgate. All the while we three followed, not close, but so that he never escaped from under our eyes. At Highgate he turned about and returned to Tottenham Court Road. Thence he departed by another line to the Bank, and, rising in and *ascenseur*, emerged upon the pavements of your City. He looked this way and that, not perceiving us who watched, walked warily to the Lord Maire's station of the Mansion House, boarded the District Railway, and did not alight till Wimbledon. It was easy to follow, but my friend, the billets, the tickets, were *une grande difficulte*. I solved the problem of tickets by my genius so *superbe*. We at first tried to take them, but *apres* we abandoned the project so hopeless and travelled *sans payer*. When asked at the barriers or in the lifts, we offered pennies, and the men who collected took them joyfully, asking not whence we came. It was *une procedee tres simple*. It is possible that these wayward uncounted pennies dropped into their own pockets. They rejoiced always to receive them. From Wimbledon we returned to Earl's Court, and then, descending by an electric staircase, which moved of itself, again found ourselves in the Tubes. I loved that *escalier electrique*; one day I will return and ascend and descend upon it for hours. From Earl's Court we went to Piccadilly Circus; there we made another change for Oxford Circus; there we again got out, and at last, after penetrating the bowels of your London, travelled to Liverpool Street. By this time it had become dark, and the spy's passion for underground travel had spent itself. He crossed the street, descended to the grand station of the Eastern Railway, and took a ticket for Burnham-on-Crouch. Exhausted, but ever vigilant, Froissart and his faithful men took also tickets for Burnham-on-Crouch.

"I will not weary you more with our wanderings, but after many hours, at ten o'clock, we at last arrived at this place. The spy was met upon the *quai* by another villain, with whom he held converse, and the pair of them, ignorant that the vengeance of Froissart overshadowed them, marched heedlessly, openly, to the river side and entered a large house of which the gardens ran down to the water. I left there my two faithful but weary ones on watch, and hastened to the *salle de police*. There an Inspector and a young *officier anglais*—a sub-lieutenant of the Royal Naval Volunteer Reserve—were awaiting my arrival with impatience. To them I told my story with the brevity that I now recount it to you. They were intrigued greatly, and the *sous*-lieutenant struck me violently upon the back and said, *ma foi*, that I was a 'downy old bird,' It was a compliment *tres 'bizarre mais tres aimable*. I was, it appeared, an old bird of the downiest plumage. I had noted the name of the house, and the Inspector seized a Directory. 'We have suspected that house for some time,' said he. There is a big boat-house at the bottom of the garden containing a large sea-going motor-boat. The proprietor calls himself English, but does not look like one. He is doubtless a snake, one whom they call *naturalise*, a viper whom we English have warmed in our bosoms.' So spake the Inspector. The Sub-Lieutenant whistled. He said only, 'Send for little Tommy; it is a job for him.' A call was sent forth, and there came into the room a scrap of an infant, habited in short pantaloons and a green shirt. The child carried a long pole and stood stiffly at attention. '*Ma foi*, do I see before me a Boy Scout?' I asked. 'You do,' replied the Sub-Lieutenant. 'This is little Tommy, the patrol leader of the Owls.' '*Mon Dieu*' I cried, 'an Owl! *Un Hibou*! Is he then stupid as an owl?' I could see that the Tommy so small frowned savagely, but the Sub-Lieutenant laughed. 'You will see presently if he is stupid. I have forty miles of coast to watch, and I do it all with Boy Scouts like this one.' '*Nom d'un chien*,' I cried. 'You English are a great people.' 'We are,' agreed the Sub-Lieutenant, 'devilish great.' Tommy grinned.

"Then the officer so youthful—his age could not have exceeded nineteen years—gave orders to the little Tommy. He was to go to the house, to enter the garden, to squeeze his tiny person into the boat-house, and watch. When the spy and his associates went towards the boat, Tommy was to warn us with a hoot—like an owl—and we were to take charge. At least so I understood the orders given in a strange sea language. Tommy saluted, and vanished. If he had ten years, I should be astonished; but he was a man, every inch of him. Wait till I have finished.

"We followed quickly behind Tommy, but saw him not, and joined my men, who still watched the house. The Sub-Lieutenant and I moved warily, climbed over the wall of the garden, and crept along the grass, soft like moss to our feet, till we could see the boat-house stand out against the dull shine of the river. There was no sign of the presence of *le petit Hibou*. Suddenly the door of the house, which gave upon the garden, opened, and four men walked down to the boat-house and entered stealthily. My heart turned to water—what a calamity if they should find and slay the pretty little Owl! The minutes passed, perhaps five, perhaps ten, and then quite close we heard the soft low hoot of an owl. The Sub-Lieutenant hooted a reply, and from among some bushes there came out that serene, intrepid infant with the pole! He joined us, and whispered eagerly to the officer. I could not hear what he said. Afterwards the Sub-Lieutenant told me that the men had entered, three had got into the boat, one remaining on land. It was a forty-foot boat, reported Tommy—who seemed of wisdom and knowledge encyclopaedic—it had a big cabin forrard, the engine was a Wotherspoon, ten cylinders set V-fashion, the power a hundred horses. So Tommy had observed and reported, and so I repeat to you. As we watched we saw the boat push out into the river, turn towards the sea; the engine so powerful buzzed like a million bees, a wave curled up in front, and it sped away for Holland like the shot of an arrow. The night was fine, the sea calm; it would complete the voyage in safety. But upon return what a surprise has been prepared for that motor-boat and its detestable owner! What a surprise, *ma foi*. I yearn to hear of the denouement.

"'We will nab the fourth man who has stayed behind,' whispered the officer, and we crept towards the boat-house. We were ten yards away when he issued forth and turned to lock the door. Then we sprang upon him. He was very quick—like the big snake that he was. He heard us, spun round, and struck two blows of his fist. The Sub-Lieutenant got one upon his beautiful nose; I got the other here under the jaw. We were shot, sprawling, upon the grass, one to each side, and the villain, springing between us, started to flee. I was struck down, but not stunned; I was alert, undefeated, eager to resume the battle. I rose to my knees. I saw the villain fleeing up the grass. Ah, he would escape! But I had not reckoned upon the patrol leader, the little Owl, the *Hibou* of a Boy Scout so deft and courageous. The spy fled, but into his path sprang the tiny figure of the Owl, his pole in rest like a lance. They met, the man and the little Owl, and the shock of that tourney aroused the echoes of the night. The man, hit in the belly by the point of the pole, collapsed upon the grass, and the Owl, driven backwards by the weight of the man, rolled over and over like *un herisson*. He was no longer an Owl; he was a round Hedgehog! I was consumed with admiration for the gallant Owl. I got to my feet, I jumped across the lawn, and fell with both knees hard upon the carcase so foul of the spy whom I had pursued all day. He lay groaning from the grievous pain in his belly, and I put upon him the handcuffs before that he could recover. The little Tommy, the Hedgehog, picked himself up, staggered to the body of his enemy, and there, leaning upon the admirable pole which he had not released in his somersaults, gave forth a hoot of victory. It was the Day of Tommy. But for that morsel of a wise Owl the spy would have escaped. I embraced Tommy, who wriggled with discomfort; the Sub-Lieutenant shook his hand, which he appreciated the more. 'Good work,' said the officer. 'Thank you, sir,' said Tommy. That was all; no emotion, no compliments, no embraces. 'Good work.' 'Thank you, sir.' *Ma foi*, what a people are the English!

"We locked up the spy. The Sub-Lieutenant told me that wireless orders had gone out to the patrols spread far over the seas. The boat, of which we had the name and description, would arrive at Holland, but upon its return on the morrow it would be seized and escorted to Harwich. If by mischance it eluded the patrols, it would be captured when it arrived in the river Crouch. All was provided for. The false news has gone to Holland, and Froissart has done good work. I ask for no reward; I will be like the English—cold, implacable. When the officer said at parting to me, 'Good work, M. Froissart, we are much obliged to you,' I replied calmly, 'Thank you, sir,' I had, you will observe, modelled myself upon the little Owl.

"And you, Mr. Dawson," concluded Froissart, wiping his face, for the effort of talking so much English had brought out the sweat upon him, "have you also succeeded?"

"Yes," said Dawson curtly, "I have also done my work, but it was not exciting. My man was no spy, and the real news about the *Intrepid* and *Terrific* will not get through to Germany."

"Saved," roared Froissart, springing to his feet. "We are colleagues most perfect. We have done work of the most good. *Embracons nous, mon ami*." Then occurred that deplorable incident which has already been related. Froissart in his enthusiasm embraced the unresponsive Dawson, and was laid out by a short-arm jab upon the diaphragm. It was really too bad of Dawson; but then, as I have said, his temper was atrocious.

* * * * *

The two battle-cruisers remained upon the shoals of Picklecombe Point all through November and well into the following month. The great salvage steamer with the arc light went away, but others remained. Work seemed to proceed, though it was unaccountably slow in producing a result. The Three Towns lost interest in the derelicts until one evening there fell upon them a blow which set them gasping for coherent speech. The newsboys were crying in the streets a Special Edition, very Special. Set in dirty type in an odd column, headed with the mysterious words "Stop Press," appeared an announcement by the Admiralty that far away in the South Seas the battle-cruisers *Intrepid* and *Terrific*, under the command of Vice-Admiral Stocky, had met and sunk the lately victorious German Squadron! It was glorious news, but the Three Towns thought little at the moment of the glory. They urgently hungered for an explanation of the inscrutable means by which two battle-cruisers, mined and cast upon the shoals below Mount Edgecumbe under their very eyes, could race hot foot to the South Seas and there lay out a German squadron. As soon as the winter dawn broke an immense crowd surged upon the Hoe gazing into blank space. The two battle-cruisers, which for a month had lain helpless before them, were gone! Gone, too, were the salvage steamers and the patrol boats. The waters which had been so active and crowded were void! Then the Three Towns understood; they grasped, men, women and children, the great spoof of which they had been the interested victims, and their approving laughter rose to Heaven. For in all that appertains to the Royal Navy every one born within the circuit of the Three Towns is very wise indeed.

PART IV

THE CAPTAIN OF MARINES

CHAPTER XV

DAWSON REAPPEARS

I had seen nothing of Dawson during my intimate association with Madame Gilbert. He had written to me copiously—for a very busy man he was a curiously voluminous letter-writer. He always employed the backs of official forms and wrote in pencil. His handwriting, large and round, was that of a man who had received a good and careful Board School education, but was quite free from personal characteristics. Dawson's letters in no respect resembled the man. They were very long, very dull, and very crudely phrased. He had evidently tried to put them into what he conceived to be a literary shape, and the effect was deplorable. One may read such letters, the work of unskilled writers, in the newspapers which devote space to "Correspondence." The writers, like Dawson, can probably talk vividly and forcibly, using strong nervous vernacular English, but the moment they take the pen all thought and individual character become swamped in a flood of turgid, commonplace jargon. I was disappointed with Dawson's letters, and I am sure that he will be even more disappointed when he finds none of them made immortal in this book. His purpose in sending them to me will have been ruthlessly defeated.

A week after Madame had vanished down my lift for the last time, Dawson—in the make-up with which I was most familiar—called upon me at my office. He also came to say good-bye, for a turn of the official wheel had come, and he was ordered south to resume his duties at the Yard. He was, he told me, taking a last tour of inspection to make certain that the Secret Service net, which he had designed and laid, would be deftly worked by the hands of his subordinates. "I shall not be sorry," said he, "to get back to my deserted family and to be once more the plain man Dawson whom God made."

"You have so many different incarnations," I observed, "that I wonder the original has not escaped your memory."

He smiled. "If I had forgotten," said he, "my wife would soon remind me. She always insists that she married a certain man Dawson and declines to recognise any other."

"So if I come south to visit you, I shall see the original?"

"You will."

"Thanks," said I; "I will come at the earliest opportunity."

"I don't say that if you call at the Yard you will see quite the same person whom you will meet at Acacia Villas, Primrose Road, Tooting."

"That would be too much to expect. But under any guise, Dawson, I am always sure of knowing you."

"Yes, confound you. I would give six months' pay to know how you do it."

"You shall know some day, and without any bribery. Now that you are here, talk, talk, talk. I want to get the taste of those rotten letters of yours out of my mouth."

He looked surprised and hurt. He looked exactly as a famous sculptor looked who, when a beautiful work of his hands was unveiled, wished me to publish a descriptive sonnet from his pen. I bluntly refused. He was an admirable sculptor, but a dreadful sonneteer. Yet in his secret heart he valued the sonnet far above the statue. In this strange way we are made.

I did not conceal from Dawson my interest in Madame Gilbert, and he rather rudely expressed strong disapproval. He suggested that for a married man I was much too free in my ways. "That woman is full of brains," said he, "but she is the artfullest hussy ever made. She will turn any man around her pretty fingers if he gives way to her. She has made a nice fool of you and of that ass Froissart. She even tried her little games with me—with me indeed. But I was too strong for her."

I regarded Dawson with some interest and more pity. The poor fellow did not realise that Madame had for years moulded him to her hands like potter's clay. She had mastered him by ingenuously pretending that he stood upon a serene pinnacle far removed from her influence. He had preened his feathers and done her bidding.

"We are not all strong—like you, Dawson," said I mildly.

I switched Dawson off the subject of Madame Gilbert, and directed his mind towards the contemplation of his own exploits. When handled judiciously he will talk freely and frankly, giving away official secrets with both hands. But his confidences always relate to the past, to incidents completed. When he has a delicate job on hand, he can be as close as the English Admiralty, even to me. He has no sense of proportion. Again and again he has recounted the interminable details of cases in which I take not the smallest interest, and has ignored all my efforts to dam the unprofitable flood of narrative and to divert the current into more fruitful channels. He looks at everything from the Dawson standpoint, and cares for nothing which does not add to the glory of Dawson. Unless he fills the stage, an incident has for him no value or concern. Happily for me the most startling of his exploits, that of bending a timid War Committee of the Cabinet to his will in the winter of 1915-1916, and of bluffing into utter submission nearly a hundred thousand rampant munition workers who were eager to "down tools," fulfils all the Dawson conditions of importance. He and he alone filled a star part, to him and to him alone belonged the success of an incredibly bold manoeuvre. I have drawn Dawson as I saw him, in his weakness and in his strength. I have revealed his vanity and the carefully hidden tenderness of his heart. In my whimsical way I have perhaps treated him as essentially a figure of fun. But though I may smile at him, even rudely laugh at him, he is a great public servant who once at least—though few at the time knew—saved his country from a most grievous peril.

In the early weeks of 1916, when work for the Navy, and work in the gun and ammunition shops which were rapidly being organised all over the country, were within a very little of being suspended by a general strike of workmen, terrified for their threatened trade-union privileges, the strength and resource of Dawson put forth boldly in the North dammed the peril at its source. In spite of the penalties laid down in Munition Acts, in spite of the powers vested in military authorities by the Defence of the Realm Regulations, there would have been a great strike, and both the Navy and the New Army would have been hung up gasping for the ships, the guns, and the supplies upon which they had based all their plans for attack and defence. The danger arose over that still insistent problem—the "dilution of labour." The new armies had withdrawn so many skilled and unskilled workmen from the workshops, and the demands for munitions of all kinds were so overwhelming, that wholly new and strange methods of recruiting labour were urgent. Women must be employed in large numbers, in millions; machinery must be put to its full use without regard for the restrictions of unions, if the country were to be saved. Many of the younger and more open-minded of the trade-union officials had enlisted; many of those older ones who remained could not bend their stiff minds to the necessity for new conditions. They were not consciously unpatriotic—their sons were fighting and dying; they were not consciously seditious, though secret enemy agents moved amongst them, and talked treason with them in the jargon of their trades. They simply could not understand that the hardly won privileges of peace must yield to the greater urgencies of war.

Civilians came north to examine the position on behalf of the Ministry of Munitions; they came, wrung their hands, and reported in terror that if dilution were pressed, a hundred thousand men would be "out." Yet the risk had to be taken, for dilution must be pressed. Dawson was hard at work sweeping into his widespread net all those whom he knew to be enemy agents and all those whom he suspected. It was not an occasion for squeamishness. With the consent of his official superiors, he picked up with those prehensile fingers of his many of the most troublesome of the union agitators, and deported them to safe spots far distant, where they were constrained to cease from troubling. Still the danger increased, and he saw that a few days only could intervene between industrial peace and war. Already the manufacture of heavy howitzers for the Spring Offensive had been stopped—by a cunning embargo upon small essential parts—and the moment had arrived for a trial of strength between authority and rebellion. He made up his mind, plainly told his chiefs what his plans were, obtained their whole-hearted concurrence, and went south by the night train. By telegram he had sent an ultimatum which struck awe into the official mind. "Unless," he wired, in code, "the Cabinet wants a revolution, it had better meet at once and call me in. Unless it does this at once I shall not go back here. I shall resign, and leave the Government in the soup where it deserves to be."

Such a message from a man who in official eyes was no more than a Chief Inspector of Police was in itself a portent. It revealed how completely war had upset all official standards and conventions.

To the Chief, his Commissioner, he opened his mind freely. "I am about fed up with politicians and lawyers," said he. "There is big trouble coming, and not a man of them all has the pluck to get his blow in first. I have always found that men will respect an order—they like to be governed—but they despise slop. What the devil's the use of Ministers going North and telling the men how well they have done, and how patriotic they are, when the men themselves all know that they've done damn badly and mean to do worse? I could settle the whole business in twenty-four hours."

"They are frightened men, Dawson," said the Chief. "That is the matter with the Government. They have been brought up to slobber over the public and try to cheat it out of votes. They can't tell the truth. When hard deadly reality breaks through their web of make-believe, they cower together in corners and howl. I doubt if you will get a free hand, Dawson. What do you want—martial law?"

"Yes. That, or something like it. If I have the threat of it at my back, so that it rests with me, and me alone, to put it into force, I shall not need to use it. But I must go North with the proclamation in my pocket or I shall not go North at all. Here is my resignation." Dawson tossed a letter upon the table, and laughed. The Chief picked it up and read the curt lines in which Dawson delivered his last word.

"Good man," commented he; "that is the way to talk. They can't understand how any man can have the grit to resign a fat job before he is kicked out. They never do. They compromise. You may put starch into their soft backbones, but personally I doubt the possibility. But at least you will get your chance. There is to be a meeting of the War Committee the first thing to-morrow morning and you are to be summoned. I told the Home Secretary that I should resign myself if they did not give you a full opportunity to state your case. I will support you as long as I am in this chair."

Dawson held out his hand. "Thank you," he said simply. The two men clasped hands and looked into one another's eyes. "It is a good country, Dawson," said the Chief—"a jolly good country, and worth big risks to oneself. It will be saved by plain, honest men if it is to be saved at all. Our worst enemies are not the Germans, but our flabby-fibred political classes at home. The people are just crying out to be told what to do, and to be made to do it. Yet nobody tells them. Don't let the Cabinet browbeat you, and smother you with plausible sophistries. Just talk plain English to them, Dawson."

"I will. For once in their sheltered lives they shall hear the truth."

For what follows, Dawson is my principal, but not my sole authority. I have tested what he told me in every way that I could, and the test has held. Somehow—I am prepared to believe in the manner told by him—he forced the Cabinet to give him the authority for which he asked, and he used it in the manner which I shall tell of. He held what is always a first-rate advantage: he knew exactly what he wanted, no more or less, and was prepared to get it or retire from official life. Those who gave to him authority gave it reluctantly—gave it because they were between the devil and the deep sea. They would gladly have thrown over Dawson, but they could not throw over the civil and military powers who supported him in his demands. And had they thrown him over they would have been left to deal by their incompetent unaided selves with a strike in the midst of war which might have spread like a prairie fire over the whole country. But though they bent before Dawson, I am very sure that they did not love him, and that he will never be the Chief Commissioner of Metropolitan Police. Against his name in the official books stands a mark of the most deadly blackness. Strength and success are never pardoned by weakness and failure.

When at last Dawson was summoned to the sitting; of the War Committee, he found himself in the presence of some half a dozen elderly and embarrassed-looking gentlemen arranged round a big table. They had been discussing him, and trying to devise some decent civil means to get rid of him. He and his story of the coming strike in the North were a distressful inconvenience, an intolerable intrusion upon a quiet life. When he entered, he was without a friend in the room, except the War Minister who loved a man who knew his own mind and was prepared to accept big responsibilities. But even he doubted whether it were possible to achieve the results aimed at with the means required by Dawson.

Our friend suffered from no illusions. "I knew what I was up against," he said to me long afterwards. "I knew that they were all longing to be quit of me and to go to sleep again. But I had made up my mind that they should get some very plain speaking. I would compel them to understand that what I offered was a forlorn chance of averting a civil war, and that if they refused my offer they would be left to themselves—not to stamp out a spark of revolution, but to subdue a roaring furnace. They could take their choice in the certain knowledge that if they chose wrongly the North would be in flames within forty-eight hours. It was a great experience, Mr. Copplestone. I have never enjoyed anything half so much."

Dawson was offered a chair set some six feet distant from the sacred table, but he preferred to stand. His early training held, and he was not comfortable in the presence of his superiors in rank or station except when standing firmly at attention.

The Prime Minister fumbled with some papers, looked over them for a few embarrassed minutes, and then spoke.

"Great pressure has been placed upon us, Mr. Dawson, to see you and to hear your report. Great pressure—to my mind improper pressure. I have here letters from Magistrates, Lords Lieutenant, competent military authorities, naval officers superintending shipyards, officials of the Munitions Department. They all declare that the industrial outlook in the North is most perilous, and that at any moment a situation may arise which will be fraught with the gravest peril to the country. We have replied that the law provides adequate remedies, but to that the retort is made that the men who are at the root of the grave troubles pending snap their fingers at the law. We are pressed to take counsel with you, though why the high officers who communicate with me should, as it were, shift their responsibilities upon the shoulders of a Chief Inspector of Scotland Yard I am at a loss to comprehend. What I would ask of my colleagues is this: who is in fact responsible for the maintenance of a due observance of law in the Northern district from which you have come, and where you appear to discharge unofficial and wholly irregular functions? Who is responsible? Perhaps my learned friend the Home Secretary can enlighten us?" The Prime Minister paused, and smiled happily to himself. He had at least made things nasty for an intrusive colleague. But the Home Secretary, suave, alert, was not to be caught. He at any rate was not prepared to admit responsibility.

"It is possible, sir," he said, "that in some vague, undefined, constitutional way I am responsible for the police service of the United Kingdom. But happily my direct charge does not in practice extend beyond England. The centre of disturbance appears to be on the northern side of the Border, within the jurisdiction of the Secretary for Scotland. It is possible that my right honourable friend who holds that office, and whom I am pleased to see here with us, will answer the Prime Minister's question. He is responsible for his obstreperous countrymen." The Home

Secretary paused, and also smiled happily to himself. He had evaded a trap, and had involved an unloved colleague in its meshes; what more could be required of a highly placed Minister?

"God forbid!" cried the Scottish Secretary hastily. "These aggressive and troublesome workmen are no countrymen of mine. It is true," he added pensively, "that when I am in the North I claim that a somewhat shadowy Scottish ancestry makes of me a Scot to the finger tips, but no sooner do I cross the Border upon my return to London than I revert violently to my English self. A kindly Providence has ordained that the central Scottish Office should be in London, and my urgent duties compel me to reside there permanently. Which is indeed fortunate. It is true that technically my responsibilities cover everything, or nearly everything, which occurs in the unruly North, but I do not interfere with the discretion of those on the spot who know the local conditions and can deal adequately with them. I am content to rest my action upon the advice of those responsible authorities whose considered opinions have been quoted by the Prime Minister."

The Prime Minister smiled no more. The wheel which he had jogged so agreeably had come full round, and, in colloquial speech, had biffed him in the eye. He fumbled the papers once more, and frowned.

"It seems to me," plaintively put in the First Lord of the Admiralty (a political chief very different from the one whom Dawson encountered in Chapter XII), "though I am a child in these high matters, that no one is ever responsible for the exercise of those duties with which he is nominally charged. For, consider my own case. Though I am the First Lord, and attend daily at the Admiralty, I am convinced that the active and accomplished young gentleman whom I had the misfortune to succeed regards himself as still responsible to the people of this country for the disposition and control of the Fleets. At least that is the not unnatural impression which I derive from his frequent speeches and newspaper articles."

There was a general laugh, in which all joined except the War Minister and Dawson. They were not politicians.

"If there is a big strike," growled the War Minister, "the Spring Offensive will be off. It is threatened now, very seriously. I am months behind with my howitzers."

His colleagues looked reproachfully at the famous warrior, and shifted uneasily in their chairs. He had an uncomfortable habit of blurting forth the most unpleasant truths.

"Yes," put in the Minister for Munitions, "we are behind with the howitzers and with ammunition of all kinds. But what can one do with these savage brutes in the North? I went there myself and spoke plainly to them. By God's grace I am still alive, though at one moment I had given up myself for lost. At one works where I made a speech the audience were armed with what I believe are called monkey wrenches, and showed an almost uncontrollable passion for launching them at my head. I was hustled and wellnigh personally assaulted. Like my patriotic friend the Scottish Secretary, I was very happy indeed when I got south of the Border. The central office of the Munitions Department is happily in London, and my urgent duties compel me to reside there permanently. I have no leisure for roving expeditions."

"This is very interesting," broke in the First Lord, who lay back in his chair with shut eyes. "There appears to be no eagerness on the part of any one of us to stick his hands into the northern hornets' nest, or to admit any responsibility for it. All of us, that is, except our courageous and silent friend Mr. Dawson." He opened his eyes and smiled most winningly towards Dawson. "Would it not be well if we gave him an opportunity of telling us what his views are?"

"I have been waiting for him to begin," growled the War Minister.

"We are at your service, Mr. Dawson," said the Prime Minister graciously.

Dawson, standing stiffly at attention, had closely followed the conversation, and, as it proceeded, his heart sank. He despaired of discovering courage and quick decision in the group of Ministers before him. Yet when called upon he made a last effort. If the country were to be saved, it must be saved by its people, not by its politicians, and he was a man of the people, resolute, enduring, long suffering.

"Gentlemen," said he, "we are threatened with a strike in the Northern shops and shipyards which will cripple the country. It will begin within forty-eight hours. I can stop it if I go North to-night with the full powers of the Government in my pocket, and with the means for which I ask. All the authorities in the North, civil, military and naval, have approved of my plans. I ask only leave to carry them out."

"Your plans are?" snapped the War Minister.

"To get my blow in first," said Dawson simply.

The First Lord again looked at Dawson, and a glint of fighting light flashed in his tired eyes. "Thrice armed is he who has his quarrel just; and four times he who gets his blow in first. How would you do it, Mr. Dawson."

"Yes, how?" eagerly inquired the War Minister.

"I have served," said Dawson, "in most parts of the world. When in West Africa one is attacked by a snake, one does not wait until it bites. One cuts off its head."

"You have served?" asked the War Minister. "In what Service?"

"The Red Marines," proudly answered Dawson.

"Ah!" The War Minister was plainly interested, and Dawson had, during the rest of the interview, no eyes for any one except for him and for the First Lord. He recognised these two as brother fighting men. The others he waved aside as civilian truck. "Ah! The Red Marines. Long service men, the best we have. So you would cut off the snake's head before it can bite."

"To-morrow afternoon," explained Dawson, "I must attend a meeting of shop stewards, over two hundred of them. They contain the head of the snake. Give me powers, a proclamation of martial law which I may show them, and I will cut off the snake's head."

"You soldiers are always prating about martial law," grumbled the Prime Minister. "We have given to you the amplest powers under the Defence of the Realm Act and the Munitions Act to punish strikers. Those are sufficient. I have no patience with plans for enforcing a military despotism."

"Excuse me, sir," said Dawson patiently, as to a child, "but if a hundred thousand men go out on strike, your Acts of Parliament will be waste paper. You cannot lock up or fine a hundred thousand men, and if you could you would still be unable to make them work. No means have ever been devised to make unwilling men work, except the lash, and that is useless with skilled labour. No one in the North cares a rap for Acts of Parliament, but there is a mystery about martial law which carries terror into the hardest heart and the most stupid brain. I want a signed proclamation of martial law, but I undertake not to issue it unless all other forms of pressure fail. I must have it all in cold print to show to the shop stewards when I strike my blow. Without that proclamation I am helpless, and you will be helpless, too, by Friday next. This is Wednesday. Unless I cut off the snake's head to-morrow, it will bite you here even in your sheltered London."

The Prime Minister fumbled once more with the papers before him, but they gave him no comfort. All advised the one measure of giving full authority to Dawson and of trusting to his energy and skill. "Dawson is a man of the people, and knows his own class. He can deal with the men; we can't." So the urgent appeals ran.

"And if you do not succeed? If you proclaim martial law and we have to enforce it, where shall we be then?"

"No worse off than you will be anyhow by Friday," said Dawson curtly.

"So you say. But suppose that we think you needlessly fearful. Suppose that we prefer to wait until Friday and see; what then?"

"You will see what has not been seen in our country for over a hundred years," retorted Dawson. "You will see artillery firing shotted guns in the streets."

The Prime Minister shrugged his shoulders, but the War Secretary turned to his pile of maps and picked up one on which was marked all the depots and training camps in the northern district. "How many men do you want?" he asked.

"No khaki, thank you," replied Dawson. "It is not trained, and the workmen are used to it. To them khaki means their sons and brothers and friends dressed up. I want my own soldiers of the *Sea*

Regiment in service blue. I want eighty men from my old division at Chatham."

"Eighty!" cried the War Minister—"eighty men! You are going to stop a revolution with eighty Red Marines!"

"I could perhaps do with fewer," explained Dawson modestly. "But I want to make sure work. Give me eighty Marines, none of less than five years' service, a couple of sergeants, and a lieutenant—a regular pukka lieutenant. Give them to me, and make me temporarily a captain in command, and I will engage to cut off the snake's head. You can have my own head if I fail."

The Great War Minister rose, walked over to Dawson, and shook his embarrassed hand. "It is a pleasure to meet you, Mr. Dawson," said he. The First Lord, now fully awake, sat up and stared earnestly at the detective. Those two, the chiefs of the Navy and the Army, had grasped the startling fact that for once they were in the presence of a Man. The others saw only a rather ill-dressed, intrusive, vulgar police officer.

"I have rarely met a man with so economical a mind," went on the War Minister, who resumed his seat. "If you had asked me for eight thousand, I should not have been surprised." He turned to the Prime Minister. "If our resolute friend here can stop a revolution with eighty Red Marines, let him have them in God's name."

"Oh, he can have the Marines," growled the Prime Minister—"if the First Lord agrees. They are in his department. And if it pleases him to dress up as a temporary captain, that is nothing to me; but I draw a firm line at any proclamation of martial law."

"Well," asked the War Minister of Dawson, "what say you?"

"I must have the proclamation, my lord," replied Dawson. "Not to put up in the streets, but to show to the shop stewards. They won't believe that the Cabinet has any spunk until they see the proclamation signed by you. They know that what you say you do."

["Great Heavens," I said to Dawson, when he recounted to me the details of his surprising interview with the War Committee, "tact is hardly your strong suit. You could not have asked more plainly to be kicked out. The flabbier a Cabinet is, the more convinced are its members of adamantine resolution."

"If I had to go down and out," replied Dawson, "I had determined to go fighting. I was there to speak my mind, not to flatter anybody."]

The silence which followed this awful speech could be felt. The Prime Minister gasped, flushed to the eyes, and half rose to dismiss Dawson from the room. He himself thought for a moment that all was lost, when through the tense atmosphere ran a ripple of gay laughter. It was the First Lord who, with instant decision, had taken the only means to save his new friend Dawson. He has a delightfully infectious silvery laugh, and the effect was electrical. The War Minister opened his great mouth, and bellowed Ha! Ha! Ha! The Minister of Munitions put his head down on the table and shrieked. Even the Home Secretary, a severe, humourless, legal gentleman, cackled. The Prime Minister, whose perceptions were of the quickest, saw that anger would be ridiculous in the midst of laughter. He admitted the First Lord's victory, and forced a smile.

"You are not a diplomatist, Mr. Dawson," said he reprovingly.

"Like Marcus Antonius," whispered the First Lord, as he wiped his eyes delicately, "he is a plain, blunt man."

The War Minister pulled a sheet of paper towards' him and began to write. He scribbled for a few minutes, made a few corrections, and then read out slowly the words which he had set down. All present saw that the moment of acute crisis had arrived.

"That is all that I want," said Dawson. "If you will sign that paper, my lord, I need not trouble you gentlemen any longer."

"I am one of His Majesty's principal Secretaries of State," observed the War Minister. "Shall I sign, sir?"

"I believe," remarked the Home Secretary primly, "that if one has regard for strict historical accuracy there is but one Secretary of State, and that I am that one."

"I will not trouble you," said the War Minister.

"I am technically responsible for the country over which I am supposed to rule," put in the Scottish Secretary plaintively. "I speak, of course under correction, but north of the Border my signature might—"

"You are not a Secretary of State," growled the War Minister, "and your seat is not safe. No one shall sign except myself, for I have no need to seek after working-class votes. Dawson and I will face this music."

"And if I decline to permit you to sign?" asked the Prime Minister blandly. "This is not a Cabinet meeting, and we have no power to commit the Government to so grave a step."

"You will require to fill up the vacant position of Secretary for War," came the answer.

"And also the humble post of First Lord of the Admiralty," murmured that high officer of State. "We are up against realities, and Cabinet etiquette can go hang for me."

The War Minister again read aloud what he had written, signed it carefully and deliberately, and rising up, handed it to Dawson. "Get it printed at once and go ahead, Mr. Dawson."

"Captain Dawson, R.M.L.I.," corrected the First Lord, who also rose and warmly shook hands with the new captain. "You shall be gazetted at once. I will see the Adjutant-General myself and give orders to Chatham."

"You have both made up your minds?" inquired the Prime Minister.

"Quite," said the War Secretary. The First Lord nodded.

"Very good," replied the Prime Minister; "I consent. We must above all things preserve the unity of the Cabinet in these circumstances of grave national crisis."

"Clear out, Dawson," whispered the First Lord.

Dawson cleared out.

CHAPTER XVI

DAWSON STRIKES

It was a little past noon, and Dawson had much work to do before he could be free to speed north by the midnight train. First he skipped across to the Yard and into the private room of his firm friend the Chief. To him he showed the potent proclamation and recounted the methods of its extraction. "I thought that I was in a company of jackals," said he at the end; "but I was wrong—two of them were lions."

"We should be in a bad way if there were no lions," commented the Chief. "Those two, and another who is dead, saved South Africa; there are one or two more, but not many. What shall you do with this?"

"We will set it up on our own private press, and run off a couple of hundred placards. The secret must not leak out; I am playing for surprises."

The Chief struck a bell, the order was given, and Dawson's priceless proclamation vanished into the lower regions.

"Now?" inquired the Chief.

"Chatham," explained Dawson, "to pick up my men—and to get my uniform." When telling the story, Dawson again and again described to me his uniform, with which I happened by family association to be intimately acquainted. He did not spare me a badge or a button. I am convinced that no girl wore her first ball-dress with half the palpitating pride with which Dawson surveyed himself in his captain's kit. When I chaffed him gently, and hinted that the stars of a captain were cheaply come by in these days, he had one retort always ready, "Not in the Red Marines." He did not value his office of Chief Detective Inspector a rap beside that temporary rank of Captain of Red Marines. He had, you see, been a private in that proud exclusive Corps, and its glory for him outshone all human glories.

He flew away to Chatham as fast as a deliberate railway service permitted, and found upon arrival that an urgent telegram from the Adjutant-General had preceded him. Dawson was shown at once to the Commandant's quarters, and there explained his requirements. "Eighty men, two sergeants, and a regular lieutenant. Not one of less than five years' service. Also a sea-service kit with a captain's stars for me. The mess-sergeant will fit me out. He trades in second-hand uniforms."

"You have the advantage of me, Mr. Dawson," said the Commandant, smiling, "in your profound knowledge of the functions of a mess sergeant."

"I was a recruit here, sir, when you were a second lieutenant. I know the by-ways of Chatham and the perquisites of mess-sergeants. I was a sergeant myself once."

"I remember you, Dawson," said the Commandant kindly, "and am proud to see one of us become so great a man. By the regulations a temporary officer should wear khaki."

"No khaki for me, sir, please," implored Dawson. "I should not feel that I belonged to the old Corps in khaki. In my time it was the red parade tunic or the sea-service blue."

"Wear any kit you please. This is your day, not mine. I have been ordered to place myself and all Chatham at your disposal, though what your particular game is I have not a notion. I won't ask any questions now, but please come and dine with me in mess when you return, and let me have the whole story."

"I will, sir," cried Dawson heartily, "and thank you very much. I have waited at the mess, but never dined with it The old Corps is going with me to do a pretty bit of work, different from anything that it has ever done before."

"That would not be easy; we have been in every scrap on land or sea since the year dot."

Dawson looked round carefully, and then whispered, "Those eighty Marines of mine are going to cut off a snake's head and stop a bloody revolution. They've done that sort of thing many times at the ends of the earth, but never, I believe, in England."

"I wish that I were again a lieutenant," growled the Commandant, "for then I would volunteer to come with you."

"You shall choose my second-in-command yourself, sir," conceded Dawson handsomely.

Captain Dawson chose his men with discrimination. All those above five years' service were paraded in the barrack square, and Dawson, assisted by the Commandant, to whom his men were as his own children, picked out the eighty lucky ones at leisure. Those who were rejected shrugged their stiff square shoulders and predicted disaster for the expedition. In one small detail Dawson changed his plans. He had intended to take two sergeants only, but in Chatham there were four who had served with him in the ranks, and he could not withstand their pleadings. When all was settled, Dawson went to the Commandant's quarters to be introduced to his second-in-command, and surprised there that officer endeavouring to squeeze his rather middle-aged figure within the buttoned limits of a subaltern's tunic. Since the senior officers of Marines never go to sea, the Commandant's own official uniform was the field-service khaki of a Staff officer. "It is all right," explained he, laughing. "I have become a lieutenant again, and am going north with you. But I wish that your friend the mess-sergeant had a pattern B tunic which would meet round my middle. My young men must be devilish slim nowadays. I have been on to the A.-G. by 'phone. He pretends to be derisory, but I am convinced that really he is desperately jealous. He would love to go too. You seem, my good Dawson, to have stirred up Whitehall and Spring Gardens in a manner most emphatic."

"But you can't serve under me, sir," cried Dawson, aghast.

"Can't I!" retorted the new Lieutenant. "If admirals can joyfully go afloat as lieut.-commanders, as lots of them are doing, what is to prevent a Colonel of Marines serving as a subaltern? I am on this job with you, Dawson, if you will have me."

"With four sergeants and eighty Marines," said Dawson slowly, "you and I could have held Mons."

"We could that," cried the Colonel-Lieutenant, who had by now completed the reduction of his rank to that of Captain Dawson's subordinate. "Nothing, nothing, is beyond the powers of the Sea Regiment!"

At about 11.30 that night the wide roof of St. Pancras echoed to the disciplined tramp of Dawson's detachment, which marched straight to coaches reserved by order from Headquarters. "Marines don't talk," said Dawson, "but I am not taking risks. I don't want to sully the virtue of my old Sea Pongos by mixing them up with raw land Tommies." Dawson and his subaltern were moving towards the sleeping-coach in which a double berth had been assigned to them, when two tall gentlemen in civilian dress slipped out of the crowd and stood in their path. Dawson, at the sight of them, glowed with pride, his chest swelled out under his broad blue tunic, and his hand flew to the peak of his red-banded cap. The Colonel-Lieutenant gasped. "Good luck, Dawson," whispered the bigger of the strangers; "I would give my baton to be going north with you."

"Colonel —— has given up his crowns," replied Dawson, as he introduced his companion.

The Field-Marshal smiled and shook hands with the sporting Commandant. "This is all frightfully irregular," said he, "but I sympathise. Still, if I know our friend Dawson here, there won't be any fighting. You have no idea of his skill as a diplomatist. He tells the truth, which is so unusual and startling that the effect is overwhelming. He is a heavy human howitzer. I envy you, Colonel."

"I have not a notion what we are to be at," said the Colonel.

"I am not very clear myself. It is Dawson's picnic, not ours, and we have given him a free hand. You won't get any fighting, but there will be lots of fun."

Meanwhile the First Lord had drawn Dawson to one side. "Good luck, Captain Dawson; you have not wasted any time, and I have the best of hopes. We had a beautiful row after you left us this morning. It did my poor heart good. The P.M. declares that if you put martial law into force, he will hand in his checks to the King. So, my poor friend, you carry with you a mighty responsibility. But stick it out, don't hesitate to follow your judgment, and wire me how you get on."

"Don't worry, sir," said Dawson, "I shall not fail. If it had not been for you and his lordship here, I should not have had this great chance. I won't let you down."

"Sh!" whispered the other. "Not so loud. We are conspirators, strictly incog., dressed in the shabbiest of clothes. We had to see you off, for I enjoyed the tussle of this morning beyond words. I would not for anything have missed the P.M.'s face when he found himself driven to act suddenly and definitely. I am eternally your debtor, Captain Dawson of the Red Marines."

"My word," exclaimed the Colonel-Lieutenant, when the visitors had slipped away like a couple of stage villains, with soft hats pulled down over their eyes—"the Field-Marshal and the First Lord! You have some friends, sir."

"I am only a ranker," said Dawson humbly, "with very temporary stars; not a pukka officer and gentleman like you. I hope that you do not mind sharing a sleeper with me?"

"I should be proud to share with you the measliest dug-out in a Flanders graveyard," replied the Colonel emphatically. The two officers, so anomalously associated, entered their berth the best of friends and talked together far into the night. And as they talked, the Colonel, now a Lieutenant, made the same discovery which had startled Dawson's two powerful supporters of the morning. In the police officer, rough, half-educated, vain, tender of heart, he also had discovered a Man. "But for me and my Red Marines," said Dawson, as they turned in for some broken sleep, "those poor fools up yonder would get themselves shot in the streets. But I shall save them, and in saving them I shall save the country."

* * * * *

It was the afternoon of the following day, just twenty-four hours after Dawson had commandeered the resources of Chatham, and the scene was a public hall in a big industrial city. In the body of the room sat two hundred and thirty-four men—shop stewards and district trade union officials—and their faces were gloomy and anxious. They had come for a last meeting with the officers of the Munitions Dept, and to declare that the men whom they represented were resolved not to permit of any further dilution of labour. The great majority of them were not unpatriotic, their sons and brothers and friends had joined the Forces, and had already fought and died gallantly, but they were intensely suspicious. To them the "employer," the "capitalist," was a greater, because more enduring and insidious, enemy than the Germans. Dilution of labour had become in their eyes a device for destroying all their hardly won privileges and restrictions, and for delivering them bound and helpless to their "capitalist oppressors." To this sorry pass had the perpetual disputes of peace brought the workmen under stress of war! Rates of pay did not enter into the dispute—never in their lives had they earned such wages—its origin led in a queer perverted sense of loyalty to the trade unions, and to those members who had gone forth to fight. "What will our folks say," asked the men of one another, "when they come home from the war, if we have given away in their absence all that they fought for during long years?" When it was attempted to make clear that the lives of their own sons in the trenches were being made more hazardous by their obstinacy, they shook their heads and simply did not believe. "We can make all the guns and the shells that are wanted without giving up our rules. We value our sons' lives as much as you do. We love our country as much as you do. The capitalists are using a plea of patriotism to get the better of us." It was a pitiful deadlock—honest for the most part; yet it was a deadlock which, as Dawson said, brought very near the day when English artillery would be firing shotted guns in English streets.

At a small table on a low platform at one end of the room sat three civilians, and a few feet away, sitting a little back, was an officer whose uniform and badges attracted the eyes of the curious. None of the workmen knew this brown-skinned man with the small, dark moustache who looked so very professional a soldier, yet Dawson knew them, every man of them, and had moved among them in their works many times. Ten of those present were actually his own agents, working among their fellow unionists and agitating with them—hidden sources of information and of influence at need—and yet not one of those ten knew that the Marine Captain upon the platform was his own official chief. The chairman rose to speak to the men for the last time, and Dawson sat listening and studying a small slip of paper in his hand.

The chairman said nothing that the men had not been told many times during the past few days, but there was in his speech a note of solemn appeal and warning which was new. The hearers shuffled their feet uneasily, for most of them felt uneasy; they were, as I have said, most of them honest men. But when the chairman had sat down, and the men began, one after another, to reply, it appeared at once that there was present an element not honest, even seditious. Dawson smiled to himself, and studied his slip of paper, for the snake, whose head he had come to cut off, was beginning to rear itself before him. Hints began to appear that there was a strong minority at least which was unwilling both to fight and to work for a country which was none of theirs—"What has this country done for us that we should bleed and sweat for it? It has starved us and sweated us to make profits out of us, and now in its extremity slobbers us with fair words." At last one man rose, a thin-faced, wild-eyed man, who, under happier conditions, might have been a preacher or a writer, and delivered a speech which was rankly seditious. "The workers," he declared, "are being shackled, gagged, and robbed. Our enemy is not the German Kaiser. Our enemy consists of that small, cunning, treacherous, well-organised, and highly respectable section of the community who, by means of the money power, compels the workers to sweat in order that their bellies may be full and their fine ladies gowned in gorgeous raiment. They pass a Munitions Act to chain the worker to his master. They 'dilute' labour to call into being an invisible army which can be mobilised at short notice to defeat the struggles of striking artisans. The attack of the masters must be resisted. The workers must fight. There is a fascinating attraction in the idea of meeting force with force, violence with violence. It is undeniable that many of the more thoughtful among the toilers would consider that their lives had not been spent in vain if they organised their comrades to drilled and armed rebellion."

The speaker paused. He was encouraged by a few cheers, but the mass of his hearers were silent. He glanced at Dawson, whose face was set in an expressionless mask. Cheers came again, and he went on, but with less assurance. "The worker's labour power is his only wealth. It is also his highest weapon. But the workers need not think of using this weapon so long as they are split and divided into sects and groups and crafts. To be effective they must organise as workers. An organisation that would include all the workers, skilled and unskilled, throughout the entire country, would prove irresistible. But as matters stand at present I do not advocate armed rebellion. I advocate and herewith proclaim a general strike."

He sat down, and there was a long silence. The die had been cast. If the meeting broke up without the emphatic assertion of the Government's authority, then a general strike upon the morrow was as certain as that the sun would rise. It was for this moment, this intensely critical moment, that Dawson had worked and fought in London, and for which he was now ready. The chairman sighed and wiped his face, which had become clammy. He looked at Dawson, who nodded slightly, and then rose.

"I call," said he solemnly, "upon Captain Dawson. He is now in supreme authority."

Dawson sprang to his feet, alert, decided, and picked up a large roll of papers which had rested behind him upon his chair. He placed the roll upon the table and faced the audience, who knew at once, with the rapid instinct of a crowd, that the unexpected was about to happen. Dawson pulled down his tunic, settled himself comfortably into his Sam Browne belt, and rested his left hand upon the hilt of his sword.—It was a pretty artistic touch, the wearing of that sword, and exactly characteristic of Dawson's methods. I laughed when he told me of it.—There were two doors to the room—one upon Dawson's left hand, the other at the far end behind the workmen. He raised his right hand, and the chairman, who was watching him, pressed an electric bell. Then events began to happen.

The doors flew open, and through each of them filed a line of smart men in blue, equipped with rifles and side arms. Twenty men and a sergeant passed through each door, which was then closed. The ranks of each detachment were dressed as if on parade, and when all were ready, Dawson gave a sharp order. Instantly forty-two rifle-butts clashed as one upon the floor, and the Marines stood at ease. At this moment the door at the far end might have been seen to open, and an officer to slip in who, though white of hair, had not apparently reached a higher rank than that of lieutenant. "It was all very fine, Dawson," he explained afterwards, "your plan of leaving me outside with the rest of the Marines, but it wasn't good enough. I didn't come north to be buried in the reserves."

"You should have obeyed orders," replied Dawson severely.

"I should," cheerfully assented the Colonel-Commandant of Chatham, "but somehow I didn't."

While Dawson's body-guard of Marines was getting into position before the doors, the workmen, surprised and trapped, were on their feet chattering and gesticulating. The unfamiliar appearance of the blue-uniformed men, not one of whom was less than five feet nine inches in height, their well-set-up figures and stolid professional faces, gave a business-like, even ominous flavour to the proceedings which chilled the strike leaders to the bone. They would have cheered an irruption of kilted recruits in khaki tunics as the coming of old friends, and would have felt no more than local patriotic hostility towards a detachment of English or Irish soldiers. But these blue men of the Sea Regiment, an integral part of the great mysterious silent Navy, had no part or lot with British workmen "rightly struggling to be free." They represented some outside authority, some potent, overpowering authority, as no khaki-clad soldiers could have represented it. The surprise was complete, the moral effect was staggering, and Dawson, who had counted upon both when he brought his Marines north, smiled contentedly to himself. He stepped forward, with that little slip of paper in his hand, and began to read from it. One by one he read out twenty-three names, the very first being that of the man who had made the speech which I have reported.

As name after name dropped from Dawson's lips, the wonder and terror grew. Who was this strange officer who could thus surely divide the goats from the sheep, who was picking out one after another the self-seekers and fomenters of sedition, who, while he omitted none who were really dangerous, yet included none who were honest though mistaken? As the list drew towards its end, quite half the listeners were smiling broadly. They could not have drawn up a more perfect one themselves, and they did not love most of those whose names were found upon it.

"Now," said Dawson, when he had finished, "I must ask all those gentlemen to step forward." Not a man moved. "Let me warn you that every man whose name I have read out is personally known to me. If I have to come and fetch you, I shall not come alone." There was still some hesitation, and then those upon the proscribed list began to move forward. They would willingly have hidden themselves, had that been possible, but to be known and to be dragged out by those hard-faced Marines would have added humiliation to terror. They came forth, until all the twenty-three were ranged up before Dawson. Then the man, whose name was first upon the list, rasped out, "What is your authority for this outrage upon a peaceful meeting? I demand your authority."

"You shall have it," serenely replied Dawson. And, going up to the pile of papers which he had laid upon the table, he drew one forth and held it up so that all might see. It was a large placard, boldly printed, a proclamation in cold, terse language of Martial Law, signed by the Secretary for War himself.

"Martial Law! This is sheer militarism," cried the first of those arrested.

"For you and for these other twenty-two upon my list it is Martial Law," replied Dawson. "But for the rest it will be as they choose themselves. Sergeant, remove the prisoners." A sergeant stepped out, the line of Marines before the door divided, and the prisoners were led away. Dawson put the proclamation back upon the table, squared his shoulders, and turned towards his audience, now silent, subdued, and purged. His plans were working very well.

"I am no speaker," he began; "I am a man of the people, one of yourselves. I have made my own way, and though I wear the uniform and stars of a Captain of Marines, I am really an officer of police, Chief Detective Inspector Dawson of Scotland Yard." He paused to allow time for this astonishing fact to sink in. So that was why he had known the names and faces of all the ringleaders of sedition! And if he knew so much, what more might he not know! Even the most innocent among his audience began to feel loose about the neck.

"I know you all," he went on. "There is not a man among you whom I do not know. You—or you—or you." He addressed those near to him by name. "We sympathise with you and have reasoned with you. But you proved obdurate. The King's Government must be carried on; the war must be carried on if our country is to be saved. And those who have given power to me—the power which you have seen set out upon these papers, the powers of Martial Law—will exercise them unflinchingly if there appears to be no other way. But there is another and a better way. You must obey the laws which Parliament has passed for the defence of the country and for the provision of munitions. Your rights are protected under them. After the war is over, your privileges will be restored. For the present they must be abandoned. Willingly or unwillingly they must be abandoned. I said just now that it is for you to choose whether Martial Law shall take effect or not. The moment those placards are posted in the streets the military authorities become supreme, but they will not be posted if you have the sense to see when you are beaten. What I have to ask, to require of you, is that to-morrow, at the mass meeting of the men which is to be held, you will advise them to surrender unconditionally, to work hard themselves, and to allow all others to work hard. There must be no more holding up of essential parts of guns, no more writing and talking sedition. Our country needs the whole-hearted service of us all. If you here and now give me your promise that you will use every effort—no perfunctory, but real effort—to stop at once all these threats of a strike, I will let you go now and wish you God-speed. If you fail, then Martial Law will be proclaimed forthwith. Make this very clear to the men. Tell them that you have seen the proclamation, signed by the Field-Marshal himself, and that I, Captain and Chief Inspector Dawson, will post the placards in the streets with my own hands. If you will not give me your promise—I do not ask for any hostages or security, just your promise as loyal, honourable men—I shall arrest you all here and now, and deport you all just as those twenty-three have been arrested and will be deported. You will not see those men for a long time; you know in your hearts that you are well quit of them. If I arrest you all, I shall not stop my arrests at that point. There are many others—many who are not workmen from whom has come money for your strike funds and to offer bail when arrests have been made. I shall pick them all up. Nothing that you can now do will affect the fate of those who have been taken from this room. Whatever loyalty you may owe to them has been discharged, and I will give you a quittance. Their chapter has been closed. What you have to consider now is the fate of yourselves and of many beside yourselves, of all those who look to you for advice and guidance. Take time, talk among yourselves, consult one another. I am not here to hurry you unduly, but before you are allowed to leave this room there must be a complete and final settlement."

He sat down. The men split into groups, and the buzz of talk ran through the room. There was no anger or excitement, but much bewilderment. They had come to the meeting as masters, strong in numbers, to dictate terms, yet now the tables had been turned dramatically upon them. No longer masters, they were in the presence of a Force which at a word from Dawson could hale them forth as prisoners to be dealt with under the mysterious shuddering powers of Martial Law. They thought of those twenty-three, a few minutes since so potent for mischief, now bound and helpless in the hands of the Blue Men from the Sea.

At last an elderly grey-locked man stepped forward, and Dawson rose to meet him. "We admit, sir," said he, "that you have us at a disadvantage. We did not expect this Proclamation nor those Marines of yours. We did not believe that the Government meant business. We thought that we should have more talk, talk, and we are all sick of talk. We are true patriots here—you have taken away all those who cared nothing for their country—and we feel that if you are prepared to use Martial Law and the forces of the Crown against us, that you must be very much in earnest. We feel that you would not do these terrible things unless the need were very urgent. We do not agree that the need is urgent, but if you, representing the Government, say that it is, we have no course open to us but to submit. If we now surrender unconditionally and promise heartily to use every effort to bring the mass of the men to our views, will you in your turn give us your personal assurance that all our legitimate grievances will be fully considered, and that every effort will be made to meet them? You may crush us, sir, but you will not get good work from men whose spirit has been broken."

"I cannot make conditions," replied Dawson gently, "but ask yourselves why I brought my Marines all the way from Chatham to deal with this meeting? Was it not that I would not put upon you the pain and humiliation of arrest at the hands of your own sons and brothers? Though I stand here with gold stars on my shoulders I am one of you. My father worked all his life in the dockyard at Portsmouth, and I myself as a boy have been a holder-on in a black squad of riveters. I can make no conditions, but if you will leave yourself entirely in my hands, and in those of my superiors, you may be assured that there will be no attempt made to crush you, to break your spirit."

As he said these words an inspiration came to him, and by sure instinct he acted upon it. Jumping down from the platform, he approached the old sad-faced spokesman, and shook him hard by the hand. Then he moved along among the other workmen, addressing them by name, chatting to them of their work and private interests, and showing so complete and human a regard for them that their hostility melted away before him. This man, who had conquered them, was one of themselves, a "tradesman" like them, one of the Black Squad of Portsmouth, a fellow-worker. He was no tool of the hated "capitalist." If he said that they must all go back to work unconditionally, well they must go. But he was their friend, and would see justice done them. Presently Dawson was handing out cigarettes—of which he had brought a large supply in his pockets, Woodbines—and the meeting, of which so much was feared, had apparently turned into, a happy conversazione. For half an hour Dawson pursued his campaign of personal conciliation, and then went back to his place upon the platform.

"Go in peace," he cried. "Come again to-morrow afternoon and tell me about the mass meeting. There will be more cigarettes awaiting you, and even, possibly, a bottle or two of whisky."

The men laughed, and one wag called out, "Three cheers for holder-on Dawson." The cheers were given heartily, the Marines stood aside from the doors, and the room rapidly emptied. The officials of the Munitions Department and the Colonel, who was Dawson's insubordinate subaltern, crowded round him spouting congratulations. He soaked in their flatteries as was his habit, and then delivered a lesson upon the management of men which should be printed in letters of gold. "Men are just grown-up children," said he, "and should be treated as children. Be always just, praise them when they are good, and smack them when they are naughty. But if when they are naughty you spare the rod and try to slobber them with fine words, they will despise you utterly, and become upon the instant naughtier than ever."

"What about that mass meeting to-morrow?" asked the Colonel.

"I shall not be there, but ten of my men will be. Have no fears of the mass meeting. The snake's head is off—by to-morrow it will be two hundred miles away—and though the body may wriggle, it will be quite harmless. After two or three hours of talk and vain threats the meeting will collapse, and we shall get unconditional surrender."

And so it happened. The talk went on for four solid hours—vain, vapouring talk, during which steam was blown off. At the end the surrender, as Dawson predicted, was unconditional.

That evening of the morrow a telegram sped away over the long wires to the south addressed to the Secretary of the Admiralty.

"Please tell First Lord that the snake is dead. I am returning the Marines carriage-paid and undamaged. My commission as a Captain is no longer required. Dawson."

Back flashed a reply from the Minister himself: "To Captain Dawson, R.M.L.I. Adjutant-General insists that you retain rank and pay until the end of the war. So do I. You have done a wonderful piece of work for which you will be adequately punished in official quarters. But you will suffer in good company."

Though Dawson thus became entitled to call himself Captain for the duration of the war, he never used the rank or the uniform again. Once more, to my knowledge, he served in his well-beloved Corps, but it was then not as Captain, but as private, during his long watch in the *Malplaquet*, of which I have told the story earlier in this book.

CHAPTER XVII

DAWSON TELEPHONES FOR A SURGEON

I have never been able to plan this book upon any system which would hold together for half a dozen consecutive chapters. I am the victim of my characters who come and go and pull me with them tied to their chariot wheels. When I wrote the first story of the "Lost Naval Papers"—which, by the way, were not lost at all—I had not made the personal acquaintance of William Dawson. When I wrote of my own encounters with Dawson and of my share, a humble share, in his researches, my dear Madame Gilbert had not met me and subdued me into a drivelling worship of her shining personality. While I was amusing myself trying to convey to the reader the frolicsome atmosphere which Madame carries about with her and in which she hides the workings of her big heart and brain, I was ignorant of the adventures of the two battle-cruisers and of Dawson's encounter with the War Committee, and of his triumph over the revolting workmen of the north. I have therefore written, as it were, from hand to mouth, more as one who keeps a vagabond diary than as one who consciously plans a work of art. It is as a diary of personal experiences that this book should be regarded. It has no merit of constructive skill, for I have never known what the future would yield to me of material. When Dawson parted with me to return south to the Yard, and to his deserted family in Acacia Villas, Primrose Road, Tooting, I did not expect to see him again for months, possibly years. But a turn came to the wheel of my destiny as it had done to his. I also was plucked from my northern place of exile and transported joyfully to the south country, whither I have always fled whenever for a few days or weeks I could loosen the bonds which tied me to the north. Now that those bonds have fallen entirely from me, and I am back in my southern home—whether for good or for evil rests upon the lap of the high gods—I have been able unexpectedly to resume contact with Dawson and to bring this, discursive book to some kind of a conclusion. It cannot really end so long as Dawson and Froissart and Madame Gilbert live and remain in friendly association with me. They have become parts of my life, and if I have not outraged their feelings beyond forgiveness by what I have written of them, I have hopes that I shall meet all of them often in the future and that they will tell me many more stories of their exploits.

* * * * *

As soon as I had settled myself in London I took the earliest opportunity of calling upon Dawson at the Yard. He was absent, but his Deputy, who knew my name, received me kindly. He explained that it would not be easy to find Dawson. "We never know where he is or what he is doing. I suppose that the Chief knows; certainly no one else. How can one be Deputy to a man who never tells one what he is doing or where he may be found?" I agreed that the post seemed difficult to fill adequately. "I wish I could chuck it as Froissart did when he went back to Paris. Have you ever seen Madame Gilbert?" he inquired eagerly. I observed that Madame did me the honour to be my friend. "So you know her, do you? She's a clinker of a woman. Hot stuff, but a real genuine clinker. She could do what she pleased with old man Dawson; make him fetch and carry like a poodle. She's the only woman born who ever turned Dawson round her fingers." I observed rather stiffly that Madame Gilbert was a lady for whom I had a very high regard, and that the expression "Hot stuff" was hardly respectful. "Hum!" said the Deputy, eyeing me with interest. "So she has made a fool of you like she has of the rest of us. Even the Chief gets down on his rheumaticky old knees and kisses the carpet of his room after she has trodden on it."

The Deputy tended to become garrulous, and I cut him short with an inquiry for Dawson's exact address. He lived in Acacia Villas, but I was without the precise number. The Deputy told me, and promised to inform Dawson of my visit at the earliest moment. "It may be to-day, or next week, or next month. It may not be till the War is over"—an expression which has come into colloquial use as a synonym for the Greek Kalends. I thanked the officer, and withdrew somewhat annoyed.

It appeared that Dawson was not far away, for a letter from him reached me two days later at my club. It was an invitation to visit his home and to dine with him on the following Sunday at one o'clock. Enclosed was a plan designed to assist me in penetrating the mazes of Tooting. That Sunday was a beautiful day in May, and I wandered down with plenty of time to spare to provide against the danger of being "bushed." But with the aid of Dawson's thoughtful plan I found Primrose Road without difficulty. The hour was then 12.15, and the house deserted. Dawson and his family were at chapel. I had forgotten what I had heard months before of Dawson's fervour as a preacher upon Truth until reminded of it by a constable whose beat passed the house. "If you are looking for Chief Detective Inspector Dawson," said he, "I can show you where to find him in chapel. He will be holding forth just now." The opportunity of seeing Dawson as he really was—known certainly only to his wife and to God—and of seeing him as a preacher, spurred me into active interest. "My relief is coming now," said the constable; "as soon as I have handed over I will show you the way."

As we walked together the policeman revealed to me the admiration inspired by Dawson in his humble subordinates. "There is nothing that man can't do," said he. "He is a skilled mechanic, a soldier—some say he has a general's uniform hid away in his house—an electrical engineer, and a telegraph operator. He has been all over the world in the Royal Navy, and could if he liked be commanding a ship now. He's the friend of Ministers and Secretaries of State. He's the best detective that the Yard ever knew, and he preaches to folk here like—like the Archangel Gabriel come to trot 'em off to Hell. I'm a Wesleyan, myself, but I often go to hear the Chief Inspector. He makes one come out in a cold sweat, and gives a man a fine appetite for dinner. He shakes you up so that you feel empty," he explained.

I observed that if Dawson were so great a stimulus upon appetite, he would not be popular with the Food Controller. The policeman, though he had heard of the Food Controller, was unconscious of his many activities, which shows how little the world knows of its greatest men. It also suggests that police constables do not read newspapers.

The chapel was a building illustrative of the straight line and plane. It was fairly large, and so full that the crowd of worshippers bulged out of the doors. Though we could not force our way inside, we could hear the booming of a voice which was scarcely recognisable as that of Dawson. Waves of emotion ran so strongly through the congregation that we could feel them beat against the fringes by the doors. "The Chief Inspector is on his game to-day," whispered the constable. "He's hitting them fine." From which I judged that the constable had in his youth come from the north, where golf is cheap. It was a disappointment that I could not get in, but perhaps well for the reader. The temptation to record a genuine sermon by Dawson might have proved too much for me. Presently the voice ceased to boom, the congregation squeezed out hot and oily, like grease from a full barrel, and I waited for Dawson to appear. "Don't speak to him now," directed my guide. "Let him get up to his house. He can't talk for half an hour after holding forth; there's not a word bad or good left in his carcase."

After all the worshippers had gone there issued forth a party of three: a man, a woman, and a little girl. "There he is," said the constable, nudging me. "Who?" asked I. "The Chief Inspector. There he is with Mrs. Dawson and their little girl." I stared and stared, but failed to recognise my friend of the north. I was too far away to see his ears, and his face was quite strange to me.

"I hope," I whispered primly to the constable, "that Mrs. Dawson is sure he is her husband."

"She ought to be. Aren't you sure?"

"Not yet; I am not near enough to see properly. That Dawson, is not a bit like those others whom I know."

"That Dawson! Those others! Is there more than one Chief Inspector Dawson?" asked the man, wondering.

"I should say about a hundred," replied I, and left him gasping. I fear that he now thinks that either I am quite mad or that Mrs. Dawson is a pluralist in husbands.

I gave the Dawson family sufficient time to reach their home, and to recover the power of speech, and then walked gravely to the door as if I had just arrived. One becomes contagiously deceptive in the vicinity of Dawson.

The stranger, who was the real undisguised Dawson, welcomed me to his home. The house was a small one and the family kept no servant. I do not know what income the Chief Inspector draws from the Yard, but am sure that it is absurdly inadequate to his services. The higher one rises, the less work one does and the more pay one gets—provided that one begins more than half-way up the ladder. For those like Dawson who begin quite at the bottom, the rule seems to be inverted: the more work one does, the less pay one gets. I should judge my own ill-gotten income at twice or three times that of Dawson—which even that cautious judge, Euclid, would declare to be absurd.

He led me to the parlour, which was well and tastefully furnished—Dawson has seen good houses—and we waited there while Mrs. Dawson dished up the dinner. "Please sit there, Dawson, facing the light," said I. "Let me have a good look at you." He complied smiling, and I examined his features with grave attention. Dawson, the real Dawson as I now saw him for the first time, is a very fair man. His pale sandy hair can readily be bleached white or dyed a dark colour. He uses quick dyes which can be removed with appropriate chemicals. His hair and moustache, he told me, grow very quickly. His complexion, like his hair, is almost white, and his skin curiously opaque. His blood is red and healthy, but it does not show through. His skin and hair are like the canvas of a painter, always ready to receive pigments and ready also to give them up when treated with skill. I began to understand how Dawson can make to himself a face and appearance of almost any habit or age. He can be fair or dark, dark or fair, old or young, young or old, at will. He carries the employment of rubber and wax insets very far indeed. His nose, his cheeks, his mouth, his chin may be forced by internal packing to take to themselves any shape. I made a hasty calculation that he can change his appearance in seven hundred and twenty different ways. "So many as that?" said Dawson, surprised when I told him. "I don't think that I have gone beyond sixty." I assured him that on strict mathematical principles I had arrived at the limiting number, and it gave him pleasure to feel that so many untried permutations of countenance remained to him. In actual everyday practice there are rarely more than six Dawsons in being at the same time. He finds that number sufficient for all useful purposes; a greater number, he says, would excessively strain his memory. He has, you see, always to remember which Dawson he is at any moment. When he was pulling my leg, or that of his brave enemy Froissart, the number multiplied greatly, but, as a working business rule, he is modestly content with six. "I suppose," I asked, "that here in Acacia Villas you are always the genuine article."

"Always," he declared with emphasis. "Once," he went on, "I tried to play a game on Emma. I came home as one of the others, forced my way into the house, and was clouted over the head and chucked into the street. When I got back to the Yard to alter myself—for I had left my tools there—Emma had been telephoning to me to get the wicked stranger arrested for house-breaking. I never tried any more games; women have no sense of humour." He shuddered. Dawson is afraid of his wife, and I pictured to myself a great haughty woman with the figure and arms of a Juno.

But when Clara—who asked kindly after my little Jane—had summoned us to the dining-room, I was presented to a small, quiet mouse of a woman whose head reached no higher than Dawson's heart. This was the redoubtable Emma! "Did she really clout you over the head and chuck you into the street?" I whispered. "She did, sir!" he replied, smiling. "She threw me yards over my own doorstep."

Between Dawson and his little wife there is a very tender affection. In her eyes he is not a police officer, but an inspired preacher. She knows nothing of his professional triumphs, and would not care to know. She, I am very sure, will never trouble to read this book. To her he is the lover of her youth, the most tender of husbands, and a Boanerges who spends his Sabbaths dragging fellow-creatures from the Pit. The God of Dawson and of his Emma is a pitiless giant with a pitchfork, busily thrusting his creatures towards eternal torment; Dawson, in Emma's eyes, is an intrepid salvor with a boat-hook who once a week arduously pulls them out. Dawson married Emma when he was a sergeant of Marines, and I think that he has shown to her his uniform with the three captain's stars. To me she always spoke of him as "the Captain," though I could not be quite sure whether she meant a Captain of Marines or a Captain in the Army of Salvation. Dawson, his Emma, and Clara are very happy, very united, and I am glad that I saw them in their own home. I am helped to understand how tender is the heart which beats under Dawson's assumed cloak of professional ruthlessness. At first I wholly misjudged him, but I will not now alter what I then wrote. My readers will learn to know their Dawson as I learned myself.

Whenever in the future I wish to hear from Dawson of his exploits I shall not seek him at his own house. He is an artist who is highly sensitive to atmosphere. In Acacia Villas the police officer fades to shadowy insignificance, even in his own mind. Then, he is a husband, a father, and a mighty preacher. He will talk of his disguises, and in general terms of his work, but there is no fiery enthusiasm for manhunting when Dawson gets home to Tooting. I shall seek him at the Yard, or upon the hot trail; then and then only shall I get from him the full flavour of his genius for detection. Dawson, away from home, is so vain as to be unconscious of his vanity; Dawson at home is quite extraordinarily modest. He defers always to the opinion of Emma, and she, gently, kindly, but with an air of infinite superiority, keeps his wandering steps firmly in the path of truth. He is, I am told, a most kindling preacher, but it is Emma who inspires his sermons.

Once only during my visit did I see a flash of the old Dawson, the Dawson of the *Malplaquet*, and of the War Committee, and that was just before I left. We were in the parlour smoking, and I was getting rather bored. Conjugal virtue, domestic content and happiness, are beautiful to look upon for a while, but I confess that in a remorseless continuous film ("featuring" Dawson and Emma) I find them boresome. There is little humour about Dawson and none at all about his dear Emma. I would gladly exchange fifty virtuous Emmas for one naughty Madame Gilbert. We had been talking idly of our sport together and of his different incarnations. Suddenly he sprang from his chair and his pale face lighted up. "Now that I have you here, Mr. Copplestone, I shall not let you go until you tell me by what trick you can always see through my disguises. Would you know me now as Dawson?"

"Of course," said I. "There is no difficulty. If you painted your face black and your hair vermilion, I should still know you at once."

"You have promised to tell me the secret. Tell me now."

I considered whether I should tell. It was amusing to have some hold over him, but was it quite fair to Dawson to keep him in ignorance of those marks of ear by which I could always be certain of his identity. He had been useful to me, and I had made free with his personality. Yes, I would tell him, and in a few sentences I told.

He gripped his ears with both hands; he felt those lobes so firmly secured to his cheekbones, and those blobs of flesh which remained to him of his wolfish ancestors. He fingered them carefully while he thought. At last he made up his mind. "It is the Sabbath," said he, "but when I am on duty I work ever upon the Sabbath day. It is now my duty to—" He reached for the telephone book, took off the receiver, and called for a number.

"What are you doing?" I asked, though I ought to have known.

"I am making an appointment with a surgeon," said Dawson.

THE END

END OF Ashed Phoenix Library'S THE LOST NAVAL PAPERS, BY BENNET COPPLESTONE

Lightning Source UK Ltd.
Milton Keynes UK
UKHW051248250219
337978UK00004B/400/P

9 780368 277368